I0780896

GRAVESIDE PRESS

HOWL

A SHAPESHIFTING ANTHOLOGY

CONTENTS

CONTENT WARNING

For a list of potential trigger warnings,
please turn to page 276 or visit our website:
graveside-press.com/cw/howl

IN SICKNESS & IN SLAUGHTER
S.H. Livernois

THE TRICKIEST PART of getting his wife clean after one of her spells was keeping the brains from clogging the tub drain.

He'd learned that the hard way, the first time Alice had come home like this. Many mistakes were made that night, least of all scouring gray matter out of a dozen tiny drain holes. Four years and many full moons later, he'd adapted into an expert. Though an expert in what, he couldn't say, but no one—he was certain—did this better than Eugene Mayhorn.

He'd unloaded Alice in the usual spot for clean-up—the claw-foot tub downstairs. It was just after two a.m. She was inert, unconscious, nude, and reeking—a primordial stench that made Eugene think of a carnivore who'd had its snout in a torn stomach cavity. The smell was like nothing he'd ever experienced *before*; it had mass, misting the air gray-green, with a sweet, rotten flavor that coated his tongue.

And it was not escaping through the open window. A light breeze drifted in, and an animal scurried past, rustling a bush, but the stink remained. Thankfully, he had a remedy for this.

With a fresh garbage bag in hand, Eugene took one step inside the bathroom, keeping a wary eye on his wife and the blood-spattered porcelain tub that cocooned her. He removed his poncho and stuffed it in the garbage bag, which he placed on the floor. He'd already laid down the plastic; it was murder, scrubbing blood from between the tiles, something he'd also learned the hard way. Walking on tiptoes, he crossed to the bathroom sink cupboard, fetched his kit, hidden behind the Comet and Lysol, and took out the clothespin and bandanna, which he fastened to his face in that order.

The stench—for the most part—vanished, but Eugene could still taste it. He gagged, though his stomach was empty. By design, of course. He always fasted on the full moon. He barely ate at all anymore, actually. Alice had noticed his frame wasting away over the months, and Eugene responded to her comments with a dismissive wave. Just a new exercise plan, he excused, and she didn't push, which was hurtful. Didn't she worry at all if he was ill?

Illness could easily explain his diminished appearance. His limbs were stringy and fragile, like a preteen boy after his first growth spurt. His clothes, the same trousers and button-up shirt he always wore, sagged off his bones, and his glasses slid down his thinned-out face. Where his posture was once erect, he now hunched a little at the shoulders. He hadn't lost any of his hair, thankfully, but the black curls, which he tamed with pomade, were streaked with gray. Wrinkles had sprouted around his eyes. He felt as desiccated as he looked, like a gentle breeze could shred him into dust.

Sometimes, he longed for it.

He put on a fresh poncho and elbow-length dish gloves and surveyed the mess of his darling wife. The blood painted all over her stout body— she was shaped more like a barrel now than an hourglass—and the (Eugene gagged again) tissue in her hair.

God, I don't want to do this.

Eugene took a deep breath and remembered what he was breathing in and cough-gagged. He moved closer, but an opposing force—instinct, he supposed— tried to push him back, as if he were approaching a grizzly bear before her first meal of the spring. He placed the folded towel on the floor next to the tub and kneeled, bending over her.

"Let's make you beautiful, Alice."

The first task was to mop up the blood before it dried, which required an entire roll of paper towels. He wiped everything, because the gore was everywhere—under her breasts, between her legs and toes, across her stomach, inside her navel, and between fat rolls, pale as uncooked dough. He merely patted her left arm, though, avoiding the fresh wound there. He cleaned the tub as well, lifting her heavy body here and there to get beneath and around her.

Eugene slapped a gloved hand on her shoulder and shoved her forward, so that her heavy breasts smacked against her thighs, and wiped down her back. Bloody rag after bloody rag went into the garbage bag, and she was pink and raw when he was done, shreds of paper towel clinging to her clammy skin.

When he was pacified, he took the wide-tooth comb in hand; this, and the next task, were among the foulest. Eugene started picking through her graying hair like she was an ape, collecting bits of brain and wiping them into a grotesque pile in the palm of his gloved hand. As Eugene worked, his mind drifted. He pondered how, hours before, these shreds of matter had generated thought and personality and memory...

Stop.

Don't.

That was a dark path. He couldn't go down there.

He sucked in a shaky breath and imagined the bits in his palm were cold oatmeal.

Next were her teeth. Over the years, coffee and tea had tinted them the color of pale urine, but they were straight and well-shaped. Alice did have a dazzling smile, which she brought out to play more often lately. Eugene carefully flossed between them; shreds of *something* came loose, and he deposited these in his palm as well. Then he scrubbed under her nails with a bristle brush, extracting more blood and more tissue.

Now came the deep clean.

He sprayed her with the shower head; little rivers of pink streamed across the basin of the tub toward the drain. Then he squirted half a bottle of dish soap all over her body and the tub, spraying both with water, not stopping until the porcelain was ivory again. He filled it with the hottest water and way too much soap and lathered and scrubbed and exfoliated his wife from head to foot.

When she was polished clean and looked like herself again, Eugene removed the clothespin and bandanna. A faint stench remained in the room, but there was little else he could do about it. Sweating and lightheaded, he drained the water.

Alice laid there, glossy and nude. With all the ugliness scoured away, Eugene could finally see the woman he married. Sodden curls of her wild hair clung to the side of her neck and collarbone, tracing the curve of her breasts. He sat down on the toilet and just looked at her, so helpless in the bath. So calm and quiet, with nothing to upset her.

In all the years he'd known Alice, she'd complained about her size—that she was too big, too hippy, too sturdy, not feminine. She reminded him of one of those Renaissance beauties with their rounded, soft curves, like Titian's *Venus of Urbino*. The ideal of womanliness and sensuality, in his opinion. The comparison didn't exactly offend her, but she never liked it either.

Though as they sailed past forty together, Alice had either stopped caring what she looked like or had decided to embrace this description, because she'd become rounder and softer. Perhaps she assumed Eugene preferred this cushiony look; he didn't but was still relieved to see her unclothed. These monthly bathtub sessions were all he was permitted these days. He sat for a few more minutes to enjoy the view, searching within her lush curves for the thinner Alice he'd married twenty-five years before.

Eugene picked up the plastic he'd spread on the floor and stuffed this in the garbage bag, laid down towels, and dragged Alice from the tub, laying her upon them. She didn't often look pitiful, but she did now—

drawn and pale and barely breathing. He checked her vitals—blood pressure, blood sugar, oxygen levels—finding all abnormal, but not critical. His throat tightened. This took so much out of her, and Eugene feared it got worse each month. There was nothing for him to compare it to, no reference he could turn to for answers. It was all guesswork. What was next? How long could this go on? No one knew.

He leaned over her, kissing her lightly on the forehead, whispering "I love you" with every ounce of strength he had.

There was one more task before the transformation was complete, and this Eugene dreaded more than picking human tissue from her hair, teeth, and nails.

The wound on her arm had shrunk a bit since he'd first spied it and would continue to heal—supernaturally fast—while she slept and recovered, but he wanted it gone *now*. He put on a set of nitrile gloves, took up a pair of tweezers, and, with both hands and instrument trembling, approached.

He gagged, eyes watering.

Dr. Eugene Mayhorn used to love peeking inside the human body, most preferably into an open chest cavity. Man, thus broken apart and exposed, was at his most vulnerable, and it was his responsibility to put the patient back together. That wasn't surgery's only appeal, though. Once he'd seen inside a human, of any gender, race, or age, he realized what the optimists and poets already knew—people were all the same. Blood and guts were a great equalizer.

But what he saw inside Alice's cut was beyond the normal, marking her out as an "other." Not an equal, though whether she was better or worse than the rest of humanity, he had no idea. If sheer strength was the deciding factor, the answer was probably better.

Eugene looked at her arm from the corner of his eye, which leaked a hopeless tear that trailed down his cheek to settle, salty and warm, in the crook of his mouth. He forced his arm to move, the tweezers edging closer, but another gag stopped him.

He breathed, slowly, steadily, and his head swam.

Again.

The cut gaped open, like a mouth sucking air. It was closer to her elbow than her shoulder, and inside, Eugene didn't see dermis or muscle. There was no blood.

No, something *poked* out from inside Alice, into the world, stark against her silken white skin—

A tuft of soft black fur.

It was the same shade as her hair.

Eugene didn't want to go near it, not even with gloved fingers, but of course, he had to get rid of it. He couldn't be in the house with her like that. He went after the wound with his tweezers again, hesitating for a half-second of disgust, and forced his mind to blank.

Duty before fear.

He held his breath.

In swift, frightened movements, he tucked the fur back into the gash, under Alice's torn skin, smoothing down any stray hairs, trying not to think about how soft and pliable the fur felt under the tweezers, or how they slipped under the flap of severed skin where he felt even more fur, unseen beneath the familiar curve of her bicep. He didn't want to concede that this creature filled the inside of his wife's body, wearing her skin like a costume.

Eugene tried not to think of these things and failed. When he was done, he collapsed on the floor next to his wife, leaning against the toilet, feeling faint and clammy. He ripped off his glasses and sat with his sweating forehead in his hands, shuddering and fighting the urge to vomit or run from the bathroom and then the house, leaving Alice to face this horror alone.

He shook his head. That wasn't an option.

From his secret bag, Eugene pulled out a suture kit he'd pilfered from work years ago, back when he still had a job. He took up a needle and thread and closed the wound, erasing the fur. Alice was a normal woman again.

Nothing was wrong.

Nothing at all.

He packed up his kit and placed it back in its hiding spot before pulling out another, bigger bag. This contained beauty products Alice used to use but, for reasons he didn't understand, no longer bothered with. Her health was frail when she recovered, yes, but once she did, Alice was ebullient, if a little distracted and flighty. Despite that, she no longer straightened her hair or wore makeup, and that was alright. He could cope with the loose layers of mismatched clothes she now wore, too. But the lapse in shaving? It was difficult, watching Alice neglect herself like that. It spoke to him of something wrong, like she didn't take pride in herself anymore.

So, Eugene shaved all that should be shaved, gave her a manicure and pedicure, exfoliated her face and applied a balancing toner and a serum under her eyes, and smeared her from hairline to collarbone with a luxurious moisturizer. He whitened her teeth and drenched her entire body with a creamy lotion that smelled of roses. When he was done, she not only looked like a cleaner version of herself, but her old self, from their old life.

From before the first time she'd changed.

He'd only seen it once, and that was enough for him. Every month afterward, when the moon waxed silver in the sky, he prayed that he wouldn't see it ever again.

The first time surprised him, to say the least. He and Alice had been laying in bed, and he was awoken by gagging—like the noise a dog makes before it's going to retch. He turned on the light and there was Alice, sitting up in bed, her chest convulsing, and it took a moment of watching her to realize *she* was making that awful, guttural sound. It was so violent Eugene had thought she was going to cough up her organs.

Then Alice stopped.

Her eyes were quivering saucers. She clutched her throat and chest. Eugene asked what was wrong, if she was okay, trying to be calm because he was a surgeon and he was used to crises, but this was his wife, and calm was impossible. Alice couldn't answer anyway.

Her jaw worked feverishly, as if chewing something too big for her mouth. She did this for a couple of minutes.

Her lips peeled open with a wet smack.

She'd looked just as surprised by this as Eugene had.

A dark shape poked out between her lips and thrust outward, stretching her mouth from corner to corner. Light from the bedside lamp caught the shape's contours, glistening with moisture.

Eugene heard two sharp intakes of breath. The shape twitched.

The sound and the sight were simultaneous. Which meant the impossible: the shape had breathed.

A sucking sensation tugged at the base of Eugene's throat. His fingertips tingled. He couldn't move. Why was his brain telling him the thing sticking out of her mouth was a nose? That couldn't be right.

Alice retched again.

The nose pushed outward and behind it came a furry snout, and the corners of Alice's mouth ripped in a spray of blood that painted his face and chest, red dribbling down her chin and her neck, staining the collar of her nightshirt.

She sprung from bed and stood in the middle of the room. The snout grew, the skin stretching at her cheeks and by her nose until it split, peeling back from her forehead, over her scalp, falling away at the base of her skull. The snout turned into a face.

The face of a werewolf.

The creature emerged from Alice's severed neck. The flesh stripped away from her shoulders, chest, stomach, and down her legs, disintegrating before it hit the floor. Like the beast had simply removed a layer of clothing, it stepped out of his wife's skin and into the world.

To this day, Eugene believed the only reason he'd survived this incident had been Alice's confusion as her new form grew in their bedroom until its head touched the ceiling. She hadn't gotten her bearings yet, hadn't realized what she'd become, and this had saved him. It had given him enough time to run, faster than he'd ever run in his life.

He should've kept running. Yes, he'd said the vows, but how much simpler would his life have been if he'd broken them that night? She was still Alice between full moons, though, and that made him go back to the house an hour later and get in the car and drive around in search of her.

He shouldn't have. Nor should he have stopped when he found her, snout deep inside someone's belly, and, when she'd had her fill, scooped up the pieces to hastily bury them. But Eugene did it because he didn't want her to get into trouble. And he loved her. He told himself that a lot when he was in prison.

I did it all for you, he thought while slipping Alice into his favorite of her pajamas—the silky, powder blue ones. He carried her into bed and lay her on the soft mattress, pulling the covers to her chin, and sat on the bed next to her.

He wished he could tell her the truth. Why she felt so ill every month. The real reason he had been gone for three years, leaving her to endure this alone. He often wondered how she'd done it without him. Eugene almost let the truth spill many times, but then the local news would run a story about the Ides Neck Beast—a rabid animal of some sort, officials believed—and he imagined his dear Alice knowing it was she who'd savaged so many innocents, and, well... He couldn't do that to her.

This knowledge was his burden to bear.

Eugene kissed her on the cheek, the forehead, softly on the lips, and told her again that he loved her and blessed her with dreamless sleep. She'd be unconscious for at least ten hours, maybe more. As usual, that gave him just enough time to clean up her mess.

There was a blood trail from the kitchen where she'd collapsed to the entry hall and out the door to the walk path; it disappeared into the grass. She'd broken one window and shattered the wooden garden ducks. A few strips of grass had been ripped up.

The damage wasn't too bad this time. Small mercies.

It was four a.m. and though sleep called to Eugene, he couldn't rest. He had to mop up blood and sweep up glass and tamp down the grass and replace the broken window with plywood. It was nearly dawn when he stuffed the garbage bag, filled to the brim with the bloodied paper towels, assorted gore, and debris into the bin inside the garage.

He grabbed a flashlight, popped open the garage door, and trudged into the woods that surrounded their house; it was just a few acres of hemlock, maple, and ash. Eugene had to make sure Alice hadn't brought her meal—or pieces of it—back home.

Once he was sure of that, he could rest.

Bleary-eyed, he scanned the forest floor, encircling his house while fantasizing about continuing to walk, crossing the invisible border between his property and the next, following the narrow peninsula to the mainland, hitchhiking to town. He'd have to change his name. This one was ruined. He imagined what he would do. Something simple, like a grocery store cashier. Nothing involving thinking or worry. Or Alice. The vision was both sad and appealing.

On his way back to the house, the moon caught his eye, pale in the western sky. He shouldn't be mad at her for this. She hadn't asked to be bitten, nor could she resist the moon's monthly call. The doctors couldn't do anything, of course; without the werewolf detail, hers was a nonspecific malady. Any sane doctor would tell Alice her "illness" was all in her head.

Eugene did a last scan of the ground with his flashlight, finding nothing amiss, and shuffled back toward the driveway. His anxiety would shift now from dread of the inevitable to the fear of being caught. He turned his eyes to the fading stars. Before Alice got sick, he'd never prayed, but in the past few years, he'd made it a regular habit. Who else was he going to talk to?

"Please, Lord, cure my wife," he begged while standing near the mailbox. "And if you can't, help us endure another month. And prepare me for the next full moon."

Halfway down the driveway, Eugene heard rustling inside the garage. In his exhaustion, he'd left the damn thing open, no doubt letting in opportunistic raccoons. After two more steps, he saw a figure emerging from the garage's depths.

For a horrifying second, Eugene thought it was Alice, revived early from her slumber, transformed again, and willing to end Eugene's suffering. The figure was tall and broad-shouldered, so he could be forgiven for thinking so.

This was worse.

It was a young man who stood in the driveway, staring at Eugene in the predawn light with an unsettling and specific kind of terror in his vacant eyes. Blood stained the front of his clothes from chest to knees and splattered his young cheeks.

Alice had consumed her dinner in front of a witness. Eugene supposed it was inevitable; werewolves in the throes of hunger weren't the most careful types.

This witness held something in his left hand. He brought it closer to his body, enlisting his right arm to drape around it protectively.

Eugene's heart twisted in his chest.

It was the bulging garbage bag he'd just disposed of moments before.

He logged a couple of details about the young man's appearance— the rounded cheeks of youth, the strong shoulders and thick thighs of an athlete— and the man sprinted right, into the yard and toward the woods.

For a few seconds, Eugene watched his figure weave between the trees, garbage bag swinging in his hand, but he didn't move. He hadn't decided whether to follow or to stay. He wasn't thinking at all. Maybe it was shock, or resignation, or bone-deep fatigue, setting in at the prospect of a conclusion to his misery.

The young man was gone now, to offer the garbage bag as evidence to someone, to tell a tale about the werewolf who ate his loved one and, eventually, point out the house and name the names.

Awakened by the brightening sun, birds began to sing. Eugene listened to them awhile, jealous of their simple lives. A shaft of light sliced across the house. He turned to the mailbox marking the end of the drive. *Mayhorns* emblazoned on the side announced his and Alice's pairing, and this, their home. Beyond, Kingthorpe Road veered off into shadow on its way down the peninsula to the mainland, and the promise of something else, if he could just find the guts to start walking.

A COAT OF MUD AND BONE
Akis Linardos

Marya shambled down Bugle Road of Dominica Island, the mud-caked face-shaped bones threaded on her overcoat *clack-clack-clacking* like marimba. She licked her gums, spreading the sweet flavor of human blood congealed between her teeth.

One, two, three blocks and now she was knocking on the mahogany door of a manor, nearly as tall as her cavern in the Caribbean. Only, the walls were not granite dripping with wonderful humidity. These were sterile marble.

The door creaked open, releasing the clamor of jubilant humans, and out came a reed-thin, wrinkled old man in a waistcoat and black trousers, reeking of expensive cologne. Shriveled like a raisin he was, and with a sullen look, like life was too much to bear for him. It made Marya wonder if a human wife had sucked the life from him or, more likely, his wicked boss.

"Your name, girl?" the old man said.

Marya grinned, presenting her sanguine-tinged teeth. "Tia Marya."

The man's eyes widened for a moment, and then he was whipping away from the door, showing Marya his back. She reached out, sprouted a long nail from her fingertip and touched his spine. From the tip she withdrew a viscous, black thread—a man's shadow stretched so thin only her sharp eyes could see the mouth gaping in despair—and dipped it into a fistful of mud. The mud shuddered and thickened.

Crunch, scrunch, crack.

Part of the mud's core turned to bone, the pale whiteness bulging from the wet dirt and slowly forming the shape of a wrinkled face. It pulsed with the vigor of a beating heart a weathered man such as him could never have had in life.

The man fell lifelessly to the floor, and the muddy bone was still.

Marya was born of a mermaid called Selenia and the seed of a man whose name remained unknown. This one her mother did not drown, but not because she did not try.

"As I pulled him under," Selenia had told Marya, "the full moon peeked from the clouds to shed silver light through the water's surface. When it touched the man, he cast a shadow so vast it covered the reef entirely."

"His human skin discarded like a shrimp shedding its shell and out came muscles and fur of a wolf." Selenia had pointed to the white scar along her fishtail. "He left me with that gift as he thrashed away from my grasp. You have the beast's blood in you, and that's why you can never join our true home in the depths."

That had hurt Marya then. She'd spent days gazing over the shoreline as her merfolk eyes pierced the dark, witnessing the quivering shadows of her merfolk kin celebrating their underwater life in lands far below. It pained her for a long time, until her heart grew numb. Or maybe she got used to the sting of isolation. Maybe witnessing the shadows of drowning sailors on the water, suffering as their lungs imploded, made awfulness seem a perfunctory matter of existing.

Her mother raised Marya in a cavern inside a lake that connected to the sea. Since Marya had no fins nor fish tail, her mother brought her fatty salmon to dig her teeth into, tasting the sea salt in the flesh and sticky innards.

"The sailor numbers have thinned," Selenia told Marya one night. "But the Goddess of the Deep hungers for drowned lungs. The men have taken to living in large buildings on the land. It's up to creatures like you, dear daughter, to bring these men from land to shore. Lure them with your charm once you come of age."

When that time came, she went into the human town as her mother had instructed, after handing her pilfered human clothing laced to reveal her shoulders but no cleavage. Cheeks puffed-up with star-shining salt to make her glimmer, seashells beneath the dress to clatter and draw attention. Pretty, innocent and seemingly powerless — as their human targets like them.

Most of the town was ramshackle save for the manor, whose towers shone like lighthouses. So bright was the contrast with the town, Marya wondered if the manor itself was sucking the lifeforce out of all the other buildings, feeding itself on their groaning foundations, corroded windows, fallen lanterns and cracked glass.

At the tavern, she sipped human ale for the first time, cool foam on her lips, vile alcohol burning her throat. In the unashamed stares of the drunken crowd that laughed and licked their own teeth hungrily, she felt tiny and exposed.

An older man approached her first. Brown, balding hair, a pig-like nose, and a potbelly bulging from a coat too clean to fit in this haven of debauchery. Other men averted their gaze like creatures giving up on prey because a beast they can't out-fight set its eyes on it. He pressed against her, sweaty skin touching her shoulder. He offered to buy the most expensive wine of this place, his mouth so close she could feel the warmth and the waft of expensive cigars from his breath. For a moment, she wondered if there was fire boiling in the back of his throat, like a dragon ready to char juicy meat before devouring.

She let the man talk of himself while he asks nothing about her. It's as her mother instructed it would go. Marya sipped the wine and spat it in secret, pretending to fix a shoe that wouldn't quite fit. As the night marched on and the man's intoxication increased, his searching hand reached her thigh and disgust mingled with the grape aftertaste, causing bile to rise on the back of her throat.

But her mother taught her how to twist words with men to have her way, and before his advances could reach further, Marya stood and twisted her mouth in a lopsided smirk proposing a quieter place for them to be alone: a cavern some leagues by the shore. His brief hesitation gave way to lecherous excitement as soon as she promised dirty things to him.

She led the man into the forest, keeping longer than arm's distance from him, exhibiting her legs in dancing grace to keep him sated as she repeated parts of whatever uttering or boast he made, to keep him talking and distracted by carnal desire: *"You made her come three times?"* and *"You have a hundred men in your employment?"* and *"You killed a mermaid on your own?"*

That last one shocked her for a moment, then admonished herself for believing it even briefly. Her mermaid mother would have a man as easily manipulated as this one at the palm of her hand.

But the more they approached the shore, something kicked inside her. This all felt wrong.

The man's stench. The way he looked at her. The way her mother looked at her skull collection, plucked from the men she drowned. The powerful looking at living creatures as if they were things to be possessed. Marya was growing sick of them all.

What if the man harmed her like her mother did those men? What if the goddess could not protect her or didn't care? She was a goddess Marya did not really believe in, after all.

A goddess of a place beneath a sea Marya did not belong to. Worshipped by a mother that would suffocate strangers over showing love to her own daughter.

If the Goddess of the Deep was real, why give Marya legs and not a fishtail? Why confine her in a cave until now?

Why did the song of the trees feel so much more alluring than the sea?

They reached a hill at the forest's end, overlooking the sea. Her own thoughts had kept her quiet and the man was now impatient. Her back turned to him, she could hear his staggered footsteps, could feel his smell of excess and self-importance leaning closer. Before his arm could reach her, she crouched abruptly and pounced away on all fours.

The man looked aghast for a moment. Glowering, he ambled toward her with lustful eyes. Slow, self-assured steps. Her throat clenched at his air of certainty. The man had said he could buy anything he pleased, and that included living things to serve him. The way he looked at her, the way he moved. He was denying her the option of refusing him.

With every step he took toward her, her heart beat thrice against her chest.

Shock him. Show him what you are. And run. Run as fast as you can.

Marya shed her fake clothes, revealing the scales covering her belly. Before the man could scream in shock, she dashed past him, heading westward, knowing he could not easily run after her.

Marya kept running until her feet hurt, then ran farther, until they hurt no more from numbness. She ran through the forest, deep into the island, away from mothers, men, and drowning shadows.

Beside a lake, Marya found a crevice inside a tree. In that crevice she kept herself warm at nights, and during the day she leapt between branches of the trees, snatching squirrels with claws that sprouted from her fingertips. These are things Marya didn't know she could do before she came to the forest. The dry animal tang of the wilderness molded something in her that was not there before. Or maybe it was, but dormant. Maybe that's what comes from mermaid and werewolf. Maybe the proper place for a creature in limbo between land and sea is a lake like this.

One day, as Marya chased after a jackrabbit, something leapt and snatched the animal from her. Marya rushed, ready to pounce on whatever stole her prey, but froze.

It was a girl.

A girl with claws sprouting from her fingertips and muscled hips to bounce from the earth. The girl was beautiful, with hair the color of summer sunset, braided in the shape of a nest for eagles. With a mouthful of rabbit innards, the girl turned and looked at Marya, and for a long moment, they stayed frozen in the chill of the forest.

"Hi," Marya said eventually.

"Hi," replied the girl, wiping the blood from her lips.

Her name was Dalma, and she had also been raised inside a lake cave, on the other side of the island. She had also spent her childhood staring with dread at water shadows, seeing more than the surface, hearing the world she wasn't allowed to have.

Marya and Dalma hunted together, feasting on squirrels and skittering tarantulas whose chitinous legs crunched deliciously between their teeth. They'd share their food, their lips touching, tongues curling over one another, swapping crushed insect legs as delicious sweets.

One hot morning, a bear came to their burrow. The girls froze.

They crawled until their backs pressed against tree bark, gripping each other's hands. The beast sniffed and stood on two legs, looming giant-tall.

The girls ran.

They leapt over gnarled roots, branches whipping their faces. Until Dalma slipped with a yelp, and the bear was upon her, dragging heavy paws and claws across her skin.

Marya halted, twisted, and pushed herself off the earth and onto the bear. She coiled her hands around the beast's neck. She sank her teeth into its fur, struggling to penetrate the thick skin. The bear flailed thick claws; she clenched even harder.

No one would hurt Dalma.

No one would take away from her the one person that had tasted a loneliness of the same flavor and understood her like no one else.

Crack.

Her teeth sank into the flesh, and sweet beast blood trickled into Marya's mouth.

The bear was now slamming her back against tree trunks, rolling on the ground. But no matter how madly the bear thrashed, Marya held on. The instinct to protect Dalma had faded now. It was no longer what drove her to hold on so tightly, to bite even harder, to thrust her tongue deep into the gamy flesh and suck with all the power of her lips.

What drove her was the blood tasted so damn good.

Marya and Dalma laid in a bed of pungent bear entrails, beneath the canopy, the song of hummingbirds singing sweetly overhead, tasting the beast's blood from one another's fingertips.

"There's something," Dalma said. "Something Mama taught me to do. When men did not want to come with me."

"You mean showing more hip?"

Dalma shook her head. "Nay, not this kind of thing. Old magic. The hoodoo kind." Dalma produced a tiny mud-caked bone shaped in the face of a man. "Touch," she said.

Marya felt the crafted bone surface.

Vibrations. Warm pulsating walls.

This was not just a bone statue. It was thrumming, beating with the cadence of a thing alive. But there was no blood pumping within it, because there were no veins, and surely a heart couldn't fit in something so small. Could it? "What is it?"

"A soul trap. A living thing's soul is within the backbone, Mama taught me. In the fluid that runs across the spine, the spirit swims, be it a beast or man. It's where the shadows come from. Shadows different from lifeless things, visible from water deep up to the surface like the ones you and I had eyes to see and envy." She paused, bit her lip, then shrugged. "Anyway, it has plenty of uses. If you crush the statuette, it will ignite a howl from beyond death. Any kindred spirits in the proximity of the sound will writhe on the ground, foam at the mouth, and go mad if exposed too long. But it takes art to pull it out without fragmenting it."

Marya hugged her legs. She pictured drowned sailors the sea washed ashore after her mother drowned them, mouths bloated and filled with foam. She'd grown tired of such imagery. Tired of the world revolving around violence, and every beautiful thing hiding venom or thorns. "What use could such a thing have?"

Dalma placed a palm on Marya's knees, and rubbed down to the ankle, relieving some of the tension. "Weapons of magic can hurt, but also protect. And creatures like us—we need defenses."

Dalma's caress relaxed Marya. She was no longer beholden to the cruel whims of her mother. And Dalma was right.

The world was cruel.

"Teach me," Marya said.

Dalma got to her feet, leaping onto the tree and pouncing on a skittering squirrel. With the tip of her finger, she sprouted the tiniest claw and prickled the flailing rodent's spine, then pinched between thumb and index, and out she pulled a sticky thread like blackened spider spittle. She scooped mud from the riverbank and formed a mound. When she placed the thread on top, the mud swelled and wrapped around it. With *crunching* sounds a bone formed within and soon it had the squirrel's face.

Dalma pointed at a skittering rat beside their tree burrow. "Now you try."

Marya pounced and snatched the rat between her teeth, but when she tried to pinch out the soul, it thrashed like a fish washed ashore and then a fissure spawned on its flesh as if it was made of glass and it burned her skin. She let go and the rat faded to dust as it dropped to the ground.

Dalma shrugged. "Try again tomorrow?"

Marya nodded. "Mm-hm."

They tucked close into the burrow of their tree, keeping each other warm with the heat of their bodies. Marya was kissing Dalma's shoulder, brushing her lips against her soft skin, when they heard the gunshots.

Now they were on their feet again, skulking from bush to bush, sneaking toward the source of the air-ripping sound.

Marya witnessed men skulking through the forest with eerie familiarity.

Her forest. Dalma's forest.

Their forest.

How dared these men come into their home?

Her mind conjured images of the things Mother's horrific tales had described, of cages, of brothels. Of men that have too much wealth to understand there are things that don't belong to them.

What would these men do to them if they got caught?

Unlike the man from long ago, these men wore no expensive cologne and polished coats. They bore muskets and eyes thirsty for blood. Her mother had also warned Marya of the muskets, but the wind-shattering speed of their bullets was even greater than she'd expected. They pierced through wild beasts in such quickness and precision no claw or teeth could ever hope to match.

"Let's go somewhere else until they leave," Marya said.

But Dalma shook her head. "Don't be afraid of men no more. Look at their skinny legs. Look how they shiver at every rustle. We can take whole bears down."

Yes, but men can take bears down, too. From a safe distance. With greater speed. What if they take you away from me? What if they take both of us away and look at us with hungry eyes and treat us as possessions?

But she said nothing, because she was ashamed of admitting she was afraid.

Dalma watched the men from behind the bushes. The girls watched as the guns seared the air and felled the beasts, waiting with an unspoken agreement to suck the delicious blood of bears the men would leave behind. Because it was known that many men hunted for sport.

Then came the rustle of leaves from behind the girls.

Dalma screamed as a man hoisted her by the hair, flailing and naked. He stared at the scales that covered Dalma's ribs, snarling as if he was staring at a disease.

Before Marya could leap on the man, she was hoisted too, hopelessly sprouting claws and flailing for purchase on the man's skin.

"Boss," the man hoisting Marya said, reeking of sweat. "It's two of them. Leprous skunks got scales like fish, as you described."

An older man approached, and Marya recognized him as the man she spared two years ago. Bald now, and a thick handlebar mustache over his mouth. Whatever enmity and disgust his face held then had twisted into something far more sinister. He had the poison eyes of someone intending to do worse than murder.

He stopped a few feet away, cocked his head, and his face split into a toothy grin. "Little half-breed made herself a nest in the forest, eh?" He spat. "Cage them. They'll make fine exhibits."

Then Marya stopped flailing her hands and instead bounced her feet from the ground and coiled them around her captor. By the time she'd bitten off a mouthful of shoulder-flesh, a bullet was searing the air and piercing through her own shoulder.

Marya toppled over along with the man.

Then it was Dalma's turn to roar and leap and coil her legs around her captor.

Marya struggled to stand. The world had twisted to a green blur of hailing bullets and the burning metal pain on her left shoulder. Her foot bumped on something. Maybe a rock, maybe a gnarly root. She was too dazed to tell.

With a splash, she was inside the lake, watching the canopy fluttering as the stream carried her away.

Marya awoke to a prickling sensation like needles on her shoulder. Something was nibbling at her wound. A rat.

Her drenched body shivering at the touch of cold wind, she twisted and shoved the rat to the ground. The fist clenched, releasing the stored rage at the remembrance of the abductors. Tiny rodent bones *cracked* and warm blood trickled down her fingers as they dug through fur into rat flesh.

Then she was erect, pressing the squirming, squealing thing to the earth and pinching the cracked spine to remove what remained of its soul. In her mind, this was no rat, but a man with a bald head and a handlebar mustache. A viscous dark string glued to her fingertips, and she pulled it out of the rodent until the rat was still and lifeless.

She scooped mud into a mound, like Dalma had, but before she could place the soul-thread on it, the thread had scattered in the wind.

"Clumsy," a voice came from the rustling bushes, so low and baritone Marya imagined it was the forest itself that spoke to her. "The untethered soul cannot be imprisoned by shaky hands. Not by fury. Not by rage."

Then the creature was in front of her. Wolfskin covering its shoulders, wolf muzzle, fangs and yellow eyes. But below was the shape of a muscled man showing black skin between thick patches of gray fur. Across his chest was a belt strapped with threads of bone and dolls made of hay pierced through with needles. And in his hand, a rabbit, dead but clean of blood.

Her rage now cowered in his presence. It was not fear as it was with the other men, not exactly. It was the feeling of looking up at the stars for the first time. The feeling of the cold sea brushing her toes at midnight. She felt safe in his presence, but also, she felt small. Insignificant.

She tried to form words but her tongue knotted. She tried to snarl and crouch to seem threatening, but her muscles didn't dare. She tried retreating but her legs were paralyzed.

The pain in her shoulder registered now, where the bullet had pierced through before she landed on water. It seared her as if that iron nested inside it still, pulsating like a second heartbeat.

She grabbed the shoulder, pressing the wet wound and took a deep breath. In her mind's eye the vision of an ensnared Dalma kicked around by savage men focused her thoughts to purpose.

"What should I do?"

The wolf-man took another step and dropped the animal's carcass to her feet. "Eat."

She wanted to say: I can't *eat*. Not now. There are men that must die by my hand. Instead what came out was: "My friend is taken. I must hurry."

"Hurry makes blunder. Eat. Recover."

Half-heartedly, she grabbed the animal, wincing at wounds she was only now starting to register. Obediently, she wrapped lips around the fur and bit into the rabbit skin, throwing hesitant glances at the wolf-man. Daring herself to meet his gaze. Failing to look for more than seconds.

"Withhold your worry," he said. "Hairless men are possessive of their toys. They won't break her."

Marya swallowed, and as the man turned to vanish: "Please, teach me. Teach me how to take her back."

"I will return tomorrow."

"They'll make her suffer today."

"If you try to rescue her wounded and half-prepared, they'll make both you and her suffer to your end of days."

He vanished into the vegetation, and Marya was left alone, sinking teeth deep into the rabbit's flesh, thinking of the vein-bulging delicate human necks of Dalma's abductors.

Horrific visions seized her dreams that night, of men taking Dalma's body apart, sawing her limbs off on a table as Marya fought to reach her. But Marya was caught in a stream, and no matter how hard she swam, the current pushed her further away.

And when she landed, she was in that human tavern again, witnessing peddlers that raised stands by the bar to sell away Dalma's arms, her pelvis, her legs as rarities to exhibit, talking up her scales as precious ingredients for the finest jewelry. Suddenly, Marya was elsewhere, on a street strikingly different from any she had ever seen. It was purple, like velvet, and it undulated. It pumped like a vein, feeding into the manor that loomed over her.

A black structure whose walls pulsated like a heart, beating louder with each moment and every quaking rumble of rock under her feet. The railing of the gates wavered, and stopping them, she noticed the heads adorning its spikes. At first unrecognizable, shifting and blurry, but soon their faces took shape.

And they all looked like Dalma.

Marya awakened screaming, drenched in sweat, with the sunlight of summer's dawn striking her eyes. Her own heart beat like the nightmare manor with its stolen heads.

Throughout the day, Marya caught thirteen rats, trying her own hand at hoodoo. For all she knew, that wolf-man was full of lies, possessing no knowledge about untethering spirits from spines. Uncaring for the hunger pangs and her aggravated wounds, she continued hunting for tiny creatures by the river as the waters turned golden by the late afternoon sun. Marya placed each captured rodent on a slate she'd heaved off the riverbank that morning, a flat and stable surface upon which to practice. Now the slate was bloodied and crusted with charcoal remnants and ash of dissolved rodents from her many fumbled attempts.

One by one, she plunged her nails into the fragile spines, hoping this practice of rodent soul-snatching could work through perseverance. Hoping the same curse would imprison those men and unleash their maddening shrieks within that manor, paralyzing the men and uncaging Dalma. But Marya's ash mound only grew bigger, and as the moon appeared overhead, she lost all hope she'd make it. Each attempt was clumsier, rushed, a bigger failure than the previous one.

Then her will expired, and she released the final squirrel that writhed in her grasp. It skittered away, into a bush or maybe up a tree. She didn't notice which, because now she was busy rocking back and forth hugging herself, digging her nails into her muscles, welcoming the pain as punishment for her weakness. She should have protected her. She should have gutted that lecherous man years ago so he couldn't hurt or own anyone again.

From beyond the thicket, a rustle.

A prick of hope. Could it be the wolf-man returned to share his secrets of manhunting? But no. Those eyes and snout were on her level, a predator prowling low. A wolf growling and eyeing her not with curiosity but calculating hunger.

She crouched, wincing as pain branched from shoulder to chest—the wound aggravated by her reckless rat chase.

Slowly, she stepped sideways, crab-like. Nearby, she'd seen the river cascade downward. A waterfall that perhaps was noisy enough to frighten simple animals.

Marya leapt for the nearest branch as the wolf pounced. She swung from tree to tree, but her shoulder flared, the scab cracking and the muscle pain stretching on every leap.

Rushing water. Three more swings, and she was floating over the spray of the cascade. Through the darkness, she crashed belly-first on a thick branch, then landed on her rear atop a boulder.

By the waterfall, an alcove: like a shrine, statuettes of bone encircled a small stone tower. *Mermaid* statuettes.

The wolf reached the edge and didn't hesitate to leap over. Marya staggered to her feet, and backed against the wall as the beast bounded past and spun around. It was snarling now. Marya recognized the determination to feed. She knew the dread of a stomach that had been vacant too long. Not even a storm could stop a starving predator, much less some water.

If only she could reason with wolves. She could promise an endless supply of meat once she'd take her vengeance. But now there was only one thing she could think of. As the wolf closed in, she hurled one of the mermaid statuettes against the boulder, shattering it.

All at once, voices of shadows from the depths assaulted her, rattling her skull and discarding any thought of the fangs she was dreading a moment ago. Her surroundings obscured by a tenebrous mist with pockets of vision. She could not tell if the wolf had fled.

Wet viscous fluid escaped her ears as her mind flooded with whispers that conjured vivid thoughts of a world before and after the corporeal realm. Deeper than the abyss. Lonelier than a hybrid's life. Stripped of starlight.

There was clapping, then silence, and finally, a hand reaching out and pulling her from a black sea she did not realize she had sunk into.

The wolf-man pulled her up by the elbow and hoisted her to the waterfall.

"Stare at the water," he said. "Focus. Remember you are alive."

The spray cooled her face. Breath came fast. Her heart beat so violently she thought it would rip a hole through her chest.

Slowly, a wave of relief enveloped her. The certainty that she was in her own body, touching ground, feeling the liquid of life upon her skin.

The memory of what she saw faded, but the sinking dread remained, leaving her a little more haunted.

Marya turned. The wolf-man had released his grip, and was now sitting cross-legged by the shrine, displacing the statuettes. It only dawned on her now that this was his shrine. These were *his* statuettes.

"You," she said. *You have caged mermaid souls.* She did not make the accusation. "What are these? Is this shrine yours?"

"No shrine. A grave. The ones who try to drown, may drown themselves when they least expect it. Hybrids find no love from either race. We must learn to fend for ourselves."

This felt wrong. But even if it was wrong, it didn't diminish its necessity. "Teach me."

He stood. "By earth and water, the flesh and bone is made." He approached her, lay a claw softly on her back, and pinched the top of her spine. "By flesh and bone, the soul's imprisoned."

Her lungs emptied, and for a moment she panicked, aware of the absence of air within her. Aware that her own heart had stopped beating.

"This is what it takes," he said. "To remove a soul, your chest must not pummel with breath and beating heart. Be steady, as if your own soul has been removed."

Marya's spine hunched. It seemed she was hanging by a thread, hoisted to the skies puppet-like. "Please," she mumbled.

The wolf-man pushed the claw back into her spine and fresh breath returned to her. Her heart pounded like a beast within a cage.

"Steady claw. Steadfast heart." He sniffed once, twice. Then shoved his hand into the earth and plucked a chipmunk from within. He proffered it to her. "Determined will."

Marya took the burrowing rodent, sat beside the dirt mound, and sprouted a tiny claw from her finger, prickling the spine with steady movements, fury both raging and tamed inside her like a beast thrashing within a cage.

The thread squeezed out of the chipmunk spine, and now she realized it was chipmunk-shaped, too, the shadow of the thing stretched to thinness. With movements as slow as the ocean waves, she placed it over the mound. The mud glued together around the thread, then formed the bone that had its face.

Her fingers rubbed the surfaces, feeling the light beat of a feeble beast's heart on the mud bits clinging to the bone.

Ba-bump. Ba-bump. Ba-bump.

The wolf-man walked away into the forest. Sharing another two words with her before he vanished into the trees.

"Grow strong."

Now she was alone, in a wooden silence broken only by the disjointed song of nightingales. The trance of his presence dispelled, it only now occurred to her that maybe this man had been the same as the one that scarred her own mother many years ago.

She clenched her fist, unleashing part of the caged fury, and crushed the chipmunk bone. Rodent shadow evaporated from it, and a weak squeal as far as rodent lungs could muster escaped its fledgling soul. With a series of small thuds, the squirrels skittering on the trees around her fell from their branches.

Marya leaned over one of the rodents. It convulsed on the ground, foam spilling from its mouth.

The scream of a being already dead is a terrible thing. Maybe the death throes of a soul are too much for living things to bear. Maybe the soul death throes of one's own kin are more terrible still.

Maybe there were things in this life more important than her fear of men.

A plan to rescue Dalma half-shaped in her mind, Marya ran across the forest, leaping over the curving roots, dodging the crooked branches. She knew the manor of the man she'd lured away long ago. She knew how heavily guarded it was then and that she'd need a way to stun the rich man's guards.

The town was an hour away.

And there were many souls to gather.

The mud-caked bones of her coat *clack-clack-clacked* across the corridors of the manor, into the parlor of befuddled humans with bloated bellies and red faces. On the long table beneath a golden chandelier, Dalma thrashed against the silver bars of her cage. Grime covered her face and her hair was fuzzy, as if she were the child of a bear and not a mermaid. When her eyes met Marya's, Dalma stopped thrashing, and an uneasy grin spread on her face.

The drunk, chuckling men seemed not to notice.

Not until Marya approached one of them from behind, laid a hand on his shoulder, and clamped onto his carotid.

Her teeth, designed to tear flesh from bears, punctured through the muscle like soft clam flesh, and the man flailed and clasped the back of her neck with both hands in a desperate embrace. The others were on their feet, chairs toppling over, pushing themselves away from the table as if the gravied steaks they'd been served would come alive and bite them.

Marya tore a mouthful of neck flesh, chewed its gamey rawness and spat it out as the man bled on the carpeted floor, hands hopelessly squeezing his mangled neck. Her eyes were fixed on the one with the handlebar mustache, who was once friendly, once enemy, and now a fearful animal pressed against a corner. He called out to his guards and soon men with muskets swarmed the room, shot without warning, and Marya covered her face with arms curtained in bone-faces. The bones shattered, releasing dark ghosts that shrieked, shrill and banshee-like until the room was covered in such resounding screams it made the humans drop and clutch their ears.

Everyone but her and Dalma.

Maybe because they were of another kin. Or maybe because the ears of the sea were used to the death throes of drowning men.

Now Marya loomed over the mustache man, stooping level with his face, allowing the fresh blood of his friend to drip from her lips as it mingled with her own saliva. "Key," she demanded, pointing to the cage holding Dalma.

As his ears began to bleed, the man's tremulous hand fumbled in his pockets and produced a rattling keychain

Marya snatched it and rushed to her beloved. She unlocked and yanked the cage-door open and kissed Dalma deep into her mouth, letting her taste the warm human blood of her captors.

Their mouths parted and Dalma said, "I was so afraid."

"Me too," Marya said. "But not afraid of *them*. Not anymore. I was afraid I'd never see you again."

Dalma caressed the shards of Marya's coat. "You did it."

"I had help. There was a man—half-man, half-beast. The rage within me. The desperation of not having you with me. It made it all effortless."

They kissed again, and parted again.

Then Marya turned to the men bleeding from their ears and shaking on the floor, throwing fearful glimpses at them. The gaze of all of them had shifted. It was the glazed gaze of ghosts. "You know what I think, Dalma?"

"What?"

Marya rubbed her lips, tongued her thumb, and took a few slow steps toward the coward with the mustache, Dalma close on her heels. "I think that perhaps we should pay our mermaid mothers the visit long deferred. And bear an appropriate present with us."

"I quite like that idea."

The man whimpered, crawling away from them. His poison eyes were now ghostly pale. "Please. Make it stop. Make the screaming stop."

"I wonder if his shadow will shiver for long, in the canvas of the sea."

Now both of them were on him, hosting him up from shoulders, dragging him out the manor kicking and screaming as his pants soaked with his own urine and the blood staining the carpeted floor.

ENTRY OF THE GLADIATORS
Hannah Rebekah Graves

"PRETTY SURE THIS place is off-limits after dark," Michelle calls to the group.

She's more than pretty sure. She's positive. The sign in the parking lot said as much. No loitering, no drinking, park closes at sun-down. Not that it's much of a park. More like a vast, empty field cut off abruptly by thick forest, and plopped right in the middle is a tiny playground set that's seen better days. Some rusted monkey bars, a lopsided merry-go-round, a pair of swings—although one of them is just a set of dangling chains at this point with no sign of its missing seat—and an old wooden climbing house, the kind with a metal slide that's given third-degree burns to many a child's butt and thighs in the blistering summers.

Abigail glances back from where she's latched on to the arm of her boyfriend, Tommy. She grins. They take a seat on the lone picnic table near the playground, hip to hip, never far from one another's side.

"Did you leave your sense of adventure at home again?" Abigail asks.

Michelle meanders up alongside the table, gaze roaming the playground and beyond, scrutinizing the dense woods that swallow any ounce of light offered by the full moon or the couple of dim streetlamps dotting the paved trail from the parking lot. She's not sure if it's the darkness among the trees or the vast stretch of tall grass swaying in the gentle breeze that makes her more uncomfortable.

"I'm just saying, I really don't wanna get murdered."

Daniel has already cleared the playground and hauled himself up into the climbing house by the monkey bars. Tommy and Abigail have tried for three months to set him and Michelle up, and nice as he might be, Michelle has dug her heels in. She's not interested in getting into a relationship that's likely to fizzle out the second they go to colleges in different states in the fall. Still, Daniel's cute, and he does have one of those smiles that catch her attention when he turns it on her. And…well, aside from the weird Amazon delivery guy who keeps trying to ask her out, it isn't like she has a line of suitors vying for her attention.

"We're fine," Abigail continues. "Look, we can see the parking lot from here. Pretty sure I can see the signs from the deli, too."

Michelle steals a look over her shoulder. Really, there are plenty of lights in the distance of businesses open late on Fifth and Main. She can't tell one sign from the next. They're all just a blur of illumination. And their proximity doesn't make her feel better.

"Uh-huh. Five people murdered in the last two years and dumped in these fields makes me feel *so* safe."

"Five in two years isn't *that* big of a number," Tommy says, watching his friend climb about the playground and seeming to consider whether he wants to join him. "I'll bet some of them were drug deals gone bad. They've busted so many exchanges here over the years, it's ridiculous."

"The victims also came alone," Abigail tacks on. "I think a group is probably too much of a hassle to murder, whether for drugs or anything else. We should probably be more worried about the place being haunted."

Silence falls over the group, interrupted finally by Tommy snickering. Abigail elbows him. "What? It could be! We should've brought a Ouija board."

Maybe they can poke fun at subjects like that, but the thought of hanging around a place where multiple people have died—much less trying to communicate with them—sends a shiver straight up Michelle's spine.

"Cold?" Daniel asks, having abandoned the monkey bars to join them at the table. He looks ready to offer his jacket, but Michelle quickly shakes her head.

At everyone's grumbling or silence over the Ouija board idea, Abigail sighs. "Y'all have no sense of wonderment or adventure."

"Believing in ghosts doesn't have much to do with wonderment or adventure." Daniel slides down onto the bench beside Michelle. "Though I guess it *is* pretty weird that all the murders happened on a full moon like tonight."

"What? Really?" Michelle's gaze jumps from Daniel to Tommy to Abigail and back again. Was this planned? They all know how freaked out she is by the supernatural, that she'd never have agreed to come if she'd known this had anything to do with it. Did they think it'd be funny? It wouldn't be the first time Tommy and Abigail pulled something like this just for a laugh. "You're making shit up."

"He's not," Tommy says. "That last murder a few months ago? Full moon. I've been keeping up on it. Some people are saying it's a serial killer, calling him the Lunar Ripper."

Even Michelle has to snort at that. "What a stupid name."

"Moon Murderer?" Daniel says.

"Just as bad," says Abigail.

"Nighttime Stalker?"

"No, Daniel, that's been used." Tommy again. "Loony Killer? Lunar Shredder? Moonlight Massacrer?"

A pause, and then Abigail: "What if... And hear me out... What if it's a werewolf?"

The boys let out simultaneous barking laughs.

"Hey, *hey*. Full moon, bodies found ripped to shreds and half-eaten. No DNA left behind. It's not that far-fetched."

Tommy rolls his eyes and hugs Abigail to his side. "Are you assuming the killer's species? What if it's a werecat?"

"Weregeese," Daniel says. "The Canadian ones. Those things are fucking vicious."

"Okay, okay. It's silly, I get it." Abigail laughs.

Their laughter does nothing to put Michelle's frazzled nerves at ease. It's stupid. She *knows* it's stupid. That this place could be haunted should *not* terrify her more than the idea they could potentially encounter a very real threat of a killer. Michelle huddles, hugging herself, trying to keep her focus on her friends and not let her gaze stray to the dark line of trees in the distance.

They've moved on from talk of murderers and shapeshifters to college. Tommy and Abigail are staying here in town, working part-time while Abigail takes classes and Tommy looks into vocational training. Daniel's got a full ride at a university two states over, thanks to his flawless GPA. Michelle, meanwhile, is bound for California with a few grants and an impressive art portfolio. Thinking about it leaves her with a tingling sensation of nervousness and excitement. She's hardly been away from home for more than a few nights, especially out of state. The entire atmosphere of her new campus, of dorm life, of society in the Bay Area—

"What was that?" Abigail asks.

They all pause to listen. Michelle tips her head, but the only sounds that reach her ears are the droning noises of crickets and frogs.

Tommy finally starts to say, "I don't hear—"

He's cut off abruptly by a very faint *honk*.

"Was that a car?" Daniel asks quietly.

Tommy snorts. "Did that sound like a car horn to you? That was like…"

"Like a toy," Michelle finishes. "Like…a bike horn or something."

Silence, save for the shift of fabric as they each turn this way and that, scanning the park for any signs of someone fucking around. It's all empty, open space up until the trees start. Nowhere for someone to easily hide. Finally, Daniel gives a nervous chuckle that starts to dissolve the unease. Clearly, they were hearing things.

"See," Tommy says, "nothing to be—"

Honka-honka.

The streetlamps flicker. All of them. In unison.

Michelle lurches to her feet. "Nope, nuh-uh, fuck this. I'm going home."

Abigail grabs her coat sleeve with a whimper.

"Okay, chill out." Tommy holds up his hands. "We don't need to go overreacting. Nothing in this park is well-maintained."

Logically, that makes sense. Logically, statistically even, there's no reason the four of them aren't safe out here. They're together, they're in a wide open space, they're not *that* far from civilization. Michelle's gaze drops to Abigail, who no longer looks like she's having fun but whose eyes implore Michelle not to leave her there.

Not like she can leave on her own, anyway. It'd involve walking by herself, and they brought Tommy's car. She'd get as far as the parking lot before she'd be stuck.

"Whatever. Let's just—"

The lights flicker once more.

Then they go dark.

Abigail shrieks, yanking Michelle's sleeve so hard she's forced to sit back down or else fall over. Within seconds, four cellphone flashlights cut through the darkness, illuminating their wide-eyed faces.

"Fine," Tommy croaks, "we'll call it an early—"

Honka-honka.

Michelle whips around, casting her light toward the woods. "What the *fuck* was that?"

The others follow suit. Even all four lights combined do a poor job of piercing the night, but as the clouds roll through the sky to let the full moon shine through, they can finally see the source of the sound.

Coming out of the woods is a clown…riding a tiny bicycle.

Everyone, Michelle included, is too startled to move.

"What the fuck…?" Abigail whispers.

Daniel slowly gets to his feet, circling around the table as the little bike crunches down the unkempt gravel path toward them. "Dude, what're you doing out in the woods like a creep?"

Honka-honka.

As the clown draws closer, Michelle can make out vague details. White skin, an exaggerated mouth painted in black and red, the stereotypical polka-dotted jumpsuit and wild hair topped off with a cone-shaped hat, black with little red pom-poms.

"Time to go," Michelle says as she stands. Abigail and Tommy get up, but Tommy's gaze stays fixed on the approaching clown, ignoring Abigail as she yanks at his arm.

"She's right, Tommy. Screw this. I don't care why there's a weirdo cosplaying in the woods; I wanna go home."

"Hold on a minute." Tommy shakes her off, stepping up alongside Daniel. Whether it's curiosity or machismo and the need to show off that makes them disregard common sense, Michelle doesn't know. Either way, it's sheer stupidity. "Hey, man! You're freaking some of us out. We're not really in the mood for whatever this is."

The comically small bike draws to a stop before them. As they readjust the angle of their flashlights, the cheery birthday party glamor of the clown disappears.

The white grease paint is weathered at the edges, white goop giving way to mottled gray flesh. The red outlining its black lips looks less like makeup and more like glops of congealed blood, clinging to the thick stitches that hold its mouth shut. Grinning, it stares at them—or at least, it would if there weren't large, black chasms where its eyes ought to be.

"I'm—I'm sorry." Michelle staggers back a step. Abigail goes with her, linking their arms together while she chokes on a sound of horrified confusion. "Our friends are just being assholes. We'll get out of your way."

The clown pulls forward a full rotation of the small tires and cocks its head.

Tommy bristles, squaring his shoulders as though trying to make himself look bigger. "Back off, man. Any closer and I'm beating your ass."

For several long seconds, no one moves.

Then the clown leaps off the bike, performing a forward flip to land before them. Its obscenely large shoes squeak when they hit the ground.

Daniel grasps Tommy's shoulder to yank him back—"Not worth it, let's go."—but Tommy shrugs him off and stalks forward with a sneer. He's afraid and Michelle knows it, they all know it, but when Tommy's fight-or-flight is triggered, it *never* turns to flight.

"Alright, asshole," he starts to say.

He puts his back to his friends as he faces the clown, ready for a fight, but his words swiftly devolve into a shrill scream as the clown makes some kind of movement Michelle can't make out. Tommy spins around, reaching for his face but not quite touching it, not with the way his right eye, along with the surrounding skin, is melting into a stream of flesh and fluid down his face. Daniel lurches for his friend, grabbing his shoulders, trying to understand what just happened.

Michelle can't look at that mess of his face, though. She stares at the clown instead. Notes its long, gnarled fingers around a large fake flower attached to the front of its jumper. It squeezes the flower, which emits a spray of what she would've assumed was water, except when it hits Tommy's retreating back, he howls again in pain and stumbles forward into Daniel's arms.

What the hell…

Daniel keeps hold of his friend to keep him from slumping to the ground. Before he can back them away, the clown crams a hand into its pocket, emerging a moment later with a small, black gun. Daniel freezes, clutching a whimpering Tommy. Abigail clings to Michelle, choking on a scream, and instinctively Michelle pushes her friend behind her despite her own heart jack-hammering in her chest.

"We don't want any more trouble," Daniel blurts. "I'm sorry. We're all sorry. There's no reason for us to tell anyone what happened here tonight, so—"

Gunfire pierces the air, stealing the breath from them all.

Abigail has her face pressed into Michelle's back, trembling.

Michelle's voice wavers when she calls out, "Daniel…?"

From the barrel of the clown's gun juts out a yellow flag with the word *BANG!* written in big red letters. Daniel twists toward them, looking down at his chest, where he clearly expects there to be a fresh hole. But his shirt is completely unmarred. Even the clown tips his head and frowns, confused. Daniel lets out a single, sharp laugh triggered by fear and nerves, melding with another pained moan from Tommy.

Michelle sees the clown moving before they do. It almost seems to vanish before reappearing directly in front of the boys with its arm raised. She opens her mouth to scream, but it doesn't make it out before that arm comes down, smashing the butt of the gun into Daniel's temple. The first time, just hard enough to daze him.

The second time, hard enough to make him drop Tommy and stagger.

The third time—

The clown slams Daniel to the ground, beating what Michelle thought to be a toy gun into his face. His nose caves first. He yowls, a sound soon gurgling with blood. Tommy, half-blind and the skin still dripping down his face, makes a feeble attempt to throw himself onto the clown's back, trying to drag the thing off of his friend.

"Tommy," Abigail shrieks, "don't!"

The clown does pause in his task, but only long enough to reach back, grab Tommy by his shirt, and shove him off with such inhuman force that he hits the ground a foot in front of the girls. Abigail chokes on a nonsensical sob that is probably meant to be Tommy's name.

Michelle steps back, preparing to run. There's no helping Daniel. He's motionless in the grass, face a mushy pulp of nothing that remotely resembles a face. But Tommy's still kicking, and Abigail won't leave him behind.

"Help me!" Abigail screams at her, crouched by Tommy. Michelle startles, moving without thinking, rushing to his other side. They each grab an arm, helping a half-conscious Tommy to his feet. The stench of burning flesh and something acidic fills Michelle's nose so strong it makes her choke and gag and nearly lose her grip. Whatever he got sprayed with, it sure as hell wasn't water.

In those same moments, the clown has straightened up. It examines its gun before tucking it back into a pocket, then puts its bloodied hands on its hips and surveys the mess that is—was—Daniel, nodding in approval.

The moment Abigail screams at Michelle for help with Tommy, though, its head snaps up. It marches toward them with purpose, beginning to pull something from its sleeve.

There is no possible way they'll save themselves if they try to drag Tommy along. Michelle releases a remorseful moan…and she lets him go. Abigail sags under the added weight, unable to hold Tommy up on her own. Before she can shout after Michelle, the clown has stepped in front of her. From its sleeve, he's drawn out a string of brightly decorated handkerchiefs. Before she can register what's happening, the clown has those handkerchiefs wrapped around Abigail's neck, choking off any attempt she would have made to scream. She claws at the fabric, at the clown's hands, gasping for air.

Michelle has set a safe distance between herself and the bloodshed, but now she's frozen to the spot, too horrified to make her legs move.

Leaving the guys was one thing, but leaving Abigail? Her best friend? She inwardly shouts at her legs to *move*, to do *something*.

With a final burst of energy, no doubt spurred on by the realization that his girlfriend is in trouble, Tommy pitches himself between the two. Immediately, the clown releases the handkerchiefs, and Abigail is knocked to the ground, gasping in a lungful of air as the color slowly returns to her face.

The clown grabs Tommy's shoulders, shoving him to his knees. Tommy sways, too exhausted, too much in shock, to know what else to do but kneel there, as the creature draws a long pink balloon from his seemingly bottomless sleeves. It gives Tommy a scowl and a shake of its head, exaggerated by its running makeup and grim smile.

Then, with speed and precision that's almost impressive even given the circumstances, the clown twists and turns and squeaks the balloon into the shape of a dog. Proudly holds it up for them to see.

It grabs Tommy's lower jaw, wrenches it open, and crams the balloon into his mouth.

Not just his mouth, Michelle realizes. His *throat*.

Tommy weakly paws at the clown's hands, but its grip is ironclad as it wedges the balloon inch by squeaky inch into Tommy's esophagus, until the cracking of his jaw is loud enough for Michelle to hear. When released, Tommy tips to his side, clawing at his throat as he fights to breathe.

The clown has already returned its attention to Abigail, though. Tommy is old news.

Abigail has begun crawling her way toward a petrified Michelle, still dragging a tangle of handkerchiefs behind her. The clown takes three large steps in its comically large shoes. In an instant, it snatches the bright bits of fabric, shoves Abigail to the grass with a foot against her back, and pulls.

It's effortless. There is no real struggle, at least not from the clown.

Abigail is another story. Michelle can do nothing but stare at her best friend's face, her eyes bulging from their sockets, blood vessels beginning to burst from the sheer force around her slender neck.

Then she's still, staring off at nothing.

And Michelle is alone.

The clown claps its hands together, traipsing the few feet toward her with a smile. The stitches holding its mouth shut pull taut. Michelle finally manages to move, but only two steps before her jellied legs give and her ass hits the ground. It doesn't stop her from scrabbling back, leaving grooves in the damp earth, dirt shoving up under her nails.

The clown tips its head as though perplexed. It stops. Considers. Holds up a finger as though it has a splendid idea. It reaches into a pocket and yanks something else out.

Michelle tries to cry out. It catches in her throat as the clown presents her with…

Flowers.

A bouquet.

It holds them out in front of her face. Michelle only stares, too shocked to understand, still waiting for what comes next. A spurt of acid. An explosion. Something. But when she doesn't respond, the clown frowns. It tosses the flowers aside, stitched mouth pulling down at the corners. It bows forward, hands to its face, covering the black pits of its eye holes as though crying.

It rebounds quickly, however. This time, it removes a bright red horn from a pocket. Squeezes it.

Honka-honka.

It balances on one foot, then the other, hopping back and forth in some grotesque idea of a dance while honking out a merry little tune.

As though it's…putting on some show for her.

Too terrified to take her eyes off of it, Michelle reaches for her voice. It comes out little more than a pitiful whine. "Just leave me alone. Please. I don't want to die. I won't tell anyone, I swear to god…"

Her would-be suitor seems to realize it won't get any other response from her, because it chucks the horn aside and again mimics crying, throwing its head back in despair.

Finally getting hit with a burst of adrenaline, Michelle pitches herself to her feet and *runs*.

She makes it six feet before the creature somersaults past her and rights itself in her path, forcing her to an abrupt halt.

It's inches from her face. Every detail seems cranked up to high definition from her fear. This close, she can see the redness around each hole in its mouth, the saliva dribbling from its lower lip. What she'd assumed to be grease paint looks more like dried blood now. Its breathing has a wet, wheezing undercurrent to it, carrying the stench of something sickeningly sweet. Something rotten. Something *old*.

It starts to open its mouth.

"Please—"

The first stitch pops. Followed by the second. And the third. Each crusty thread snaps as its jaw opens wide, until all Michelle can see are rows and rows of yellow, sharp teeth. Endless. And somewhere in the infinite chasm of its mouth, she can hear it:

Honka-honka.

It's quite the feast. The balloon boy is gamey and stringy, but his friend and the women taste plump and divine. It sinks its teeth into arms and legs and abdomens, tears out intestines and slurps them down like spaghetti.

It saves Michelle's heart for last.

All too soon, the morning is looming. The clown must relinquish the rest of its feast, collect its things, and leave. Back onto the bicycle with one last honk before riding away into the woods.

The sun has begun to rise. With it, the clown feels bits of itself slipping away. Its nose shrivels and rots off, nothing more than ash before it touches the ground. The huge shoes fall apart at the seams. Hair comes out in big, greasy clumps with scalp still attached, leaving behind short-cropped brown hair.

By the time he reaches his destination, he's just a man, naked and cold and disoriented. He stares blearily ahead at his truck—an Amazon delivery truck, currently decked out in battery-operated twinkle lights. He doesn't remember doing that. Of course, he doesn't remember doing a lot of things.

But he remembers enough.

He crawls into the back of the truck, clumsily pulling on his uniform before collapsing behind the steering wheel. Staring off at nothing as his brain tries to catch up with his body. It's always such a slow process.

But reality dawns, as it always does.

"Not again…"

He bows his head, sobbing into his hands.

So much for asking Michelle out on a date.

A DAMNABLE LIFE
C. W. Stevenson

GERMANY: 1589

"Father," Herel began as he clutched a fistful of robes tighter to his body. The breeze had a maddening chill this day. "We cannot linger if we are to make it in time."

Father Konrad swished his hand without a care at the young priest's comments. He stared down from their place on the mountain path at the Rhine Valley below. From their vantage point, clear of any obstruction, a vast forest of spruce and pine trees populated the landscape. Despite the saddening gray of rain clouds blotting out the sun, the sight was enough to break the heart of any man.

Father Konrad made the sign of the cross and muttered a prayer to himself, likely something having to do with the Lord's generosity of providing them with such a picturesque path and his genius behind the world's design, as the young priest had witnessed him do several times. Their escort through the countryside, two men-at-arms of the Baron von dem Bongart, followed Father Konrad in making the sign of the cross. They'd done so since their journey had begun.

Young Father Herel shook his head. He found the hypocrisy infuriating. While in the view of Father Konrad, the two acted as saints, but away, they cursed and drank in abundance.

"Herel," Father Konrad called, his voice raspy with age. "Just look at it."

Herel dismounted from the pack mule and stood next to the old priest, letting out a deep sigh. He'd started running out of patience several leagues back. He'd no wish to spend time on the road longer than necessary. After all, time was of the essence. A man was to be executed.

Following the untimely death of Bedburg's priest to a summer fever, the task had fallen upon Father Konrad and himself to take confession of the Bedburg townsfolk and that of the man they had sentenced to die. A curious case, truth be told. Father Konrad hadn't the heart to tell Herel of the man's terrible crimes, but he'd overheard their escort whispering about it near the abbey's hearth the night they'd first arrived to fetch the priests. They'd mentioned Bedburg as a "cesspool of death" and quite possibly the very "entrance to hell".

"Neither sheep nor shepherd are safe. Not until he is *struck* down by His servant's hands."

Blasphemous talk, Father Konrad had determined.

If the man was indeed a murderer, as a Catholic, even he was entitled to a confession, something the man had apparently asked for. Baron von dem Bongart, Lord of Schloss Paffendorf, and the elders of Bedburg had permitted the killer his small ask—a decision that must have stemmed from their devotion to God, Father Herel had said. But, in accordance with the request, the elders had given orders to the escort to tell the priests to "Make haste so that this evil may be upended." They had not, thanks to Father Konrad's slow step and ever slowing mind.

"What man can say he has seen God when they have never seen sights such as these?"

"A question for the mystics, Father," Herel replied.

"Bah," Konrad said, waving another hand. "The question is answered here and now. God has presented Himself through the very magnificence of this land. Take heed, young man, the proof of His existence lies before us."

Herel nodded, unable to remind Father Konrad he'd repeated a variation of the same words at every stop. He glanced back at their escorts, bored by the look of it as they passed a small bottle any time they thought the priests weren't looking. Because of their unsavory task of escorting, Herel did both men a favor by shooting them a quick glance before Father Konrad could take notice. The old priest would not take kindly to drunkenness, especially so on a journey to do His work. Quickly, the men wiped their mouths and stowed the bottle beneath one of their cloaks.

Herel took hold of Konrad's frail shoulder. There was nothing left of the stocky man who'd taken him in from the streets of Cologne. Herel's parents—both drunks—had given into thievery, resulting in their executions and Herel's new life as an orphan. If it hadn't been for Father Konrad's tutelage, Herel might have followed his father and mother in short order.

He was grateful to Father Konrad, and grateful to be by his side here, doing God's work together. It was the first time he would be venturing from the abbey and the surrounding village. But no longer was he the boy Father Konrad had found, but a man, ordained by God, and he would see His work done.

"Come Father," urged Herel. Slowly, the old man turned, walking stick in hand, and led them down the dark path to Bedburg.

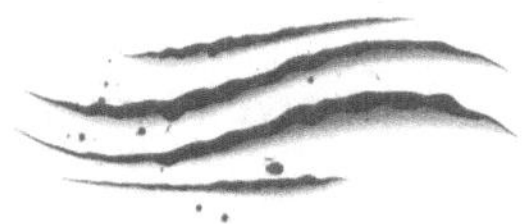

Outside the town, the trees thinned, giving way to bare fields. In the distance, an occasional man could be seen out near a herd of baying livestock, or smoke rising from a cottage, but aside from those few instances, life seemed nonexistent around Bedburg. The only folk on the road did not so much as make eye contact with Father Herel and the others as they crossed paths.

A strange land indeed. But then, it was wet, cold, and gray, and the last harvest was long past. Perhaps the folk had reason to remain indoors.

Off to the side of the road, a pyre lay smoking. Although no blackened corpse could be seen, Herel was sure it was not long gone.

Family members must've taken what remains were left for burial, Herel thought. *Or wolves.* Here, where lambs were aplenty, wolves would never be too far away. In front of the pyre, Herel took notice of a charred sign that'd fallen over. He couldn't make out the words.

"Poor wretch," Father Konrad remarked.

Their escorts remained silent, making the sign of the cross without mirroring Father Konrad. As the others walked onward, Herel peered down long enough to read what was written in blood on the charred sign.

Father Herel muttered the single word to himself, "Witch."

As evening came, their escorts brought them to an old farmhouse outside Bedburg. Behind the house, the adjoining fields lay barren save for grass and soil. Smoke rose from the chimney and the smell of meat cooking inside made Herel's stomach rumble. For their journey, Father Konrad had brought along only stale bread and some apples. His old age was truly beginning to show these past few months.

Father Herel's heart began to race. The farmhouse in the dark, the blackened pyre they'd encountered on the road, the looming presence of a murderer nearby—he was beginning to wish he was back in the abbey.

"Where is the accused?" asked Father Konrad.

An alderman approached from the open door to the farmhouse. Or perhaps he was a man of some local power as Herel compared his fine clothes to that of the retinue of villagers who had followed them past Bedburg. More than his clothes, the man's obese stature spoke volumes of his social place amongst the scrawny and malnourished villagers.

"Chained," he said. "In the back room. But I would speak against this, Father. There has…been a change of heart among the elders of Bedburg. This abomination deserves no confess—"

"That," interrupted Father Konrad, "is between God and the man."

Dipping his head in reverence and out of respect for the old priest's words, the fat man pointed at the door situated at the end of the hall.

As the two priests came closer, Herel noticed the door was some kind of metal. Surely this wasn't the community's makeshift cell? And a queer place to put one, away from the nearby towns, in an old farmhouse.

Then, an odd sound caught Herel's ears. Sniffling.

When he looked back, the alderman had tears in his eyes.

"*Our own neighbor*, Father. He is a most veritable devil. *Do not* believe his lies. The wolf cares for nothing but the taste of flesh in its jaws. Witchery, cannibalism, and incest, Father. This devil has been charged with all three."

"Incest?" asked Father Konrad.

"His own *daughter*," the man said, as if he were pleading. "The young witch is being held close by, in the town."

Herel gently patted the man's shoulders with an awkward tap and prayed over him. Then Herel asked, "What is your name?"

"Oswald, Father."

"Oswald," he began. "Your troubles are over, my good man. Any malevolence caused by your neighbor is in the past. We now must look towards forgiveness, even before he is punished for his crimes. It is our duty, as followers of Christ." Herel surmised Father Konrad could not have said it better himself, judging by the old man's grin. It felt good to make him proud.

From the way Oswald trembled and how the gooseflesh was protruding from his arms, it was apparent where Oswald's tears had truly come from... *Fear*.

"*Peter*." Oswald spoke the name like a dirty secret. "His crimes are beyond forgiveness. By this time tomorrow his body shall break, and it shall burn." Oswald stormed away then, leaving the priests outside the prisoner's door. The villagers made way for the nobleman as he went by.

Father Konrad broke the silence. "You go in," he whispered. "Get his confession and get out. These people might have burned him tonight were it not for our arrival."

Herel was taken aback. Before his days devoted to His work, Father Konrad had been a warrior. He'd even kept an old sword hanging from the back of his chamber door, serving as a daily reminder to no longer live by the sword, an oath he'd kept for half a century. He was the bravest man Herel had ever known. But he, Herel? Alone, with a murderer? Herel searched for a reason to convince the old man otherwise, but he could find none. He'd do his duty, as a loyal servant of God. He *would* find his courage.

Herel nodded. Looking back up at Father Konrad, he asked, "If what Oswald says is true, Father, why give confession to such a beast?"

Father Konrad was already near the door where the crowd awaited. "We deny no man's confession if he asks, Father Herel. A murderer he might be, but a creation of our Lord he remains."

"Where are you going?" Herel asked almost frantically, not yet ready to be abandoned.

"I must pray with this community. The word of God is sorely needed this night. I will put them on the path of righteousness once more." As if sensing his trepidation, Father Konrad added, "Do not fret, you heard yourself from the alderman that the man is in chains."

Herel said nothing, staring into the darkness toward the prisoner's cell, the metal of the bar glinting lightly from the soft tinge of torchlight. The fear of the unknown struck him hard, sending chills across his arms and down his spine. The knowledge that such evil could be lurking so close at hand, directly on the other side of that godforsaken door, it made Herel feel as though Satan himself could be there, waiting. Ashamed of his own faithlessness, finally, he met Father's Konrad's eyes.

"I…" he began to say, but he didn't have it in him to refuse the man. He *would* enter that room, he *would* give absolution to the killer, or demon, or whatever he may be. But for the life of him, he could not stop shaking.

Father Konrad frowned at the young priest. "My dear, dear Herel. Have faith, and all will be well. Look to the Lord for guidance, as there is nothing inside that room that can withstand His might."

"Yes, Father." Herel bowed, and the two men made the sign of the cross. Father Konrad walked away, towards the people, towards the light. Herel then turned and looked to his own dark path.

Do not falter. He is with me. God is with me. Protect me, please, protect me.

Unsure of what crazed soul he'd find beyond, Father Herel lifted the heavy steel bar. Then the door creaked open.

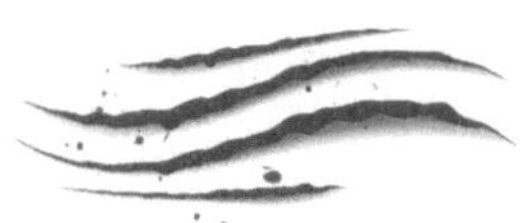

The room was dark, maintaining the appearance of a proper dungeon. It smelled of feces and rot. A rat scurried across the floor, bound for a hole in the wall. The prisoner sat in the darkest corner of the cell, where the rising moon had failed to touch through barred windows. In the room's silence, Herel felt uneasy. The only sound was that of his own heavy breathing. He fought to control it by reciting scripture in his head, but still, the fear of the unknown lingered.

Finally, after what seemed like an awkward amount of time without even the squeak of a rodent, the chains rattled. It was quiet, but just enough for Herel to determine the prisoner still lived. Approaching where the dark figure sat, dark smears of blood across the floor were present from the moonlight coming into the room. Herel stepped across the mess.

"*Father?*" came a whisper.

Herel stopped, taking notice of the link of the chain that hung down from the wall. After judging its length, he took a step backwards. Only the man's ankles were shackled.

A chuckle emitted from the shape in the corner and the chains rattled once again. "Another hour and I might smell of roasted pig."

"Apologies," said Herel. "Father Konrad is quite elderly, and as you can imagine, our journey took longer than expected."

"And where is this *Father Konrad*?"

Herel wiped beads of sweat from his brow and upper lip, drying his hand upon his robes.

"He is taking confession and blessing the townsfolk outside, and that of the nearby villagers who also have come to—"

"To see the death of the beast, no doubt," interrupted Peter, chuckling to himself once again.

A strange fellow this Peter surely was, to laugh as death knocked at his door. Herel had seen Father Konrad take confession of countless scoundrels, thieves, murderers, but he'd never witnessed the likes of this one before. With his back against the wall, Peter appeared totally at peace. He breathed calmly, his chest heaving in and out. Strange indeed.

"Would you stand for me, Peter? If you are able?"

Wearily, slowly, the accused pushed with his stub on the floor while his remaining hand clutched to what might be an injured leg. Father Herel shook his head at the cruelty of the townsfolk.

Leaning against the hard stone of the wall behind him, the killer stood upright in the darkness. "It's Mr. Stubbe. But you may call me by my Christian name, young priest."

"Indeed," said Herel. "I am Father Herel. Peter? A name of one of the apostles. If I may, Peter, do you consider yourself of my faith?"

"No. I am no Catholic."

"Ah, Protestant then. Well, be that as it may, Father Konrad has assured me you will be given confession, regardless."

Even in the gloom of the cell, Herel could see as the white of the man's eyes met his own, brows downcast, and a mouthful of teeth in preparation to snarl.

"I," he said sharply, "am no Protestant."

Herel swallowed bile that had reached the top of his throat. He fought down the urge to turn and leave. Every second alone with this man was uncomfortable, and ever more confusing.

"I do not understand." It was all he could muster.

Pushing himself from the wall, Peter limped forward a few steps, and stopped until he was standing in his own blood. Now, as he stood in the light of the moon, Herel took in the full view of the murderer. He was a stocky fellow with large, round shoulders. He definitely was not the monster Father Herel had imagined he would find behind that metal door. And he was bald, save for a few long strands of hair that fell chaotically around his head. If there was a troubling feature about this supposed killer, it was not his dark eyes, or the shadows that surrounded them, but his hand. His missing left hand.

"I don't believe in your God. I don't believe in the ramblings of old men. What I believe is more real than your fairy tales ever will be." Peter spat the words menacingly enough, but the poor state of this man had caught Father Herel completely off guard.

"Then why," he swallowed his growing fear, "why request confession?"

Peter looked out the barred window behind him. "The men and women out there do not care to hear of my innocence. I had priests sent forth so that I may be *heard*. Here, in Bedburg, they tend to burn those they do not wish to understand."

"Like the witch?"

"Yes," replied Peter. "She was a healer. A foreign woman with no husband, no children, and no God she worshiped, as far as I know."

"And you?"

"I worship nothing but the land I work. I own much of this land, my sweat and blood stand testament to that. There are aldermen here who would see my land be theirs. It is that simple. They will divide it amongst themselves and reap the fruits of my labor after my death."

"And what of your daughter?"

Peter glared at the priest. "What of her?" he asked, his tone laced with threats.

"You have made her your mistress." He stated it as a matter of fact, but to the priest's surprise, Peter did not deny it.

"And what law in *my* holy book did I break? I have none."

"There is but one *true* holy book, and you have broken its laws."

"*Your* holy book. If it is a crime to love, then I will face the consequences. Be it death? I would not agree the bodies of myself and that of my beloved should burn for a love so pure. As for the other crimes…they are lies, a conspiracy to rid me of my land. I am no *wolf.*"

"Then why do they convict you of such lies? Why are they so certain?"

"They put me on the rack!" Peter screamed, causing Herel to take a step back. "I told them whatever they wished to hear to stop the pain! Everything, untrue!"

Horrified, Herel made the sign of the cross. A confession by torture was no confession, Father Konrad had taught him as much. If this man was indeed innocent, then the townsfolk of Bedburg and the aldermen were the ones in need of a trial.

Taking a breath, Herel stepped back towards the door.

"I will consult with Father Konrad, and I will look to free your daughter, if I can." *Keep faith,* he wanted to say, but he remembered it would fall on deaf ears.

"I am innocent, priest!" Peter yelled after him. "Innocent! The true wolves of Bedburg are beyond that door!"

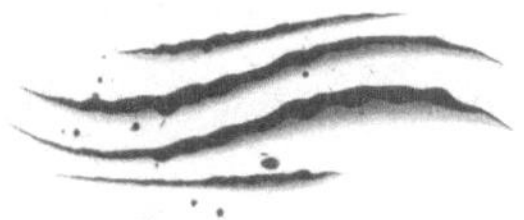

"We have come not to make judgment, Father Herel," Father Konrad said. Slowly, he dipped his fingers into a bowl of holy water and made the cross on a young woman's forehead. As water dripped from her brow, the old man blessed her.

"Do the laws of man take precedence over the laws of God?" Words from the book, and words Father Konrad was fond of saying.

"No. But, we are told to respect the laws of man. It is not our place here to play judge and jury over this man's crimes."

Herel nodded his head, disappointed he was powerless to persuade his greatest teacher.

Then Konrad tilted his chin upward with a frail hand. "Do not despair, Father Herel. This is no innocent man. For twenty years, these people have been plagued with the loss of their livestock in the night, found mutilated in their fields. Men, women, and children have gone missing, leaving nothing but a torn piece of bloody cloth to bury. When this man was caught, the nightmare ended. By his own tongue, he confessed to his dealings with the devil, who he said gave him power to turn from man to beast. He has willfully slept with a succubus who takes possession of his own daughter. He has torn babes from their mothers' wombs and picked out their small beating hearts. 'Dainty morsels,' he called them."

Unconvinced, Herel asked, "Was this all said while being stretched on the rack?"

"To my understanding, Mr. Stubbe refused to comply."

Unannounced, Oswald had come up behind the priests. "And now the beast will burn, along with that of the succubus," he said.

Oswald smiled wide at them both, a most unsettling smile, now that the truth had unraveled itself. A torn community, plagued by death, and most of all, by the lies of its elders, and with no one to stop the executions to come. Powerless, even with God on his side, Herel shed a tear for the innocent, then another for himself.

The girl, Peter's daughter and supposed mistress, would not see either priest. So not knowing what else to do, Father Herel prayed. He prayed all into the darkest hours of the night and into the next day. He visited the small church in Bedburg, where he prayed more. He prayed until dusk, only stopping at the flicker of several torches as they flashed outside the windows. The mob was on their way to witness the deaths of the wicked, or so they thought.

And so Herel followed them, praying for their souls as they walked.

A thick mist draped itself across the field where the townsfolk had gathered, somewhere close to Schloss Paffendorf, as Herel could see firelight through the trees surrounding the field emanating from the battlements and ramparts of the castle. Clouds covered the moon, but with the torchlight of the many villagers who'd come from miles around, there was not a blade of grass that could not be seen.

Herel searched for Father Konrad amongst the crowd, only finding him as his eyes caught Oswald helping the old man along. Oswald greeted Herel as he approached, giving him his twisted smile. Herel looked away, not bothering to acknowledge the man. Taking Father Konrad by the arm, the priests made their way to the front of the crowd.

A dozen yards in front of the assembled townsfolk, the executioner, fit with a black hood over his head and a long ax over his shoulder, walked in between two large cartwheels where several strands of rope also lay.

"If you haven't the heart to watch," said Father Konrad, "then look to the heavens."

Herel shook his head. "I must watch," he said, "or I fear for my own soul."

Father Herel knew *he* hadn't condemned the man, but had he done enough to convince anyone the prisoner might be worthy of life? That he just might be innocent of his crimes? Punishment for incest would be required, but did Peter Stubbe and his daughter deserve death?

Father Konrad looked disappointed at the young priest as they met each other's eyes, but to Herel, it was nothing compared to his own disappointment in the man who he'd believed to be the most righteous of God's servants in this land.

The crowd began to murmur, and the murmur turned to shouts as the two prisoners were brought forth. Men, women, and small children spat, kicked, and chucked stones at the accused as they passed.

"Murderer!" someone yelled.

"Bastards!" a toothless woman cackled. "Send them both to hell, the wolf *and* his bitch!"

Peter's daughter stared with bulbous eyes as they placed her gently atop the wheel, tying her ankles and hands in such a way so that she lay spread out. Then, the same was done to her father on the wheel beside her.

The executioner spoke no words as he approached the innocent girl. He flipped the ax head so that the blunt end stared down at her. Her eyes remained closed as the ax came down.

As the first bone cracked, the crowd roared their approval, and did from thereafter. With each strike of the ax, blunt metal met skin and bone, and the girl screamed in anguish for mercy. Peter yelled curses of revenge and death, but mostly he sobbed as he watched his daughter, his *lover*, be broken before his very eyes.

The sickening crunches were enough for bile to climb to the top of Herel's throat as his stomach began to churn. He looked around as the crowd raised their hands in triumph, their distorted faces gleaming with mad grins as they praised God, and Herel wondered for the first time with real concern if it was the same God *he* praised. *Is He not supposed to be merciful?* Herel put his hands to his lips as the bile came up, and he coughed as the sour wetness came through his lips.

After the executioner had broken her limbs, some of which took more than a single swing, he was handed a red-hot pincer.

"*We must stop this*," Herel muttered, but no one was listening.

After the clothes were torn away from her body, the young woman lay exposed upon the splintering wheel as she sobbed through the pain of her broken bones. The executioner began peeling flesh before she could utter another cry.

Herel stepped forward, raising his hands as he pleaded to the crowd, "Stop this! I beg of you! In God's name…*stop!*"

But his pleas were met with laughter as someone yanked him backwards. "Hold your tongue, priest!" It was Oswald, his eyes filled with hate. The bigger man held on tight to one of Herel's arm. "You won't ruin this for us!"

With a shove, Herel was sent sprawling backwards. There'd be no saving the condemned. They were in God's hands now.

As the third piece of flesh tore free, Herel caught the scent of cooked meat, melted skin against the hot metal. It disgusted Herel that, aside from all the horror he was witnessing, he could not deny the enticing smell of the cooked flesh. Pinching his nose, he reluctantly continued to view the bloody spectacle through tearful eyes.

Ax in hand once again, the executioner beheaded the girl and her body continued to shake in convulsions a few moments after death. Blood spurted from her neck as the crowd cheered with glee.

"Now!" presented the executioner. "The Wolf of Bedburg!"

Further cheering erupted as the blunt end of the ax came down, splintering a knee.

"God!" Peter screamed.

It came down again, this time crushing bone and flesh where the forearm met the elbow.

"*God!*" Peter screamed again.

Herel gritted his teeth at the terrible crime taking place. The crowd watched hungrily, like a pack of wolves.

"No," Herel said. He couldn't stand it any longer. This was *not* God's work.

Pushing villagers aside, Herel did not stop until he was only a few feet in front of the executioner.

"Take me!" Herel begged.

But the executioner ignored him. Instead, he raised the ax and brought it down hard upon Peter's other arm.

Herel fell to the ground, his head bowed. He reached out toward the executioner's boots with desperate hands. "Take me!" he repeated. "In God's name, take me!"

Strong hands lifted him upward. Oswald and two others began dragging him back toward the crowd as he fought, but it was to no avail. His weak, flailing fists did little against Oswald and his men.

"To interfere in a lawfully sanctioned execution is a crime, priest!" Oswald turned to one of the men beside him. "After the monster takes his last breath, fetch me my whip. Father Herel will face justice!"

They continued to hold Herel, making sure his head was facing toward the tortured screams of Peter and the headless corpse of his daughter beside him. Again, the ax came down, and again, each time the cracking of Peter's bones emitted another cry from his lips as he screamed the one name Herel thought Peter would not utter. "God!"

But as the ax continued to fall, this time making contact with a wrist, another noise came from Peter...

Laughter.

The ax shattered the bones below his stub in the executioner's attempt to stifle his cackling. But Peter continued, literally sobbing cries of sick joy.

"Look!" Peter exclaimed, with an expression of pure wonder and insurmountable happiness. He pointed with a twisted finger to the heavens. The crowd did as Peter bid, mostly with confusion at the man's fit of euphoria.

As the clouds moved across the sky, the moon shone full and bright, lighting the field and surrounding countryside. Herel couldn't remember seeing the moon so bright.

A young girl beside Father Konrad screamed and pointed at Peter on the wheel.

Another crack, and Peter's leg snapped *back* into place.

Herel watched in horror as the man's bones began to mend.

Face contorted, Peter continued to laugh as gritty, dark hair sprouted from his skin and his body thickened with muscle. His mended limbs bent but did not break, and he grew with every passing second. His laughter grew, too, until a snout produced a howl that would chill the snowy peak of any mountaintop.

Standing upright, loose rope hanging from one clawed hand and a furry stub, the Wolf of Bedburg roared across its hunting grounds, thirsty for blood, for revenge, for *sport*…as it always had.

BIG DOG
Scott Weisser

Never enter the room—that's my rule. Not when I'm in this kind of shape. If I don't take the first step, I can't take the second, and then nothing bad will happen. Right?

It's so important to set boundaries.

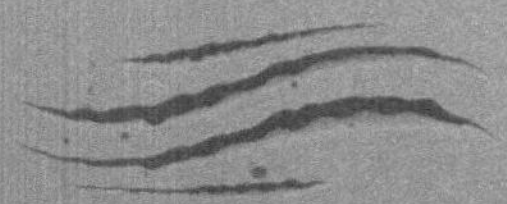

Sam is screaming again. It's late and I'm exhausted but my son needs me. I pull on a shirt and stumble down the hallway.

"Sam, what is it?" I ask. "What's wrong?"

What's wrong? is the sort of thing mothers ask at times like this. It's ingrained, but for me the question is a formality. I already know what Sam's going to say.

"Big Dog," he cries as tears slip down his cheeks. "Big Dog was here."

I take Sam into my arms and hold him tight. I try to comfort my sweet boy.

"It's okay," I say. "Everything's going to be okay."

I'm supposed to be writing down these episodes in a journal listing date, time, and whether there was anything unusual about Sam's day. That was the original plan, at least, after what happened at preschool.

Sam told the other kids about Big Dog. Then came the pictures.

All of Sam's finger paintings were in black and red—black for the creature's fur, red for the blood. Sam's teacher, Miss Taylor, called me in for a meeting. I told her that Sam had been having nightmares.

"He becomes absolutely terrified and there's no consoling him," I said, sounding all the right notes of parental anguish. Miss Taylor nodded sympathetically.

"Even with everything that's been going on, I'd say that's more than just a nightmare," she said. "That sounds like a night terror."

Miss Taylor gave me the name and number of a child psychologist. She assured me that Sarah Bennett was well regarded and had great rapport with children. I called to schedule an appointment the next day.

Sarah and Sam hit it off well, as expected, and I was told there probably wasn't anything to worry about. Sleep terrors affected about forty percent of all young children, according to Sarah.

"It *is* a little odd that Sam's episodes are so cyclical," she said. "There's usually no set timetable for when they occur."

We talked about sticking to a regular sleep routine and, most importantly, not letting Sam watch the local news. Then we scheduled another session to see how things were going—to "touch base," in Sarah's words.

"That one will just be for us grown-ups," she said.

I know Sarah and Miss Taylor only wanted to help, and it's not that I'm hostile to good intentions. People mean well. They just don't understand.

Sam isn't having night terrors. He's frightened on certain nights, yes, but that only makes sense. Big Dog? Sam's right. I suppose it does resemble an especially large canine.

My son is afraid, but there's no reason for him to be. My love for him has been stronger than any hunger. I've proven it again and again.

Besides, what kind of monster would harm the flesh of her flesh?

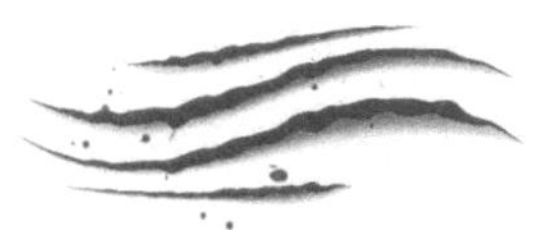

Before Sam, I never thought I would love anyone as much as his father. I didn't think a dream like Robert could ever come true, especially for someone like me.

Robert and I met at a party. We started dating soon after and were married the following year. We wanted to spend every moment we could together, just the two of us, and what few friends we had soon fell out of contact.

I'd never been happier. We had a little place out in the country and were making a shared life for ourselves. We understood each other, or as much as any two people can. Robert kept no secrets from me and I only kept one from him. He found out what it was on our last night together.

Please believe me when I say I was careful and quiet. Robert slept like the dead and I'd done this before, many times. I'd walked almost to the end of the driveway when I heard my husband's voice behind me.

"Going to meet someone by the light of the full moon?" he asked.

"Robert, what—what are you doing up?" I said. "What are you doing out here?"

My indignant husband drew closer, step by step.

"First, how about you tell me what's going on," he said.

I tried to be rational, for Robert's sake.

"Please, this isn't what you think," I said. "I promise you—I swear—I'll explain everything later. But you have to let me go. *Now.*"

"Hmm…that word. 'Go.' Where exactly *do* you go?" Robert asked. "What do you do? Wait, wait, let me guess: you're investigating those gruesome livestock deaths that have the farmers so riled up. My lovely wife, a lone nocturnal avenger hot on the trail of The Cattle Killer." He grinned. "Ha! Did I guess right? Do I win a prize?"

He never heard a word of reply from me, but he had eyes to see.

And then I had no secret to hide from my husband ever again.

We hadn't gotten close to anyone in the area where we lived, and it wasn't hard to leave. Who could blame me? Who could fault the grieving young widow who wanted to be far away from the scene of her husband's violent death?

Neither of us knew it at the time, but Robert had given me a precious gift.

I found out I was pregnant with Sam just two weeks after I killed his father.

It's not hard to start over, really, or even to disappear. These days there's nothing unusual about a mother raising a child on her own, either. It was just the two of us, Sam and me, and that's how I thought it would always be. Until Sarah.

I knew someone else was hunting in the area; the scent of blood in the air was strong. I had no idea who it was, though, until Sarah came into our lives.

There's a certain feeling when hunters meet for the first time in daylight. A recognition, if you will. It's unmistakable. At our follow-up meeting about Sam, Sarah apologized for all the earlier clinical talk, all that silly business about night terrors. Other than the one who'd introduced her to this life—Sarah survived the attack her friends didn't—she had never encountered another of our kind before. She'd needed to be sure.

"And are you?" I asked.

"Yes," she replied.

I couldn't remember the last time I blushed.

The three of us have been so good together. Sarah's schedule allows her to be with Sam until I'm off work, and then we can all enjoy the rest of our day. And on special evenings, when little Sam is sound asleep, Sarah and I make the most of what the night has to offer.

Sam is so happy that Sarah is a part of our lives, or at least he was. Lately, he's been clingy and needy. Jealous. Like the professional she is, Sarah is taking it in stride.

"Sam's just going through a phase where he needs his mother's reassurance," she says.

She's right, I know, and I want to be a decent mother to my child. I do! I know how good I can be, but sometimes it's hard.

I've been thinking a lot about Sam, the boy I check in on every night, no matter what night it is. My son is so loving and trusting. He keeps no secrets from me and I only keep one from him.

Lately, though, I have more and more questions. I wonder if this sobbing child will ever be ready for what lies ahead. Sam's just a few short years away from a big change. I want to prepare him for his new life, but can I? Will he even appreciate his gift, his birthright?

I'm beginning to have doubts.

Awful things are happening under the full moon, if you believe our local media, and the public demands action. The authorities hint at extraordinary measures. Frustrated men with guns are forming groups and making plans.

We need to leave soon. Sarah and I are talking about moving to a larger city, somewhere with more people with fewer connections to each other. A place where "awful things" happen every day and don't get much attention at all.

Sarah wants what's best for Sam. She has the kindest heart. Before Sarah, I never thought I would love anyone as much as my son. I didn't think a dream like Sam could ever come true, especially for someone like me.

Sarah is standing in the doorway to Sam's room. She's in her robe, fresh from the shower after our night out.

"How's our boy?" she asks.

"Just a bad dream," I say. "Isn't that right, Sam?"

"I…I guess so," my little mouse answers. Oh, Sam. Sometimes I could just gobble him up.

"Things are going to change," I say as I hold him snug. "Things will be different very, very soon. I promise."

Sarah watches us and doesn't say anything. Normally she loves it when Sam and I cuddle, but not tonight. Something's wrong.

I think she knows I would never break a promise to my child.

Sam is screaming again. Big Dog was here, and not like before. I broke my own rule, you see. I finally took the first step.

Maybe one day Sam will paint a picture of our last night together, the night when I failed him and Sarah didn't. She has the kindest heart, and the sharpest teeth.

Maybe one day Sam will paint a picture in black and red.

Black for the creatures' fur, red for the blood.

FOXGLOVE MANOR
Vincent West

Nestled deep in the embrace of a shadowed wood, an ancient manor stood in a state of disrepair. Years ago, there would have been an entire group of servants, maids, and groundskeepers to maintain the property both inside and out. Now there was only Daniel, and he alone could not compete with the manor's size, the seasons, or the gradual decay that inevitably came with the passage of time.

Daniel didn't often stop to reflect on exactly how long he had been at Foxglove Manor. Time slipped away when each day followed a similar routine, leaving him in a lull that gradually became hypnotic. He woke, dressed, ate, and set himself to work. He swept the floors, tidied the most obvious bits of dust, and tried to stop the vines and weeds from overtaking the yard entirely.

Most consuming of all his work were the plants from which the manor took its title from: the beautiful rows and rows of flowers that crept closer day by day. Most of Daniel's time was devoted to keeping the foxglove healthy but contained, carefully shielding his skin from contact with worn leather gloves. Sometimes, in his lowest moments, Daniel wished to set the entire field of it aflame, but he knew that was just heartbroken rebellion.

Besides, he worried what might happen if he did. He needed it, after all; he couldn't forget that. Reminders of its cruel necessity came from the basement he visited every morning, noon, and night, and the sharp, shrill sounds that would summon him if he was late.

Thankfully, today's task of polishing the windows was a benign, even enjoyable one. Grand, gorgeous sheets of glass illuminated the manor with enough warmth to ward away the chill of isolation. When the sun shone inside, brilliant and radiant, Daniel could remember first stepping foot into this place. Seeing the light catch on the shelves of books, glinting against their golden labels, he'd felt the same enchantment that first made him want to stay here forever.

He felt lucky then; he still felt lucky now. He simply hadn't expected the cost that came along with it.

Content he'd managed enough outside, Daniel turned his attention to lunch. He washed his hands, scrubbing at the dirt stuck in the worn calluses that hadn't existed before he became the manor's keeper, and wondered idly about how much he must have changed since he came here. That desire brought him here initially: the desperate urge to change.

"You won't make for a pretty wife," his mother warned him once as they stood together in the kitchen. "So you have to be other things. Do you understand?"

She hadn't meant this unkindly, although it had stung at the time. She had wanted Daniel to be taken care of, and knew that this child, with their stout posture and chore-weathered hands, had fewer options than most. Daniel didn't care if his skin lost its softness, or if his limbs gained thickness unbefitting of a young girl. It felt comforting instead, in much the same way emotion swelled in his chest when he first swept his hair up in a cap, keeping it out of his way as he helped his father gather wood, and a passing stranger called him a boy.

He didn't dare voice it. He took his mother's lessons because an unpretty wife must be charming in other ways. She had to cook, clean and be on her best behaviour. Daniel used one of his mother's recipes now, slicing potatoes in one long, single line: a deftness his mother insisted on despite how no husband would see it.

When his parents grew ill and passed, Daniel took odd jobs and pressed his luck in exchange for rooms and boarding. He wore his father's clothes, hid his hair, and posed himself as a working hand. He became a perfect employee, being careful as he could. He survived on his own for a good time like that. Sometimes the work moved on; sometimes the pay dried up—but only once did Daniel get caught. There wasn't an uproar like he'd expected, maybe because quietly kicking him out spared a scandal. Either way, he couldn't feel too embittered—if he hadn't been on the street, he wouldn't have met Rowan.

Seeing Rowan for the first time had been like stepping into a dream. Daniel had frozen where he stood, watching as Rowan spoke adamantly with a shopkeeper. His fair hair was neatly kept, shining golden against the dark cloak cascading down his shoulders, deep blue like the waves of a tide. He wore a billowing white shirt underneath, and his fingers glittered with jewels. Never had Daniel seen so much finery in one place, and he couldn't fathom how the shopkeeper kept a clear enough head to turn him down.

"I'd have to make such a long journey every time," Rowan said, hands pressing together like a prayer. "I would be happy to pay for everything to be delivered."

"I already told you," the shopkeeper replied. "That isn't going to happen. Stop wasting my time."

The shopkeeper turned away, leaving Rowan in a huff, and all at once, Daniel understood.

"No one will go to Foxglove Manor." How he found his voice, he wasn't sure, but when he raised it, it didn't tremble. Rowan's stare rooted him to the spot. His eyes glinted like emeralds, almost unnatural in their sharpness, but Daniel held his ground. "No one ever does."

Rowan regarded him for a moment, his gaze making a deliberate trail up and down Daniel's body. Dressed in dirty clothes, with all his meagre belongings stuffed into a worn sack over his shoulder, Daniel wasn't an impressive sight. Rowan didn't have a speck of dirt on him and Daniel put it together: only someone with a great deal of money to their name would dare try to occupy the recently emptied manor.

It happened like clockwork: someone new and naïve, with ample wealth, came with lofty goals of reshaping the manor into something elegant and noble. However, they didn't account for how no one in the nearest town would so much as speak to them and treated them as if they carried the plague. Cut off from resources and workers, they eventually packed up and left, until another bright-eyed and heavy-pocketed fool replaced them. This man would be like all those who came before him.

Unless.

"But I can work for you," Daniel said. "I know how to keep a house running. I can come to town to pick up whatever you need. You can ask around, but I guarantee no one else will come to you on account of the manor. They all think it's haunted."

Rowan tilted his head, fair hair spilling to one side and a jewel dangling from his ear. "Do you?" he had asked, his voice ringing like a bell.

Knocking came at the manor door, hard and demanding, and Daniel's knife slipped with an abrupt snap back to reality.

In all his time here, this had never happened. The sound felt like a war drum: thudding and insistent, matched to the now spiked rhythm of Daniel's heart. No one ever dared to come here; there was nothing worth risking the fierce reputation, unless—

Unless Rowan's trespasses had finally caught up to him.

To *them*.

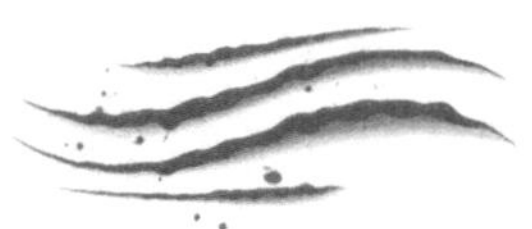

It started off like a storybook. Daniel had followed Rowan to the manor, and together they worked away at the ruin and grime. Once they began, it wasn't quite as daunting as Daniel feared. The interior was mostly a victim of age, and it took no time at all to clear the layers of dust and make it presentable. Against Daniel's expectations, Rowan did his own share of labour, sorting through the belongings of the manor's old masters, discarding ruined books and mouldy clothes. The outdoors, however, were an entirely separate ordeal. It took weeks to hack away the weeds clogging the entryway and to upturn enough soil to start a proper garden.

"Be careful of the foxglove," Rowan warned right away, "or it will make you sick."

Rowan was unlike any other employer Daniel had known. At first, he blamed it on their isolation: with no one else to speak to, Daniel sufficed to occupy Rowan's time. Keeping his head down had been essential to Daniel's survival, so he was pleasant but quiet, speaking when spoken to and tending to his own tasks. It did occur to him that perhaps he'd misjudged this. Running into Rowan when the town was braced to make him an outcast certainly felt like a twist of fate. However, it did mean he was isolated here with Rowan, who had ample time to study his mannerisms, to watch him work, to find out that Daniel was not entirely the man he presented himself as.

If anything stood out, Rowan made no sign of it. He spent his days in the manor buried in books, studying something Daniel could not understand. He ventured deep into the woods, but clearly not to hunt or forage for anything practical, and Daniel didn't make himself bold enough to inquire. He'd honour Rowan's business if Rowan honoured his.

"Daniel," Rowan asked one night, nudging his dinner with his fork, "why did you come here with me?" He'd never asked before, perhaps too reluctant to pry against Daniel's quiet demeanour and too grateful to question his hard work. When Daniel didn't answer right away, Rowan offered a smile. "You're not afraid of a haunted manor?"

Daniel shrugged, considering leaving it at that, but his jaw worked and he compelled himself to speak. "I don't think it's haunted," he said. "I think it's…like a circle. Maybe one terrible thing happened to someone who lived here a long time ago, so people got an idea in their heads. Then the next people came along, and they're treated funny because of what came before. That makes it hard to live so they have to leave. Then the story gets more power. It builds with the next person and the next."

Daniel hadn't said so many words to Rowan at once before and tried to dismiss the gravity with another shrug.

"I'm not worried about ghosts. I'm worried about other people."

Rowan watched him for a moment, and his smile widened. "I hope you're not worried about me."

Daniel shook his head and Rowan glanced at his food, avoiding Daniel's gaze with an undeniable shyness.

"Good."

But Daniel did begin to worry. As Rowan spent more and more time in his books, Daniel wondered what exactly he was looking for. Rowan hadn't come here just to make this manor his home—it was far too grand and inconvenient for one person. Daniel approached the subject, mildly enough, and Rowan's pale cheeks turned rosy.

"Should I want more company? I quite like it being just you and me."

Daniel didn't know what to make of that. Surely, he misunderstood or was getting daft in his own isolation.

However, bit by bit, Rowan opened to him. Like Daniel, he had no family left and his loneliness showed through. He began following Daniel about during the day, just to be in his space. He insisted on cooking for Daniel regularly, instead of the other way around. He brought Daniel cool tea when he laboured in the sun.

Eventually, emboldened by the way Rowan hung in his orbit, Daniel found the nerve to pry. It seemed unfair, given his own share of secrets, but at last he asked: "What are you looking for at Foxglove Manor?" When Rowan didn't meet his gaze, Daniel continued. "People buy a haunted property because it's cheap. Which is fine, to try to make a living, but I know you're after something else."

Rowan paused, his hands smoothing out his fine clothes, taking time before he spoke. "You may call me mad, but I'm here for magic." Before Daniel could respond, as if fearing the judgement of his persistent practicality: "Let me show you."

The library was a collection of Rowan's dedicated work. He had drawn up a map of the manor, the woods, and noted all the little oddities and potential secrets. There was a journal of a former lord who spoke of spirits (the ethereal and the liquid both). There were odd patches of ground where nothing grew. There were myths and whispers of madness when the former owners vacated, and then again on those who came before, going back at least four generations. He showed Daniel his books, speaking of his findings adamantly, until—shamefully—Daniel admitted he could not read them.

Rowan sat on the library floor, countless texts spread about him, all comparing some similar theme. He tried to share some revelation, and Daniel meekly shook his head, having to confess his own ignorance. Glancing up at him, Rowan's emerald eyes looked terribly weak, and Daniel wondered if Rowan thought him to be a fool. Instead, Rowan started reading aloud. He spoke of the woods surrounding them and his voice flowed over Daniel like running water, cool and shivering up his skin.

He described a shrieking chorus of voices who robbed the former lords of their sleep; sightings of unnatural creatures undefined in any literature; a daughter stolen away into the wood without a trace. What he spoke of wasn't beautiful, but his voice made it so. Rowan didn't believe this was a haunting: he thought there was something special here. He rhapsodised, kneeling among his research, and Daniel found it difficult to disagree with the conclusion.

Daniel was a fool for what he did next, but he couldn't help himself. His hand moved to the back of Rowan's neck, tangling in the soft gold of his hair, and he bent down to kiss the crown of his head.

Rowan went so still at first that Daniel was certain he'd made a mistake. Then, faster than he could measure, Rowan threw his arms around Daniel's middle, and the two of them fell among Rowan's careful research, apparently uncaring for whatever secrets it held.

Whatever thread that kept Rowan restrained snapped and he kissed Daniel on every bit of skin he could find. He smothered his face, the underside of his wrist, and the place where his collar dipped. Before Rowan went too far, Daniel stuttered in an effort to explain, but Rowan merely shook his head, golden hair tossing side to side.

"I don't care. Danny, do you have any idea how wonderful you are?"

No one had ever called him that before.

The first night they spent together left Rowan fast asleep but Daniel wide awake. He sat up in the plush, spacious bed in Rowan's room, admiring the sight of golden hair against the soft material of the sheets, and could not move past his disbelief.

His serenity was pierced with an unearthly sound: a scream that shot Rowan upright. Daniel took his arm, centring him, and eased him back against his pillow.

"It's just a fox."

"They sound horrible," he said, and Daniel couldn't disagree. As they carried on, the barks became more apparent among the shrieks, but the effect was no less chilling.

"I hear them often enough up here," Daniel said, privately amused that Rowan apparently slept too heavily to notice. "I wonder if that's where the ghost stories came from."

Rowan looked at him in an odd way then, his eyes sparking with certain recognition, and he suddenly smiled at Daniel like he'd been given a gift.

"When you go into town, I want you to stop by a metalworker," Rowan said. "I need traps."

The request itself wasn't strange. The manor did have its share of vermin due to the years of neglect, but nothing beyond the average. Daniel believed he was quite thorough in keeping things under control, but Rowan apparently thought otherwise. When Daniel mentioned what they owned already, Rowan shook his head.

"These are different," he said, entrusting Daniel with a slip of paper that he could not read. "I need them to be silver. The chain too. Don't forget it."

Daniel thought it strange and so did the blacksmith, who glanced at the note, but he accepted payment nonetheless. Once everything was prepared, Rowan had Daniel set the foothold trap up around the edge of the foxglove.

For a while, Daniel almost forgot about it. Everything carried on as it usually did: Daniel tended the garden, he cooked, and Rowan devoured his books and made his notes. Days were spent working on their separate tasks, and in the evenings they came together and could scarcely be separated. As the weeks went on, Daniel thought they might live like this forever.

Until the trap caught prey and shattered the dream like glass.

A foul, shrill scream sent Rowan running from his dinner. Daniel had never seen him move so quickly and barely kept up with him. Their quarry was thrashing about in the flowers that shared its name, its leg crushed in the teeth of the silver trap. Try as it might, the fox could not break loose. It flailed and shrieked with a terrible voice that grated against Daniel's bones.

But Rowan was laughing.

That sound haunted Daniel worse than the fox's cries. A dark, cruel triumph shone in Rowan's posture, and for a moment Daniel did not recognise him. Gathering his wits, he grabbed the nearest thing he could find, his hand clasping the axe he used to gather wood. He approached and Rowan turned on him with shock.

"What are you doing?"

"Putting it out of its misery," Daniel said, weary but resigned. His father had to teach him this kindness when he was young, though it never felt easier for him. When Rowan stepped between him and the trap, Daniel mistook the protest for the same childlike naivety.

"You can't kill it. I need the chains. Hurry."

Daniel hesitated for only a moment before he obeyed. Even as he did, his body wanted to object with every step, the silver chain heavy in his hands. The fox's shrieks had faded into whimpers by the time he returned and as Daniel stared uneasily down at it, Rowan took control. Snatching the chains, Rowan threw them over the fox, looping it around its heaving body.

"Rowan," he said, watching him pull the creature toward the house, his chest twisting miserably. "Rowan, stop this."

Rowan didn't hear him. He dragged the fox to the manor's basement, its fragile body thumping on every step, and Daniel watched in numb disbelief as he shackled it to the wall.

"Rowan," he repeated, his voice raising. "Don't be cruel; it's just a fox!"

Rowan whipped his head up to meet his gaze, his emerald eyes alight with fire, and his smile was something terrible.

"No, it's not."

For the first night in a long time, Daniel stayed in his own bed. Rowan didn't even seem to notice or care, too preoccupied with whatever accomplishment he thought this cruelty represented. He stayed with the fox for hours and Daniel couldn't stomach accompanying him. It was late at night before he heard the door to the basement close, and Rowan retired to his room alone.

Restless, Daniel rose and filled a bowl with water. He couldn't free the fox without Rowan knowing, and with this newfound fervour, he did not know what Rowan might do if Daniel committed such an act of defiance. He could, however, offer the creature something for its suffering.

Quietly as he could manage, he descended to the basement. These stairs worried Daniel, and he hadn't managed the time to repair them. With every step, he watched his feet, which left him completely unprepared for when he raised his eyes to the sight chained to the basement wall.

Where there was once a fox, there was a woman. Her hair lay around her naked body in long, thick waves of red, and her eyes gleamed golden. Her ankle wept red from the trap's teeth and her body slumped weakly as if the chains surrounding her carried an impossible weight.

Daniel froze at the bottom stair, fixed to the spot for a moment too long before horror inspired him to act. Perhaps he should have felt more fear when he approached her, but concern flooded over his sense of self. She took the bowl greedily in her hands when he offered it, drinking it down in deep, desperate gulps, and Daniel could not help staring at her.

She smelled like fresh soil and rain, her golden eyes unnatural and piercing. The tips of her fingers and toes were stained black—perhaps with dirt, but something told Daniel otherwise. The colouring set into her skin like the marking of a fox's coat.

When she drained the bowl, she wiped her mouth on the back of her hand, studying Daniel with a small smile beneath her wild hair, and Daniel's chest twisted miserably.

"Miss. What is this?"

"Magic," she said, her voice carrying a ragged hiss, "the sort that will drive your friend mad; same as any who came before him."

Daniel thought of the terrible sound of Rowan's laughter, the cruelty in his demands, and shook his head. He couldn't confess to understanding, but panic called him to action, setting his hands to the trap. She stilled him with a touch, the gesture rattling the chains that bound her, and her golden eyes bore into his.

"I won't get far like this," she said, glancing at her pierced ankle. "If you wish to help me, I need the foxglove."

Daniel stared at her, realisation dawning, and he shook his head again. "Miss, I won't let you kill yourself."

She laughed quietly, the sound yipping and moving her chest in little jerks. Leaning closer, she squeezed his arm. "I have no plans to die here," she promised, and Daniel found that he believed her.

Quietly as he could muster, he left for the field of foxglove. More than once, he stopped, certain he heard Rowan stirring, but nothing came. With gloves of his own, he carried a bushel down and set it before the woman chained beneath their home. At her request, Daniel carefully untangled the chains from around her and—with a moment of hesitation—released the trap.

She did not scream, though her face twisted up so terribly that she once again seemed bestial, the moment so brief that Daniel might have imagined it. She went for the foxglove right away. Before Daniel could protest, she plucked a bell with her bare hands and placed it on her tongue.

Her eyes fluttered as if tasting incomparable sweetness, a soft sigh of relief exhaling from her chest. She took another, eating the petals like tiny delicacies, and the wound closed tighter with every bite. Daniel watched with transfixed awe, and once she was well enough to stand, she towered over him with a height unapparent when she had been trapped beneath the silver. Her hair fell around her like fire, and she smiled at him with pointed teeth.

"Danny."

Rowan stood at the top of the basement stairs, emerald eyes wide in disbelief, and suddenly the woman was gone. The fox that took her place ran past Rowan's heels with impossible speed, but he chased her nonetheless, heedless to how Daniel called after him.

"Leave her be, Rowan," he said, shouting into the wide silence of the woods at night, "for pity's sake—"

Once she reached outside, she was gone. There would be no catching her in the dark. She was free and she knew it. Her shrill, yipping laugh echoed as Rowan snarled in frustration in the open doorway.

"How could you do that?" Rowan's face flashed with an unfamiliar fury. "I had her, Danny! I was so close!"

Daniel said nothing, looking at Rowan and not truly seeing him. This wasn't like him. This wasn't the same person who read Daniel books or learned his favourite meals. It was as if something had infected him— madness like the woman warned.

"How could she run?" Rowan buried his hands wildly in his hair, pacing back and forth. "Even if you let her loose, she was hurt…"

Daniel clenched his jaw, as if willing it to seal shut. Despite himself, his eyes drifted to the basement where unused foxglove remained, his head haunted by the way she'd swallowed poison like medicine.

Catching his gaze, Rowan descended the basement stairs, and Daniel's heart began to pound. "Rowan, please leave it," he said, but Rowan was already studying the stem plucked of all its petals. Rowan was too clever not to realise the implication and Daniel did not know how to stop the wheels from turning.

"I'm sorry I shouted, Danny," Rowan said, though he would not look at Daniel. He stared at the foxglove unwaveringly. "By letting her go, she showed you all her secrets."

Rowan pulled a petal loose and Daniel could not stop him before he placed it in his mouth. His eyes drifted closed and he uttered the same little sound of satisfaction that the woman made before him. Encouraged, he took another, and another, and Daniel's pulse raced.

"Rowan, stop," he pleaded, but Rowan could not hear him. He plucked one stem completely empty before immediately setting on another, as if overcome with fierce hunger, and Daniel set his hands on Rowan's shoulders. When he tried to dissuade him, Rowan shrugged him off, and Daniel raised his voice for the first time. "Rowan, that's enough—!"

With an unfamiliar strength, Rowan threw Daniel from him, clearing a path to run up the basement stairs. Staggered, Daniel hurried after him, not fast enough to stop him. He found Rowan kneeling amongst the foxglove, shoving greedy mouthfuls past his lips, filling his cheeks like some starved animal, dripping spit and half-chewed petals when he couldn't slow enough to swallow.

Daniel threw his arms around him and found Rowan rooted to the spot. It took every ounce of Daniel's strength to tear him from the field, and Rowan howled like a wounded creature, his hands grasping out uselessly to claw towards the foxglove. Mind racing, Daniel could only think of one solution. He dragged Rowan, who screamed and wailed and kicked, to the basement, and chained him in the same silver that'd held the woman captive.

Outside, he could hear foxes laughing.

The knocking at the door persisted and Daniel abandoned his cooking to answer it, hesitating before he left the knife behind. He wiped his hands restlessly on his shirt, feeling clammy in his skin, and the sensation doubled when he opened the door.

The woman who was also a fox stood before him. Her wild mane of hair hung long enough to brush against her ankles, her stained fingertips curling around the doorframe to hold it open. She smiled when she saw him, her lips dark and her teeth sharp.

He should have kept the knife.

"May I come in, Danny?" she asked, with politeness unfitting of her wild demeanour, and Daniel didn't think he could refuse her.

He stepped aside—not because he felt at her mercy, but oddly, the opposite. He felt that she truly bore him no ill will. Maybe he was soothed because she addressed him by a name only Rowan ever used; a name Rowan now moaned through a lopsided mandible, the end of it peaking into an animalistic shriek. As she entered, she raised her chin to glance around the manor.

"Didn't think you'd come back," Daniel said, and she smiled at him over her shoulder.

"Neither did I," she replied, showing her pointed teeth. "How is your friend?"

Daniel's eyes drifted to the basement. Something told him that she didn't really need to ask. After the foxglove, Rowan changed. His golden hair turned rusty, his emerald eyes cracking into gold, and nothing Daniel tried could slow the steady way his body betrayed him. Rowan begged to be let back at the flowers and Daniel refused. Rowan tried to fight his chains and Daniel didn't dare free him. Rowan grew upset and his body grew with him: a mangled, extended maw, gnashing teeth, sharpening nails—none of it building to a proper shape, just a confused mess of man and monster that begged for Daniel's help in the same breath as snapping its jaws.

Rowan wouldn't eat. Daniel thought it was stubbornness he might stamp out, but when he threw up anything Daniel guided past his lips, he realised he fought a losing battle. Every day, he collected the foxglove and let Rowan have his way, devouring it shamelessly like an animal at a trough.

"The way he acted that night… That isn't him," Daniel began, and the woman hummed.

"He can't be blamed," she said, more forgiving than Daniel anticipated—but then again, her wounds had closed like nothing happened at all. "The foxglove is infectious. Afraid that it will one day wilt away, like all the other old magics, it calls out, singing promises of power and pleasure." She paused, winking a golden eye at Daniel. "But you don't seem to hear it, do you, Danny?"

Daniel chose not to answer. "What's happening to him?"

"The same thing that happened to me," she replied. "The same thing that happened to the others who came here, searching out a secret."

"What is it, really?" he asked, out of exasperation rather than curiosity—a cruel sense of defeat.

She considered Daniel for a moment before he earned her smile, revealing the points of her teeth. "I can't claim to have an answer that will satisfy you." She trailed one blackened finger across worn wood, as if trying to remember how it felt to be surrounded by four walls. "But I can tell you what I know."

Daniel nodded, guiding her to the sitting room. Taking a seat across from him, perching like a bird rather than a human being, she told him about her time at Foxglove Manor.

She had been a single maid to an aspiring lord and, much like Daniel, she had been utterly devoted to managing the Manor. She blamed this busy schedule for her fate. Too preoccupied with her work, she was naïve to the threat against her. She didn't notice the new lord's slowly budding obsession. She didn't realise what he came here for. She was a fool right up until the end: when he dragged her out of her bed one night, threw her out in front of the Manor, and began shoving flowers down her throat.

"He read the books about magic here, fables of shifting shapes and spells," she said, her coal-dark fingers braced on her knees. "Finally, he realised the source, but he was too cowardly to test the theory himself."

An icy dread settled into Daniel's stomach as she described being locked away, her torments studied and her changing body prodded for results. Her pleas were denied, no mercy granted despite her begging, and when he finally allowed her another meal of foxglove, she descended on him with her newly grown teeth.

"Your lord is cleverer than mine," she said, smiling as she cupped her chin in her black palm. "Mine didn't know about the silver." She gazed at him with her odd eyes, piercing through the core of him. "You're not responsible for what happened," she said as if freeing him. "From here, he comes with me, and he either learns to stomach it or he suffocates."

Daniel went very still. At first, he wasn't sure if he heard her correctly, and then fear twisted miserably in his chest. Did she think him foolish for staying this long, or did she assume he was here from misplaced obligation?

"And if he stomachs it?" Daniel asked, his voice quiet. He didn't dare pry about the other option. "What then?"

"Then he's one of us," she said, as if it were the simplest thing in the world. "Among brothers and sisters, and beasts that will now speak with him in a common tongue. He'll be able to take our common shape and run with us. We don't tire. We don't feel real harm. We live forever—as long as the foxglove blooms."

For all the horror, the reward was like a fable. This was what Rowan came here for; he desired this above all, and he would have it.

"And if it stops blooming?"

"Danny." She clucked her tongue, as if disappointed. "You know the answer to that already."

Rising to her feet, the woman made for the basement, and Daniel didn't dare follow her. Soon, she emerged, Rowan's beastlike form hobbling after her. Daniel stared, feeling trapped as dreamlike, and Rowan's shuddering, yipping form did not seem to recognise him—or perhaps felt simply too ashamed to meet his gaze.

"Will you come back?"

Daniel did not mean to say it, but it came out regardless, and the woman smiled. "You can taste it yourself, if you'd like to join us," she said, and then they were gone.

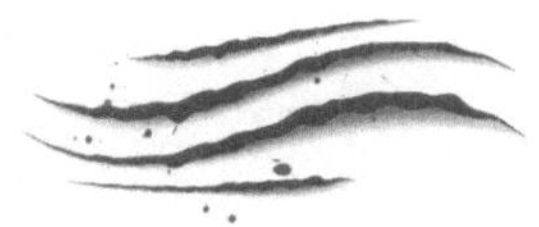

Daniel allowed himself that first night to weep, mourn, and exorcise the grief from his mind and body alike. The next morning, he rose with the sun and he went to work.

He had to tend to the grounds. He had to keep the foxglove neat, watered and sweet. It was only at his most desperate that he considered the suggestion from the woman—tasting it himself and joining the strange folk of the wood, if only for the chance to see Rowan again— but caution stilled his hand. He didn't know if he would stomach it, or succumb, and what would he do, if the other foxes came for him and he learned Rowan failed? What would immortality be worth without Rowan?

Was that even something he wanted? After so much time, living as he'd lived, making peace with this body and what it meant to exist in it… did he want to see it changed, moulded into something else entirely? At one point in his life, Daniel would've said "yes" without a thought, but then…

Then he'd met Rowan, who saw him, embraced him, and loved him, and…and his skin didn't feel so ill-fitting anymore.

Besides, as she said, someone had to keep the foxglove in bloom.

Daniel worked away at Foxglove Manor, listening to foxes laugh when the evenings grew late, and more than once he imagined the sound to be his name.

THE LAST BUS OUT OF BLACK MOUTH CANYON

Michael A. Reed

TARYN WAITED IN line to board the Human Safety bus. It had clearly been an old tour bus in a past life. Baby blue paint peeled off the sides, revealing a rusted metal frame. The gray aftermath of the word "Welcome" stretched over its hood. Beneath the pale moonlight, tired and spewing black exhaust, the vehicle looked as unwell as the people forced to ride it.

Smoking a cigarette and hanging out the window, the bus driver assessed the passenger line. He was stern and refused to look anyone in the eye. Neither did the gunman who'd checked everyone's identification documents.

Taryn didn't fault them, though. She didn't want to be here, either. This drive to Black Mouth Canyon was the final trip of the month, an emergency action certified by the governor, or president, or whoever made these choices. To spite her mother, she had delayed getting tested, and this was her last chance.

It was a waxing gibbous night, after all, a fact that every major news channel, radio station, and critical alert test wouldn't let Taryn forget.

When Taryn reached the front of the line, the gunman took her papers and examined them with a probing finger. He read the details of her incident. The party. The attack. The bite.

"Board," the gunman said without ever looking up. He adjusted the rifle slung over his shoulder and stretched his back. He yawned. Tonight was nothing more than a routine for him. Annoyed and weary, Taryn climbed the bus steps, unable to shake the feeling that she was cattle. An animal. Then again, she might be.

She sat in the middle of the bus and wished she had her music. She could bring nothing with her except for the clothes on her back, and she might not go home with even that. The bus doors closed, the hydraulics hissed, and the bus rumbled down the gravel road towards the canyon, away from society.

Taryn looked out the window and watched the shapes of desert bushes, Joshua Trees, and rock mounds pass by. Eventually, the night thickened and she couldn't distinguish a tumbleweed from a chasing shadow. Alone with her face pressed against the glass, fresh fear crept into her chest. What if she never came back?

All the passengers slept except for a man across the aisle from Taryn. He wore a dusty checkered suit coat and leaned against the window with his arms strewn over the seat tops.

"Are you worried?" the man asked, breaking the silence. He kept talking when Taryn didn't answer. "No one would blame you for being afraid. Nobody wants to be mangy."

"I'm not mangy," Taryn snapped, although she didn't know that.

"The chances are low," the man said, not unkindly. He reached his hand out and Taryn shook it weakly. "I'm Damon, by the way."

"Taryn." She turned back to the window.

"Less than one percent," Damon said, perhaps hoping to ease Taryn's worries. "Not even one in every hundred." He looked around the bus. "Probability would suggest that none of us are mangy."

A brown highway sign blurred in the bus headlights. Black Mouth Canyon, twenty miles.

"Who bit you?" Damon asked.

"Some guy," Taryn answered, reluctantly accepting that Damon wasn't going to leave her alone. "I don't know."

She really didn't have any idea who had bitten her. She and her friends had snuck out to a party. It all happened too fast. Her mom had already threatened to kick her out of the house if she wasn't able to control herself. They didn't have enough money for the pills or a panic room installation.

"A full moon party, I bet," Damon said.

"That isn't your business," Taryn said. She rolled her eyes and slumped further into her seat.

"I get it." Damon chuckled to himself. "There is something exhilarating about being out during a full moon. The danger of it. Not knowing what could happen, even though nothing usually does."

Taryn scoffed, but she didn't disagree. "Is that how you were bitten?"

"Yes," Damon said. His stare made Taryn uncomfortable and when he didn't elaborate, she turned back to the window. She didn't want new friends, anyway.

Above, the moon gleamed and Taryn swore she could see--no, practically feel--a green hue circling its edges. Pulsing. Reaching. Asking.

The Black Mouth Canyon Facility appeared from behind the canyon walls. According to the pamphlets handed out at Taryn's school, the government's Human Safety division repurposed an old mining project by constructing a rugged fabric building overtop the original tunnels. From the pictures, Taryn thought it would have been bigger, but it was more of an oversized barn than anything.

When the bus stopped, the gunman ushered the passengers off and led them to a table beside a tent. People in lab coats scurried around like a disrupted line of ants. They passed each other equipment and clipboards, occasionally stopping to whisper something imperative enough to send them running off again.

One of the facility employees, a woman with curly hair and dimples, guided Taryn by her shoulders to sit in a folding chair. According to her name tag, the woman's name was Saanvi.

"When were you bit?" Saanvi asked, her pen ready.

"Last month," Taryn answered. "At a party."

"A full moon party?" Saanvi huffed, clicking her pen several times as she looked Taryn up and down. Her frown reminded Taryn of her mother's reaction, only Saanvi hadn't thrown a bottle of olive oil at her.

"Did you know the biter?" Saanvi asked.

"No."

"Have you experienced any symptoms?"

"Like what?"

"Intrusive thoughts. Anger. Sensual urges."

"Ew, no."

"Hair growth or hair whitening. Headaches. Diarrhea. Heart palpitations. Shortness of breath."

"Seeing colors?" Taryn asked. When Saanvi's eyes widened, she wished she hadn't said anything.

"What color?" Saanvi asked, her face stiff.

Taryn imagined the moon wrapped in green lights and how she didn't look away. Couldn't look away. "Purple," she lied.

Saanvi wrote something down, then studied Taryn's face for the truth. "Discoloration can sometimes be a serious symptom. Come with me."

She walked away and Taryn obediently followed. They entered the facility through an open loading gate large enough to fit semi-trucks. Inside felt unnaturally warm and smelled like a wet dog. The tented roof had been fitted with an enormous dark tarp that blocked the moonlight and shaded everything in dull red.

Saanvi stopped in front of a metal cage with bars marred by teeth marks.

"Please sit," Saanvi said, the suggestion more of a command. Taryn sat on a metal bleacher that could've been ripped straight from a ballpark.

She looked around the open facility and watched many of the other bus passengers take seats in front of similar cages.

"It looks like it's you and me again," Damon said as he sat down next to Taryn. He smiled warmly and patted the top of her hand. Taryn recoiled and wondered why his skin felt so cold.

"What is the cage for?" Taryn asked, even though she had a pretty good idea.

"Mangy tests," Damon said. He leaned back on the bleachers, smiling smugly. If he was nervous, nobody would ever know it. Taryn wished she could stay calm like that.

"A formal activation of your lycan infection," Saanvi corrected. She pulled two rubber gloves over her hands. "Earl will explain the procedure. Please save your questions until the end."

A short, balding man stood from a computer desk beside the cage. He jogged over to the bench, holding pamphlet copies.

"Feel free to read through these as I explain the process," Earl said, his face pink and sweaty. "You've both been bitten by a lycan and will experience your first full moon transformation tomorrow night. We will use the drug Lykosadol to prematurely activate your Lycanthropy condition."

Saanvi prepared a needle as long and thick as a soft drink straw. The sight of it sent shivers down Taryn's spine.

Earl painstakingly navigated the medical pamphlet like a flight attendant explaining how to buckle up for a plane crash.

"It is the Human Safety's responsibility to ensure you are not a danger to society. Your transformation will be short and temporary. You will likely have no memory of the moment, but you may feel sick once it is over. Any clothes or jewelry you are wearing will be damaged, if not completely destroyed. Each cage is equipped with a curtain to guard your decency."

"Decency." Damon laughed at the word. "And what if we are a mangy dog? What happens if we try to bite your face off?"

"A mangy lycan will do more than that," Saanvi said, her words cold matters of fact. She obviously didn't like Damon's nonchalance. "We will kill you should that be the outcome."

"Not to worry, though," Earl said, trying to keep the instructions civil. "The chances are—"

"Low," Damon interrupted.

He turned to Taryn and winked. She hated that he imagined them as friends just because they rode the same bus. Yet something about his cool demeanor calmed her nerves. Maybe it was the warm green glow of his eyes.

"We will explain the post-exam steps and society reentry guidelines once your transformation period has ended," Earl said. "Who would like to go first?"

Taryn thought it would be better to get it over with, but before she could raise her hand, a high-pitched howl echoed throughout the facility. Someone's transformation test had begun.

Her blood froze in her veins and she clenched her fists. She remembered her first visit to a theme park, how excited she'd been until she heard grown adults screaming as they hurdled above her. She never did ride a rollercoaster.

"I don't mind," Damon said, raising his hand. He looked over at Taryn and grinned. He knew she was afraid. For whatever reason, he tried so hard to make her brave.

Saanvi and Earl prepared the cage. They double checked the steel shackles and tested the chains. The whole process looked more like medieval torture than modern science.

Damon leaned so close to Taryn that she could smell the grime on his suit coat. He cupped his hand around her ear and whispered, "I heard these tests aren't always accurate."

Before Taryn could ask what he meant by that, Damon left the bench and walked into the cage. He slipped off his coat and handed it to Earl, then Saanvi covered his wrists and ankles with cotton pads. Each shackle closed with an audible snap that made Taryn blink.

"Don't worry about me," Damon said. "It's standard procedure."

The cage door closed. Saanvi stuck the oversized needle into Damon's thigh and pumped the Lykosadol into his body. Damon's smile twitched and his head drooped. His breathing quickened and he started groaning.

Taryn watched wide-eyed as Damon changed. His face narrowed as his jaw extended, his teeth growing long and sharp. Taryn heard Damon's bones bend and tendons burst. His chest grew twice its size; the buttons of his dress shirt popped off and dinged against the cage bars. His trousers split and his clawed toes tore through his dress shoes. Damon's heels rose off the ground, arched and ready to pounce. All the while, a gray coat of hair sprung from his skin, quick and sharp, like a macro time-lapse video of grass growing in a field.

Saanvi stood ready with a second needle. From Saanvi's determined stance, Taryn assumed it was a lethal injection should Damon become mangy.

Damon tipped his head back, now more wolf than man, and howled. Saliva dripped from his chin and he fought against his chains. After a few minutes of thrashing and snarling, his coat of gray fur began to shed. He shrunk down to the size of a normal man, his wrists and ankles bruised by the shackles despite the doctor's best efforts.

Saanvi relaxed and took a deep breath. "Test complete."

Earl opened the cage, unshackled Damon, and dragged him back to the bench. Together, Earl and Saanvi exchanged notes and stared into the blue glare of the computer.

Damon sat up, naked except for his ripped pants, and smiled weakly. "Not so bad."

"What did it feel like?" Taryn asked. She tried to ignore her burning anxiety—and the unending howling that echoed within the facility.

"Do you really want to know?" Surprisingly, Damon had already caught his breath, and the color had returned to his face.

"Please," Taryn said, desperate to know

Unable to keep her legs from shaking, she never felt more like a child. Now that the howling had started and the moment of her own transformation was inevitable, she convinced herself that she needed Damon. Needed someone or something to tell her everything was going to be okay.

Like that night at the full moon party, when the lycan attacked and Taryn hid behind her friends. More than being bitten, they were mauled protecting her. They would never be the same. No prom dates. No graduation. For keeping Taryn safe from the lycan, they were rewarded with eating food through a tube, perhaps never to walk again. Taryn was still bitten despite their sacrifice. But Taryn didn't regret it.

Someone else had to face her fears.

"Before it happens, long before, it is cold inside," Damon said, his voice low. "Not your stomach. There is a place somewhere in the middle, something like a second heart. It is untamed and waiting in the tall grass of your own life. You want to let it out because you know it will make you strong. It will protect you from the whole world, but more than that, it will save you from yourself."

Damon placed the back of his hand on Taryn's forehead. His hand was cold like before, but his touch was hot enough to sting her skin.

"Who are you?" Taryn asked, her heartbeat racing.

"Mangy doesn't mean bad, Taryn," Damon said. He licked his lips, and his stare made her want to run and never come back.

When Earl grabbed her arm, Taryn yelped. "We've been calling your name," he said, his pink face now red.

He guided Taryn to the cage and locked her in place. Damon's fur, scattered like shredded rose petals, surrounded her feet. She thought she would be afraid of the cage, but she welcomed it now. Her instincts—animal or human, she could not tell—told her that Damon was dangerous. She hadn't seen it before, hadn't detected the dog inside him. She needed bars between them.

Saanvi prepared another batch of Lykosadol while Earl checked Taryn's restraints. Neither of them realized something was wrong with Damon. Finally, Earl closed the cage.

Damon stood from the bench, smiling as he always had. His teeth were sharp and his tongue pointed. His eyes were black cauldrons spilling over with poisonous emerald smoke. Whatever happened next, he wanted Taryn to watch.

"Doctor Saanvi," Damon growled. "Thanks for the Lykosadol."

When Saanvi heard the predator masked in Damon's voice, she whirled around to face him. It was too late; he had already mutated. Unlike before, his transformation was quiet, a subtle change in his muscles and the lengths of his fingers. His stringy fur hung from his back in patches like swaths of weeping willow leaves.

He swiped Saanvi across the chest and she fell backwards with a heavy thud. Damon took the syringe of Lykosadol from the ground and stuck it into his neck. He moaned with pleasure as the drug coursed through his blood.

Earl cursed and ran, but he didn't get far before Damon pounced on him. Taryn wanted to look away, but she couldn't. Damon ripped Earl's skin away like shucking a corn, then tossed his body aside.

Damon came to Taryn's cage, pressing his snout between the bars. "Do you think I'm mangy?" The words grumbled off his tongue. He had practiced speaking in this form, Taryn realized. He had taught himself.

An alarm blared. Bright flashing lights overtook the red hues within the facility. Everyone ran in different directions, yelling and pointing at Damon's terrible wolf body.

"I don't know," Taryn said. She could barely hear herself over the alarm. "I don't know what that means."

"It means you can't be controlled." Damon didn't flinch when the Black Mouth Canyon guards shot him in the back. The silver bullets worked their way out of his flesh and fell to the ground. His wounds healed almost instantly. "They are afraid of that. Everyone wants you to do what you're told. To be a good dog."

"Are you going to kill me?" The question spilled out of Taryn's quivering lips.

Damon grinned. His horrible teeth were shark-like: tight with too many overlapping layers. Then he ran away, slashing and ripping people into pieces with ease, killing whoever tried to stop him. Soon, all the facility guards were in full retreat.

He saved her for last, Taryn thought. He would come back once he had killed everyone in Black Mouth Canyon, then take his sick, sweet time gnawing on her bones. She writhed against her chains and yelled for help.

Saanvi appeared at the cage door, her face screwed up in pain. Blood soaked through her white lab coat. She opened the cage, then sank to the floor, holding her wounded chest. When she had the strength, she stood again and released Taryn from her shackles.

"The shuttle bus is parked on the backside of the building," Saanvi said, wheezing through her pain.

Taryn wrapped her arm around Saanvi to help her walk. She wanted to run and leave the doctor. Her chances were probably better if she did, but she didn't want to be a coward. Not again.

Together, they hobbled to the back of the facility, carefully stepping over Damon's dead victims. She recognized some of the other bus passengers, as well as the gunman who had checked her papers. They were corpses now. Slippery obstacles blocking Taryn's way.

"Here," Saanvi croaked. She pointed to an emergency door. Taryn opened it by kicking the push paddle. Just as Saanvi promised, the Human Safety bus was parked outside.

"What the hell is going on?" the bus driver asked. He hadn't left the bus since their arrival. "I heard screaming. Nobody is picking up their radios." When he saw Saanvi's injury, he turned pale and his cigarette tumbled from his lips.

"We have to go," Saanvi said. The bus doors screeched open. Taryn helped Saanvi up the steps and they collapsed onto a seat. Speechless, the driver revved the engines and steered the bus around the facility and onto the dirt road that led back to the city.

Behind them, still butchering anyone he could find, Damon howled. His murderous wailing caught the wind and traveled alongside the bus for miles.

"He was mangy," Saanvi mumbled. "I don't understand how he hid it." She fumbled through her lab coat pockets, looking for something to help stop the bleeding. Lykosadol injections fell from her pocket and rolled along the bus floor. She tried to reach them but didn't have the energy.

"How do you know someone is mangy?" Taryn asked. She picked up a syringe and turned it in her hands.

"They don't see the world like us," Saanvi said. She reached out her hand for the syringe. "A mangy lycan can't be trained. That makes them dangerous."

Taryn looked out the window. The moon was a blazing green rock spinning in the night like an ever-watching wolf's eye. A wolf she knew by name. From somewhere buried inside her, in a corner of her heart she didn't know existed, a cold fire stirred. She stopped trembling and did something she hadn't done in so long: she smiled.

She held the syringe out for Saanvi to take. As the doctor went to grab the medicine, Taryn thought of Damon and how he ran wild, destroying the things that hated him. He had seen something in Taryn that nobody else had. Her mother, her friends, her teachers, the doctor beside her—they couldn't see it curled in her bones. She was hungry for a better life. *Starving* for it.

Taryn took back the syringe, reveling in Saanvi's shocked expression when she removed the plastic lid. She could smell her blood. Her fear. Calm and controlled, the master of her own choices, Taryn held the syringe over her leg.

"Maybe I want to be dangerous," she said, a glint of the green moon reflecting within her stare.

HOW AFRAID
Devan Barlow

"I HEARD THERE'S BEEN a sighting," the pharmacist said as he packaged her prescription. "Over in the city."

Helen handed him the payment and took the bag, keeping her hands as far from his as possible. He wore elegant black leather gloves. She wondered if he thought they kept him safe.

She placed the prescription in her purse with a sense of temporary relief at not having to think about her meds. Until the next time they ran low, anyway. Even now, when most people had stopped going to the doctor entirely, fearing touch, she couldn't get her pills without a prescription.

"Get home safe," the pharmacist said as Helen walked outside.

The parking lot was empty. She let herself breathe the autumn-tinged air until the feeling of being simultaneously too warm and too cold abated. It would take at least an hour to get home. All the closer pharmacies were permanently closed by now. As she drove back to the city, she reflected on the conversation. The pharmacist was wrong. There hadn't been any sightings. There were no dragonflies near.

But still, when she got home, she raced inside their building, her heart dancing frantically.

An unfamiliar woman stood in the hall. Helen hesitated.

"I've just moved in," the stranger said, with the sort of hopeful-but-wary smile that had become so common these days. "I'm Jaclyn."

Moved in. Funny how certain phrases stayed around. No one monitored who lived here, no one collected rent. There weren't enough people left for that.

Helen estimated about three dozen people lived in the building. Occasionally, someone would feel brave and slip notes under everyone's doors, suggesting they have a meeting. Whoever went to the meeting would stand far from everyone else, and they'd have halting conversations about what needed fixing, and who might know how to do so.

But if this newcomer, however she'd found this place, went into the safety of an apartment and never left, none of them would judge her.

"Hello," Helen said awkwardly. Then she gave up on conversation, quickly unlocked her door, threw herself inside, and locked it behind her. When she looked through the peephole, Jaclyn was still in the hall, her eyes on Helen's door.

Rose's head poked around the corner, distracting her. "Welcome back." Her eyes followed the small bag Helen removed from her purse. "Glad they could fill it."

Helen mumbled agreement, then swallowed one of the pills with water. She started making a cup of tea to counteract the inevitable tiredness that would set in over the next hour. She was never sure how much the tea helped, but it was comforting.

"Did you have much trouble getting home?" Rose spoke in a casual tone, which Helen recognized as her sister's attempt not to add to her anxiety.

Helen shook her head. "Just the usual."

The dragonfly checkpoint at the city's boundary didn't care about seeing identification, or even seeing her face. All the guards cared about was the touch test. Testers bore a faint dusting of silver on their shoulders. The dust the dragonflies left on those they favored, the ones who helped them find prey in exchange for not being taken themselves. The news claimed all the favored had been found and forced to serve at checkpoints. Yet there was no official number of how many of the dragonflies' favored existed.

Every time Helen went through the checkpoint, she knew the person whose hand she was about to touch wasn't a dragonfly. Yet she always shook.

They called each creature a dragonfly, as if each was only *one* and not hundreds working together. Forming the shapes of the humans they'd killed. Helen didn't remember the last time she and Rose touched skin to skin. Even with one another, habit ruled.

She looked at the news. There was, in fact, a reported dragonfly incursion in the city.

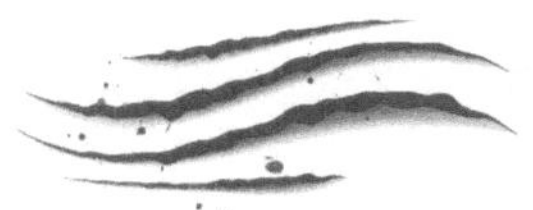

Rose had reached out first, ending a silence of two years. That silence was Helen's fault, though Rose never mentioned it. She just called and said she heard about the lab closing, taking Helen's job with it, and asked how her sister was doing. A week later, Helen moved in. Thankfully, enough people were still alive and willing to subscribe to Rose's music videos to keep the two of them afloat.

When they were little, Rose always knew when Helen wasn't okay. When she needed a room that was less crowded, or a few minutes to stand outside with no obligations but breathing. Helen would feel Rose's hand on her wrist, and Rose would angle her head toward wherever calmness waited. She'd smile a little, like they were going somewhere exciting but couldn't let anyone know.

The month after she'd moved in with Rose, Helen's former apartment building was overrun by dragonflies.

Helen wasn't sure if she and Rose were close anymore. She didn't know if they could be. But they were safe.

Noises woke her in the night from the almost-sleep that was often the best she could get, skimming just above slumber as thoughts and fear propelled her. The noises were the familiar clicking and displaced air of the front door opening. She got out of bed, hands shaking as she grabbed the box of matches on her nightstand. It wouldn't be much, but the dragonflies didn't like fire.

She cast her flashlight beam into the rest of the apartment, but it landed on nothing.

"What's wrong?" Rose blinked from the doorframe of her room, headphones draped around her neck. She preferred to work at night, snug inside the studio Helen never entered.

She already felt like she was intruding by being in the apartment and didn't want to annoy Rose by interrupting her work.

Helen looked toward the door, which was still closed and locked. "Didn't you hear that? The door opened…"

But Rose shook her head. "You must have had a dream."

Helen frowned. Rose knew how poorly she slept. "Would you even have heard? With your headphones on?"

Rose pursed her lips, concerned. "Go back to bed, Helen."

Because their sleep schedules were so different, sometimes a few days would go by where Rose and Helen barely spoke.

Helen was responsible for a lot of silences, actually. She'd always been scared of people forgetting about her, of going unnoticed where she wanted to be liked or even loved. But even scarier was the thought of making herself remembered and not being welcomed. So she stayed quiet and was never entirely surprised when others did the same.

She kept expecting Rose to get angry at her. Rose never did. When Helen pushed the issue, Rose only said she was glad to have her sister back. That silence, two years long, was the one Helen felt the worst about. But Rose knew so much about her, and for a while every time they talked Helen had remembered every mistake, every time she'd needed rescuing.

She was fine. Everything was fine. It wasn't anyone else's business when she barely slept, or when she kept to herself.

Now Rose had rescued her again.

Over the next few days, the dragonfly struck several people in the city. All of them gone, their faces and forms now part of the dragonfly's catalogue of shapes they could assume.

All it took was a touch.

Helen watched theories build up online, tracing paths and making predictions, with the previous deaths serving as markers.

The dragonfly was close.

She kept seeing Jaclyn.

She'd leave the apartment and catch hints of her neighbor's pale hair disappearing around the corner. Or she wouldn't *see* her but couldn't shake the feeling she was being watched. Sometimes she saw Jaclyn outside, a stark figure against the dying trees. Prey for any dragonfly.

In one of Helen's dreams, Jaclyn extended her hand, but then it turned into a dragonfly's wing, flickering madly.

Jaclyn had arrived the same day Helen heard about the dragonfly in the city.

The dragonflies had started appearing two years before. After the first few dozen victims, a team managed to catch one. Rather, they caught the hundreds of dragonflies that swarmed together, visible only in the moment between the creature touching a new victim and the moment they assumed that victim's form. The only time they gave themselves away.

Helen had worked in the building where that team's lab had been. For every scientist who ignored her at the front desk, there was one who was friendly. Like the sweet biologist from the third floor, who'd always checked to see what Helen wanted when he went to get coffee for his team.

That team had been the one examining the dragonflies.

The day the work was to begin, one of the administrators sent Helen out to buy more ink for the printer.

She returned to find a cordon, and panic.

Rose went to get groceries. Helen was stuck in that awful state where she was too exhausted to do anything, but knew that if she went back to bed, she still wouldn't sleep. She'd just think about that noise in the night, and the dragonfly who kept taking victims.

A few minutes after Rose left, someone knocked on the door. Softly, as if they weren't sure they wanted to be heard.

Through the peephole, Helen saw Jaclyn.

Realistically, Jaclyn was there because she had a question about the heat. The night before had been cold enough to leave frost, and the building's heat had been dying for a while. Shawn on the third floor had thankfully been willing to clean the boiler, and it helped some, but the thing needed replacing. Helen had called the property management company a year ago and was rewarded with a prerecorded recitation of holiday hours for a holiday long past. She didn't know if the employees had fled, or if they'd encountered dragonflies.

Jaclyn probably had a simple question. With so few people left, they needed to help each other when they could.

Helen cracked the door open. "Hi."

Jaclyn let out a breath and then said, "I think your sister is a dragonfly."

She should slam the door. Why didn't she slam the door?

"I tracked the dragonfly here after it reached the city," Jaclyn said softly.

Helen couldn't speak.

Jaclyn lowered her voice. "Is she home?"

Helen shook her head and started closing the door.

"She left five nights ago." Jacklyn moved to be seen in the diminishing space between door and frame.

Five nights ago. Helen's chest warmed. The uncomfortable heat spread up her shoulders and neck, burning her cheeks. Five nights ago was when she'd heard the door open. When Rose had claimed she heard nothing. Why would Rose go out in the middle of the night? Especially with a dragonfly loose...

Helen curled the hand not holding the door into a fist, resisting the urge to bite her lips until they bled. "You've been watching us."

Jaclyn nodded. "Since I got here." There was no hesitation or shame. Of course there wasn't, Helen realized. Jaclyn claimed she was tracking a dragonfly.

"What would you do?" she asked before she could convince herself not to. "If she was?" Could dragonflies even be killed?

Jaclyn's face went grim.

Helen shook her head before she could answer. "No. This is impossible."

"Wait!" Jaclyn pleaded, looking around herself tensely. "She's using you to help her stay hidden. I don't know how much longer she'll let you live before—"

"Before she makes me one of them," Helen finished. Would it quench her fears, she wondered, to become something impossible?

She shouldn't be listening to this. Rose couldn't be a dragonfly. They were safe.

Yet Helen unclenched her hand and picked up the box of matches she kept on the table near the door. Then she opened the door further.

Jaclyn closed her eyes briefly, as if considering. Then she held out her hand, palm up. "I'm real," she murmured. "You can trust me."

Helen knew she should run. The apartment would keep her safe. She brushed her thumbs against her palms, the scrape of dry skin against dry skin like an indictment of her judgement. She extended her hand.

"Helen?"

Rose stood at the end of the hall, looking at them with surprise. But... Helen blinked, tiredness wrapping around her like a thick, suffocating scarf. There was a wariness to Rose. Everyone was always wary. Around strangers, you had to be.

Rose approached slowly, her eyes sizing up the few centimeters of air that remained between Jaclyn's and Helen's palms.

Helen twitched her fingertips forward until they touched Jaclyn's. Jaclyn's fingers were cold, as if she'd been outside without gloves. Helen pulled away and stared at her hand. But it didn't change. *She* didn't change, and neither did Jaclyn.

Yet Rose was staring at them with an expression Helen didn't recognize.

Until Rose disintegrated.

Where she'd been, now only uncountable dragonflies teemed. They sounded harsh, like thousands of mouths grinding their teeth. They swarmed faster than thought, enveloping Jaclyn in a deluge of glittering silver. Jaclyn disappeared behind the wildly beating wings in patches until there was none of her anymore.

Helen watched, horror making her too warm and too cold and too *stuck*. A shriek boiled up in her throat, but before it could leave her mouth, Jaclyn was back. Reassembled out of the small winged shapes.

Her skin pulsed with soft flutters, all those frantic minds collaborating on this artifice of a person.

Helen had never heard of them reforming into multiple people. Yet some dragonflies remained, and they shaped themselves into Rose, whose face seemed newly free of a tension Helen hadn't noticed before.

Shouldn't she have noticed?

Helen backed up, but she wasn't fast enough. The creatures followed her into the apartment. In the shapes of her sister and of one who'd thought to track monsters.

Helen wondered how afraid a dragonfly ever felt.

Then she lit a match.

THE MARZIPAN DOG
Octavia Cade

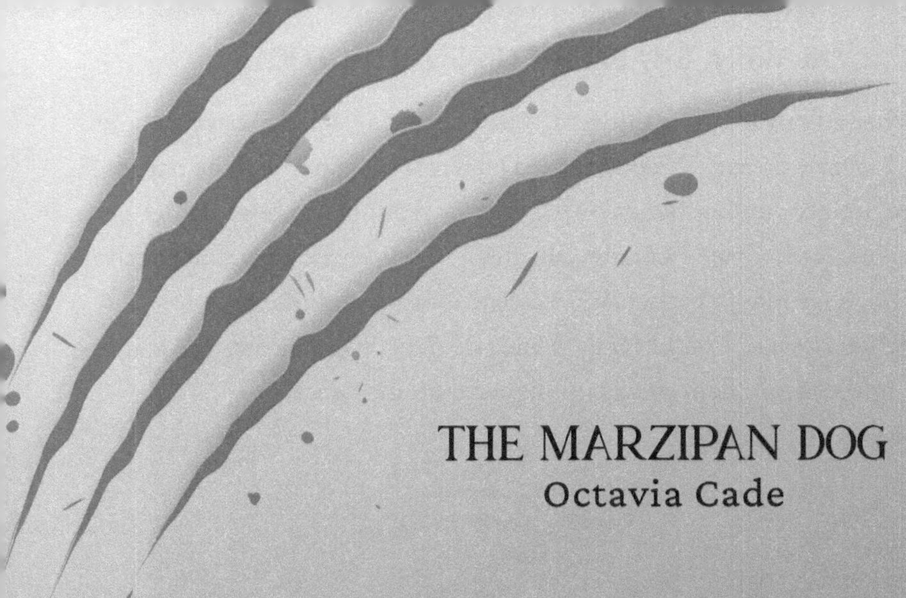

THE MARZIPAN DOG was not a Christmas present, but he arrived at Christmas time, with hairy breath and claws that clicked on the kitchen floor. Beth's parents kept him in the garage as a surprise.

"But it's not Christmas yet," she said as they pressed a small box into her hands. Not a box done up with ribbon that went into twirls when it was scraped along a scissor blade, but one that slid open easily, with paper that made crinkly sounds when Beth ripped it off. Inside, the chain was heavy in her hand. Longer than a necklace, with a clip at one end and a loop at the other; Beth slid her hand through the loop and knew what it was.

"He's here!" she cried. "Is he here? Is he really?"

Then the door opened with the slow catch on carpet that she was used to, followed by quick heavy footsteps, the sound of happy breaths, and Beth fell to her knees with her arms out. The Marzipan Dog came to her, all floppy-eared and the back half of him wagging from side to side, the solid thump of his tail knocking against her ribs like a heartbeat.

"The people who trained him thought you might like to have him a bit early," said her Dad, laughing. "Give you time to get used to each other, they said. A bit unusual, but I reckon they just wanted shot of him. Probably to get out of feeding him over the holidays."

"What colour is he?" said Beth. The coarse fur, the fat, happy snout all said *Labrador* to her. The dog settled by her feet, let her feel the harness he wore, let her run her hands over his body from tail to nose tip, let her scratch his furry belly, obliging. He made deep, satisfied grunts when Beth's fingers found a particularly ticklish spot behind one leg.

"He's chocolate," said Mum. "A nice deep brown. His ears are a little darker, and one of them pricks up higher than the other."

"I can feel," said Beth.

"I can't believe you're here," said Beth, whispering into her pillow. The Marzipan Dog rolled over her feet, having heaved himself onto the bed. When Beth reached down, she could feel his head under her hand, hear his deep breathing above the footsteps in the corridor, the footsteps coming towards her. "I can't stop thinking they're going to take you away," she said. "That they'll tell me it's all a mistake and your real owner's waiting for you."

The door swung open and there was a crash, the smell of warm milk, as Beth's mum saw the Marzipan Dog curled up on the bed and dropped the Milo she'd been carrying.

"Mum?" said Beth, alarmed.

"It's nothing," said her mother. "Don't worry. I thought I saw something, but it was just the dog. Are you sure you want it on the bed?"

The Marzipan Dog was greedy. There was no getting around it. He was hard-working and patient and loyal and unfailingly good-tempered, even when Beth stood on his paw by accident. But he was, unmistakably, a greedy dog, and that was how he got his name. "His *proper* name," as Beth put it. She refused to call him Libby—"It's a terrible name, he's not a bitch"—and his real name, Libra, was just too embarrassing.

"At least they didn't call you Aquarius," said Beth, sitting with the dog's head in her lap and running her fingers over a Braille page in one of her schoolbooks. "That would have been humiliating for both of us."

He was renamed when Beth had been rolling marzipan for a Christmas cake. She liked to make little figures out of the remnants—snowmen, mostly because they were easiest and could be trusted to turn out recognisable. "Funny decorations to have in summer, though," she said, passing them over to her friend.

Aisha sat on the other side of the table, as far from the dog as possible. She was painting faces on the figures, giving them scarves and rows of buttons like caterpillars. "It's not my holiday," she said. "Snowmen are no stranger than the rest of it."

And Beth, who would have complained, would have teased her back and poked fun until they finished in sticky-fingered giggles, said nothing. It was obvious to her that Aisha was trying, trying as hard as she could. Behaving as though things were normal seemed like it would take away from that. As though Beth didn't recognise the effort.

In the absence made by abnormality, Libra sneaked marzipan from the table and, almond-mouthed, was given his new name.

"It's your fault we have to go to the shops," said Beth. "You were the one who ate it all."

The Marzipan Dog gave a guilty little whine.

"Don't blame me—I don't want to go," said Beth. Aisha had sports practice, so Beth was left to find the replacements herself. "The lady behind the counter's horrible. She always sighs like dealing with me's too much trouble. Like I'm being lazy, not getting milk or marzipan or whatever myself." But this time, there was no difficulty—just a small and ugly squeal, and the soft patter of feet beside her, again and again, as if doubled.

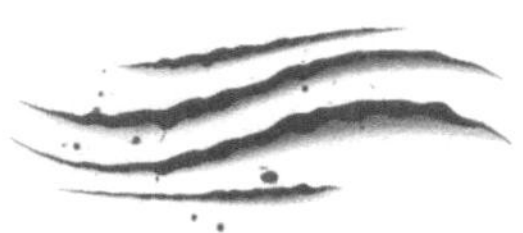

"I don't know what I'm supposed to do," Aisha had said when she first came round after the Marzipan Dog's arrival.

"Just let him sniff your hand, like this," said Beth, and demonstrated. But Aisha was shy, unaccountably shy, it seemed, and it wasn't until Beth took her shaking fist in her own hands and held it out for sniffing that Beth realised why.

"I'm sorry," she said. "I didn't think."

"That's alright," said Aisha. "I can do it. Just don't go expecting me to pet him or anything. And no licking."

"Let me put my hands around yours," said Beth, and wrapped Aisha's clenched fist in her own, felt the Marzipan Dog's whiskers brush against her skin and heard the dog snuffle at the mixed scent of them together. He kept his tongue to himself, and Beth was grateful.

Aisha didn't say anything, but Beth heard her washing her hands after, over and over.

Aisha's little brother Azmi didn't get close enough to touch. He came over one night to be babysat, brought by his sister so she and Beth could listen to music together while they watched him. Beth introduced him to the Marzipan Dog, but when the fur beneath her fingers thickened, Azmi began to cry so that he had to be taken away again.

"I could bring him round to your place sometime," said Beth. "Show the kid there's nothing to be scared of."

There was an awkward pause. "I wouldn't," said Aisha. "Service animals are one thing in theory, but..."

"It's okay," said Beth. "It is. It's fine. It's not like I need him to get round your house, anyway." And she didn't: Aisha's parents were nearly as solicitous as her own; going on twelve years of visits and sleepovers meant their house was familiar ground. Aisha's dad had even put a braided rope railing on the deck stairs for her, and her mother made sure to take her around and introduce her to every new piece of furniture she bought so that Beth wouldn't trip over it unawares.

She could always walk there with her cane.

"I'll just have to come over to yours more often," said Aisha. "'Till you're sick of the sound of me." Aisha's hair was smooth in her hands, and thick. Beth liked to brush it out, to braid it into coils and wind it round her head. If she couldn't see the fine strands, she could feel them, silk against her skin and smelling faintly of oil, and when her comb caught in the tangles, she could work them out with her fingers and brush until there was nothing left for the comb to catch on. That it would be covered by Aisha's headscarf did not disappoint her. If Beth couldn't see it, it was only fair that other people couldn't see it either.

"They'd totally be jealous if they could," said Aisha, complimentary, and Beth beamed as her hands skimmed and plaited.

This was something she could do without help, something she could do without a guide. The Marzipan Dog sat away from her, an absence of body against her leg. That was mostly because Aisha was wary of him still and didn't like having him too close. She would sit on the floor with him, her back against the sofa and having her hair tugged by strands, but she wouldn't share the leaning of him, wouldn't cuddle up to him as Beth did. Yet when they sat together, Beth could hear the faint snap and swallow of the Marzipan Dog, the muted *thump* of his tail on the carpet from the warm spot over by the window.

"Are you feeding my dog?" she said, amused.

"It's those big eyes," said Aisha, the bowl balanced in her lap and her head tilted to one side so that Beth could better reach the hair above her ears. "In that ugly, ugly face."

"I didn't know he ate popcorn," said Beth.

"That creature eats *anything*," said Aisha. "And he catches very well. I'll say this for him: he has the manners not to come eat from my hand. I couldn't stand the slobber."

"It's only drool," said Beth.

"It's disgusting, that's what it is," said Aisha, and threw more popcorn. "Filthy, nasty thing. If he ever tries to lick me, I warn you now. I'm going to scream."

Thump, thump.

"That's why he stays away, then. He probably couldn't stand the shrieking," said Beth, and tugged another braid into place.

He couldn't stand it, but he caused it. Somehow, Beth knew, he caused it. Usually the Marzipan Dog sat silent at her feet in class and snoozed, and sometimes she had to nudge him with her foot when he began to snore. She didn't like it when he snored, because there were girls sitting next to her who would make fun of him, make fun of her.

They always did, and always just loud enough so that they could be heard by Beth and Beth alone. One day they started up again, and the Marzipan Dog was not asleep, and his weight on her foot changed, became cooler and harder and had the press of scales against her bare leg, and the stench of salt water and mud rose up about her and there was screaming then, and shrieking, and the thump of feet on the floor and then the teacher was beside her, soothing and gentle and fur was soft against her leg again and the Marzipan Dog panted at her knee, panted happily and with satisfaction.

If Aisha stood a little distant from her now, she still walked with Beth on the way to school. Usually they took Azmi with them, but lately he followed behind, following with others, and Beth could feel the tension in her friend. It was familiar to both of them.

"There's always someone," said Beth, and for a moment it was as if nothing was different between them.

She'd get the easier time of it, usually. The other kids would tease and be unkind sometimes, but spent more time making fun of Aisha's headscarf than they did Beth's cane, and of the two objects, it had never been hers that they grabbed. And now the Marzipan Dog was there—and even if the comments continued, no-one would ever try to grab him. The Marzipan Dog, Beth was sure, would fight back, and when Aisha was with her no-one would risk getting too close to tease her either.

That would have been enough, in its way, if Aisha didn't have to put up with the rest of it—except the teasing came this time from the boys who had always been on her side before, the boys who had sisters who wore scarves of their own.

"What are you doing with that dog?" one said to Beth.

"He's a service animal," she replied.

"I didn't mean the Labrador."

And Aisha said nothing, nothing. Just took Beth's arm and steered her away from the calls and the jeers even when Beth didn't want to go, when she wanted to turn around and scream at them.

"Don't walk away when I'm talking to you, bitch!" she heard. The boys were back behind them again, and she held the lead of the Marzipan Dog tense in her fingers.

"Just ignore them," said Aisha, under her breath, before she swung about herself. "Come away from them, Azmi. You'll be late for school."

"I'm not a dog!" Azmi piped up, his childish voice loud as if he were trying to sound more grown up than he was, as if he tried to impress boys a decade his senior, boys who were more interested in Aisha than her little brother. "You can't tell me what to do!"

"Tell that to Mum and Dad," said Aisha, and there was a soft smack and a gasp and Beth heard a little rattle like a pebble had fallen at her feet.

"Shan't," said Azmi, but he sounded young again now, and uncertain.

"Aisha," said Beth. "What's happening? What's going on?"

Aisha pulled her aside, quickly, as if out of the way, and there was the sound of more pebbles behind her. And then Beth understood, and anger rose in her like a wave, and the Marzipan Dog whirled around and broke free of her hold, broke free of the harness and lunged away from her. He snarled a deep, savage sound that Beth had never heard him make before.

She tried to catch him as he burst away from her, but her fingers couldn't grip the heavy fur and then there were startled shouts, the sound of feet running away, and Azmi screaming and screaming.

There was a knock at the door.

"I don't want to talk about it," said Beth. She sat in her room, cross-legged on the floor, the muzzle of the Marzipan Dog resting in her lap.

"It helps, sometimes, to talk," said her dad. "Or to listen, even. It wasn't your fault."

"I know."

"Can I come in?"

"No," said Beth, and rolled her eyes when she heard the handle rattle. "Why ask if you're only going to ignore me?" But the pressure lifted off her leg, a sudden loss of fur and warmth, and the door opened just a fraction and stilled as the Marzipan Dog shifted beside her, shifted with a soft low scrape of leather, with a hint of breeze and unfurling, and the door snapped shut again.

"I'm sorry about the brat," said Aisha. "If it's any consolation, Dad smacked his arse and lectured him about respect and showing kindness to living things. I suppose he meant the dog, but he could have been talking about you."

"Oh, ha ha," said Beth. She picked at her feet, at the pink roughened skin that came from sudden bursts of new activity. "I think I've got a blister."

"Serves you right for being so lazy," said Aisha, who was on the netball team and even did cross-country, sometimes, although she complained about it.

"The Marzipan Dog wants to explore," Beth replied, defensive. "It's much more fun with him than with a cane, or hanging on someone's arm."

"I know," said Aisha. She was silent for a long moment. "Azmi's making you a card... to say he's sorry."

"That's... nice," said Beth, uncertain, and sceptical as well, though she would not say so.

"Mum's making him," Aisha admitted. "It's not really something you can get down at the shops. 'I'm sorry I was nasty to your pet'. He's going to bring it round later and apologise."

"Are they making him do that, too?" said Beth, and Aisha hummed, a small affirmative sound.

"Try to be nice to him," she said. "For me. He's not a bad kid, you know that. And I know you don't understand it, but he's really scared of your dog."

It was Beth who was silent then, who was caught between loyalties of her own. "I don't think he's the only one," she said.

Beth lay in bed at night, her palms resting on fur. "I'm not scared of you," she said. "My doggie, my doggie." A doggie with fur that smelled of marzipan, that shaped beneath her fingers, that formed as she felt.

"I wish I could see you," she said, but Beth could not see anything, not ever, and her eyes were in a body other than her own and they were not blind to her, or to anyone.

There was a long silence as Aisha considered. Beth held the Marzipan Dog steady beside her and under scrutiny, but the fur beneath her fingers was only fur, and the weight of his body against her was only warm, only soft and solid at once.

"He looks like a dog to me," said Aisha. "He looks like what he's always looked like."

"You haven't *felt* him," said Beth. "Around other people, I mean. He *changes*. I'm telling you, he's not a normal dog."

"Beth," said Aisha. "Beth. He doesn't change. I can see him as well as I see you, and I can see him at school, and I see him when we go out, to the pool or the beach or when we go dancing. And he might be wet or stinky or excited, but he's just a dog."

"You haven't felt him," said Beth again.

"Don't ask me to," said Aisha.

His tongue was warm and wet and forked, frigid and flickering and slicked with nectar. It smelled of meat and loyalty.

"I love you," said Beth. "My doggie, my doggie. *I love you.*"

The Marzipan Dog growled a deep, soft rumble that echoed. Beth felt it in her bones, felt the vibration through the harness, and when she knelt beside him to hold him back, his shoulder had grown above hers and the fur beneath her fingers was coarser than it had ever been.

"Get behind me, Azmi," she heard Aisha say, and the sound of the little boy sobbing echoed as a counterpart to the Marzipan Dog.

The dog was solid against her, solid and strong with muscles that made pillars of his legs and no matter how much she pulled at him, Beth couldn't shift him, couldn't haul him away and into silence. "He's too big," she panted. "He's grown too much!"

"It's exactly the same size as it was yesterday," snapped Aisha. "It's just the same."

"I promise you he's not," said Beth. "He's different; I can feel it. I can't see it either, but other people can. They don't like him, Aish. He scares them."

"He's scaring Azmi," said Aisha, and she did not say anything about herself.

"Azmi's not seeing a Labrador," said Beth, and the choked wails coming from the corner of her bedroom convinced her that she was right. Beside her, the Marzipan Dog's growling altered, just slightly—an undertone of satisfaction, of pleasure and power and fear. "Az, when you threw stones at him, what did you see? What were you throwing stones at?"

"The bad thing," Azmi cried, and his voice was muffled, somehow, as if he was trying to stuff both fists into his mouth. "The bad dog thing!"

"There's silver in my jewellery box," said Beth. "On the dressing table. That necklace you borrow sometimes. Take it out, give it to Az."

"No," said Aisha. "No. This has gone far enough." There was a long silence, broken only by the sound of crying, and Beth felt the floor vibrate beneath her knees, felt the Marzipan Dog shift against her slightly, as if something was coming towards them. Then his head dipped, just a little, as if someone had rested their hand on his head. The growling faltered, the echoes against Beth's chest no longer constant, but broken, uncertain.

"You are just a dog," said Aisha. "A spoilt, fat, grumpy dog. You're not any bigger than you were before. You don't feel any different. You don't look any different." The pressure lifted and the Marzipan Dog seemed to shift against Beth, to become softer, smaller, and the growl was lighter, almost a whining. And then it was gone.

"I'm taking my brother home," said Aisha. Her voice was closer, louder, as if she had bent over to look the Marzipan Dog dead in the eye. "If that animal wants to try to stop me, it can go ahead, but if it does, I'll touch it again, and this time it won't be just a pat."

Beth dreamed of darkness and deserts. The ground beneath her feet was hard and gritty and there was sand in the air, abrading her skin. She was alone. She was always alone. In the distance she could hear whining, a faint thin little sound that echoed as if off dunes and empty spaces, but though she called and called, the Marzipan Dog did not appear, and she was left to wander, powerless, without even her cane, and there was no-one to protect her.

"Hello?"

Beth had fallen asleep, curled around the Marzipan Dog, and her eyes itched and ached from crying. She'd woken to the vibration of her phone, clutched in one hand and half-pillowed under one cheek.

"Aisha? Is that you?"

There was a long silence, wherein all Beth could hear was the whuffle-snore of the Marzipan Dog. "I nearly didn't call," said Aisha. "I've been so angry. And Azmi was so scared."

"I'm sorry," said Beth. "I'm so sorry. I know you don't believe me, but—"

"I believe you," said Aisha. "I know you're sorry. I'm sorry, too, that I didn't believe you about... about the other. I've been talking to Azmi, now he's calmed down a bit. He's a nuisance sometimes, but he's not a liar. Neither are you. If you say it's changing, that it's not a dog underneath, I believe you."

Tears pricked Beth's eyes, warm as blood. "Thanks," she said, sniffling, and turning over on the bed until her back was pressed up against the back of the Marzipan Dog, and she faced away from him. "I can't explain it. I don't know why it's happening. I don't know why you can't see it."

"I think it's turning into the thing that frightens people most," said Aisha. "Not all the time. But if you're upset, or scared, well... It's your dog. It probably thinks it's protecting you. It knows it's supposed to help."

Beth snorted, and it was more watery than usual. "Some help," she said, and thought of spider legs and leather-wings and scales. Of freedom and confidence and defence. "What about Azmi?"

"Azmi sneak-watches too many horror films," said Aisha. "He knows he's not allowed. Serves him right."

"What about you?" said Beth. "You said he's never changed for you."

"It never needed to," said Aisha, and Beth remembered, suddenly, the shaking fist her friend had held out to the Marzipan Dog when they first met, the set tone, the careful distance she kept between them. Remembered, and remembered she had thought it mere revulsion, mere restriction.

"Aish," she said. "*Aisha.* Why didn't you say anything?"

"You're my friend," said Aisha. "My best friend. You needed it. And I thought: I love you more than I was scared of it. And I don't hate it any more, I suppose. I'll never like it, but I'm not afraid. So tell your beast if he werewolfs out on my kid brother again, I'll kick its fat arse. And I'll *enjoy* it. Don't think I won't."

Thump. Beth felt the bedspread shake, the rapid thrashing of tail. The Marzipan Dog was awake again and listening. She reached behind her, felt the warm, furred flank, the gentle nosing at her hand. *Thump, thump.*

"He hears you," she said.

Beth lay in bed, the Marzipan Dog hard up against her and warm, friendly beneath her fingers. Protective. Beth cuddled up against him, into his big solid body and felt the heartbeat beneath the fur, the heart that had stood between her and hurt, between her and gossip and meanness and stones. She thought of Aisha, who had stood between as well, and heard again the deep snarling growl of the Marzipan Dog as his new giant body had pulled the leash from her fingers—but this time, this time, she felt satisfaction as well as fear.

"Not Aisha," she said to the Marzipan Dog, into his fluffy, floppy Labrador ear. "And not Azmi, not ever again." She thought of Aisha, and the pulling off of headscarves, and the bullying, and the boys calling her an animal when Beth could not see to defend her. "But the rest of them," said Beth, nuzzling deeper into the fur. "The rest of them, Marzipan, are fair game."

And the Marzipan Dog shifted against her, the thud of his tail solid against the bedspread, and made a small, happy growl like a purr in his throat.

CREPI IL LUPO
Elysia Rourke

A HOWL CHILLS MY bones to the marrow.

It's Raksha pawing at the door. There's a layer of fresh snow on her coat. How long was she outside? I check the clock; it's well past midnight. My dinner, untouched in the kitchen, has gone cold.

Raksha shakes, splashing snow on the hardwood and my bare shins, before settling on her bed at the foot of my desk. I hope she hasn't been up to mischief. There's been an influx of dead house cats in town. The township suspects a coyote, but my husky has always yearned for the hunt.

I return to my desk and flip through my notes. On the last page, a long-awaited breakthrough, scribbled in blue ink before Raksha interrupted my thoughts.

Lycomania.

I studied medicine to ease the terrors looming in the dark corners of my boyhood bedroom—oppressive shadows that threatened to swallow me when the original Raksha died, my first pet. Every dog I've owned since has been named for her, the companion who pushed me to conquer death, to devote my life to her destruction. Science promised an answer for everything, a cure.

Two weeks ago, the first case arrived in my ER.

Rudy. Twenty-two. The kid had no history of mental illness or substance abuse, but my nurses found him shivering in the waiting room, salivating, his blood pressure through the roof. He'd recently landed the lead at Puck's Playhouse.

Stress-related.

I told him to rest and sent him home. Some patients present differently, I assured the staff. There was no cause for alarm.

Two days later, he came back.

This time, he claimed he'd been possessed by a wolf. He prowled around the waiting room, inconsolable, screaming and crying in heavy, airless sobs. In the exam room, he told me the skin on his chest was tightening, that something inhuman wanted to burst through. He craved raw, blood-soaked meat straight off the bone.

Look, he said. *Hair that wasn't there yesterday.*

So, I thought. *Rudy's a loon.*

I knew it wasn't fair, but I was exhausted. We were overworked and understaffed. I wanted to support his mental health, but animalistic urges were outside my pay grade. I prescribed the highest dose of antidepressants available, tracked down a ten-year-old pamphlet containing local support services, and sent him on his way.

The next time Rudy took over the ER, he brought his friends.

Dolph and Lupita and Tala and Connor. All thespians. All howling about insatiable urges, lengthening teeth, strange body hair. They lunged at the other patients, baring their teeth.

We got them a room.

As a group, they were lean and fit. They ate well. But the way they growled as they performed a uniform lope behind me en route to the exam room felt choreographed. I reminded them, one at a time, that hospital narcotics were locked in a timed safe.

I took a blood sample and ran a toxicology report, but they all passed. They were the first clean troupe since the invention of the theatre. The nurses urged me to send them away. The howling was unnerving the other patients. We weren't equipped to deal with those sorts of delusions. The Royal up on the hill would be a better place for them.

But I was unable to sleep, twirling the mystery over and over in my head. There was a paper to be written. I couldn't let another doctor write it, not when my patients' bizarre but graceful gait reminded me so much of Raksha. I studied her each night, wondering as her sleeping chest rose and fell under my palm, how the players captured canine movement with such accuracy.

So here I am, unable to sleep combing through medical journals. I thumb through the DSM.

And there it is.

Lycomania.

Rare, but not unheard of, with less than fifty cases on record since the late 19th century. I find no evidence of group outbreaks, but it wouldn't be the first time a gaggle of artistic types has caught a similar mental bug. It's bipolar disorder, schizophrenia, or a psychotic episode from undiagnosed depression.

I can test for those things. I can *prescribe* for those things.

I pat Raksha on the head and slam the book closed. *Good dog.*

A week later, a padded envelope arrives. It's a ticket to opening night at Puck's Playhouse with a note from Rudy: *We'd love for you to join us.*

I don't care for theatre, but I'm a scientist. I have a paper to write. I need to know what about this production caused the eerie, albeit temporary, mass hysteria amongst the actors.

I arrive early. Too early. A few overeager guests and relatives loiter in the lobby, but the auditorium is empty. I find my seat—burgundy velvet with wooden armrests—and fold my jacket over the back. The seat groans as I sit, announcing my presence to the empty place.

I check my watch. Over an hour to go. I came straight from work. Only Raksha awaits my return home. The theatre is large and silent, the opposite of a buzzing hospital. Even the surgical theatre feels populated, alive. This room is dead. Hollow.

Someone barks my name.

Startled, I look over my shoulder, searching the empty room.

"Over here!"

Rudy waves to me from backstage, clinging to the blood-red curtain. He beckons me up onto the platform with a grin. I abandon my jacket and follow him into the wings. There is the percussive sound of toes on plywood, like raindrops before a storm. The actors are preparing.

"Thanks for coming, Dr. Callahan," Rudy breathes.

His eyes are smoky, and he's wearing furry grey leggings. I think I spot fake eyelashes. His bare, unshaven chest is dewy and sparkles under the theatre lights. There's glitter residue on my palm from our handshake.

"Call me Peter," I say. I can't help but find myself attracted to him, this beautiful creature standing before me. My fingers long to reach out and stroke him, to see if those leggings are bristly and smooth like Raksha's fur. I imagine myself curling up next to him, drifting off into a comfortable night's sleep. Instead, I clear my throat. "Should you be warming up?" I gesture to the familiar company.

"My character arrives late in the show," Rudy says. "There's plenty of time."

The other actors stretch backstage, wearing animal costumes. Their faces are painted with exaggerated make-up, though none as stunning in their simplicity as Rudy's. Lupita and Dolph, a rabbit and some other rodent, perform dramatic yawns as they balance on one foot, tipping until the fake ears in their hair almost touch the stage. Connor balances an enormous set of antlers on his scalp and Tala wears a mess of beige and white feathers with a magnificent towering headpiece. The two are jump-squatting and roaring, stretching their faces with their fingers between each leap. They'll need to emote for the back of the room, but the way Tala tugs the corners of her mouth makes my skin crawl. I can't help but imagine her lips tearing apart, her mouth stretched into a ghoulish grin.

I turn to Rudy, examining his strange costume again. He's turned from me, calling to a stagehand dressed all in black. A tail hangs limp between his legs.

Rudy guides me deeper behind the curtain. I swallow against the darkness, preferring the theatre lights. "Let me introduce you to our director. Peter, this is Remus Rossi."

The black-clad man from the wings shakes my hand. His massive palm envelops mine. He doesn't look like your typical theatre director. He's young and sports a thick, tangled beard, and he peers at me with slits for eyes that sit atop plump apple cheeks. A mop of curly black hair covers his forehead.

But what's most alarming is his sheer size. He towers over me. Rudy looks like a child next to him. If he's the leader of their pack, he's a dire wolf.

"Congratulations on the production," I say.

Rossi's voice is soft, leashed, as though he fears losing it. "I have you to thank, good doctor. You have returned my actors to me." His words curl. English is not his first language.

"I ought to be thanking you," I say.

"For what?"

"The ticket."

His bushy eyebrows pull together before a nudge from Rudy sends a smile of recognition cracking across his face. "Yes, you're welcome. Perhaps you might want to try out for our little company one day?"

I frown at the actors, taking in their muscled legs and arched backs. They're stretching now. "I doubt it."

"You may think differently after the performance." Rossi places a meaty hand on my shoulder and pinches. His eyes glaze, his knuckles turning white. I struggle not to yelp as his fingers grind against bone.

"I'd better get back to my seat," I say, noticing the way the other actors have paused their rehearsals to watch us. Everyone seems tense. Except Rudy.

"Enjoy the show," Rossi says.

"Thanks. Break a leg?" I grimace, hoping they don't realise how unfamiliar I am with their craft.

Rossi laughs. "In Italia we say, *crepi il lupo.*"

"What does it mean?""May the wolf die." Rudy grins, slapping me on the back. His teeth glimmer under the theatre lights. "Which is why you're here, isn't it, Peter? You've killed the wolf in us."

"I suppose." Sweat beads on my collar. I wish I could loosen my tie. "Well, gentlemen, *crepi il lupo.*"

I excuse myself with a shiver. As I descend from the stage to reclaim my seat, the whisper of performers follows me, a soft chant buried in breath.

Whatever creature has curled around my neck trails a menacing claw down my spine.

"Crepi."

It is a contortive dance. A mass of limbs and flesh. Decency tells me to look away, the obscene way they blend and mingle, individuals devoured by the whole. They stomp a percussive line for a simple vocal track that sounds more like a patient reeling in my ER than singing. An upright bass keens over their inhuman movement, strings tighter than the tendons in a clenched fist.

I've seen those movements before, the way their bodies pulse and roll; full-body spasms under the surge of a defibrillator. A body near death. It isn't a thing to be celebrated, but the audience gasps with each new position. It's an unsettling sight, but I'm not looking for unsettling.

I'm watching for the wolf.

One moment, they are insects scampering on hands and feet across the stage. The next, they have morphed into a giant fish, gasping for breath on shore. They toss each other through the air, and the feathered one takes flight as a bird. It is only upon landing that I see the gait return, the drop to four-leggedness.

My stomach sinks.

There is grief behind the performance, like delivering bad news after unsuccessful surgery. A longing in their inability to stand upright.

A fight with death. The same war I wage.

Lights flash. Between scenes, we are bathed in darkness, listening to the hum of their prowl. When the scene continues, their arms move as one and they become a many-headed beast. At other times, when they fall out of unison, I see a flickering fire.

When Rudy twirls onto the stage, he is impossible to miss. He shines like a star under the lights. The play is almost over. I'll soon be heading home to Raksha, putting this strange experience behind me.

The animals scatter. A predator nears.

Rudy leaps with pointed toes. He digs his claws into the stag—Connor—and drags a red ribbon across the stage.

The audience applauds.

The ravaging has begun. Rudy moves from player to player, teeth flashing, eyes aglow. The ribbon is unconvincing, but there's a drama to it that tears at my chest all the same. The fallen actors roll to their knees in a graveside prayer.

I have seen the she-wolf, Death, whom these people applaud. She is neither beautiful nor kind. Not in my line of work. Not when each Raksha goes.

When Rudy has consumed the many-headed beast, he turns to us and opens his mouth, showing the long canines that weren't there an hour prior.

The theatre plunges into darkness, as though Rudy has swallowed us all.

There's polite applause. My eyes struggle to adjust to the blackout.

Programs rustle as we wait for an announcement, some sign that the performance is complete or the lights have failed to rise. There's no calming voice from the rafters, no light to usher us out.

In the darkness, I imagine I hear the tear of flesh. Something inhuman, clawing its way out. My mouth sours, my teeth too heavy for my gums. My whole body has gone numb.

The room closes in on me like a casket. I need air.

I whisper apologies as I climb over my seatmate, pawing toward the exit.

A relieved gasp flows from my chest like a drowning victim expelling water as I grab for the door. I anticipate the lobby, the burst into the fresh air, the short drive home. I'll speed to escape whatever chases me, this creature buried in my chest.

The doors don't move.

Locked.

Locked *in.*

The room erupts in howls. Six pairs of glowing yellow eyes descend upon the theatre, bringing the play to the aisles. There are screams, then gurgles, and the sick crunch of a body relieved of life. Blood splashes on the floor, dumped all at once.

The players moan as their skin sloughs away and the wolves emerge.

I've made a mistake. Dismissed their case too soon. I claw at the door, knowing it is futile. Panic threatens to overtake me, but I breathe and dash for the stage, hoping to bundle myself in the curtain until order is restored.

"Peter," Rudy chants, his voice wet with their sick libations. "Come out. Join us."

My shin catches the sharp lip of a chair. I curse through the pain. I've torn the skin. Badly.

"All the better to hear you with, Peter," Rudy sings. "Do you remember that story?"

I haul myself over the front row. Ignoring the wetness on my pant leg, I vault onto the stage. Almost there. There are no props, no set pieces. Nothing to hide behind. The curtain is tucked away.

It's too late.

"I see you, Peter."

I tear backstage, but the lights are out there as well. I feel my way along the hallways, searching for a dressing room. Any place to hide from the massacre.

Rudy's nails click on the linoleum as he stalks me, like Raksha on the hunt. I slam into a dressing room. The light switch is useless. Blindly, I fumble with shaking hands to slide the chain into place.

"It's a delightful story."

My fingers slip.

"It's so hard to get a proper diagnosis these days, isn't it?"

I slide the chain into its track.

"You could have helped my friends."

I throw myself into the corner of the room, smashing through a discarded pile of props. My fingers slip around a gun. Probably made for the popular Agatha Christie mysteries this theatre usually hosts, not that I've ever seen one. I'm pretty sure it is made of rubber. I point it at the door anyway.

"Peter!" Rudy screams, the final syllable of my name drawn out into a howl. The door shakes and the chain snaps.

He is all wolf now. The skin has torn from his chest, his handsome face devoured by a snout and piercing canine eyes. He grins when he sees me cowering, pointing the gun and clutching a program like a shield over my heart. Blood drips from his chin. "Rossi started this, yes. But you enabled it, didn't you? Let it go on without treatment. I came to you— begged you to help me. Do you want to beg me now, Peter? To tell you how the story ends?"

I shake my head.

"I resisted, too, at first."

His eyes fall to the pistol and he smiles that magnificent and terrible smile for me one last time, a peal of laughter sliding past his blackened lips.

"Oh, Peter. You don't believe in werewolves," he snarls. "But you believe in silver bullets?"

For some reason, I think of Raksha, the dog who never dies. I can't recall how many iterations there have been, how many have come and gone.

"Think of what you could do," Rudy croons. "As one of us."

That's how it always goes. I wake one morning and Raksha is young again. My life continues unchanged.

I lower the gun, taking a deep breath, wondering if I'm doing the right thing. I give Rudy a curt nod. "How does the story end?"

I'll do anything.

He pounces and sinks his teeth into my cheek, my neck, the tender crook of my arm. His bites are shallow, almost tender as he presses into me, exactly how I imagined. His body heaves with ecstasy, my veins flooding with his curse. I pull him close, breathing in the sweet scent of grass and musk and fur.

It will be over soon, this play. I can drive home to Raksha. I wonder if she'll notice anything different.

Rudy's teeth sink into my thigh.

"Good dog," he breathes, as I throw back my head and howl.

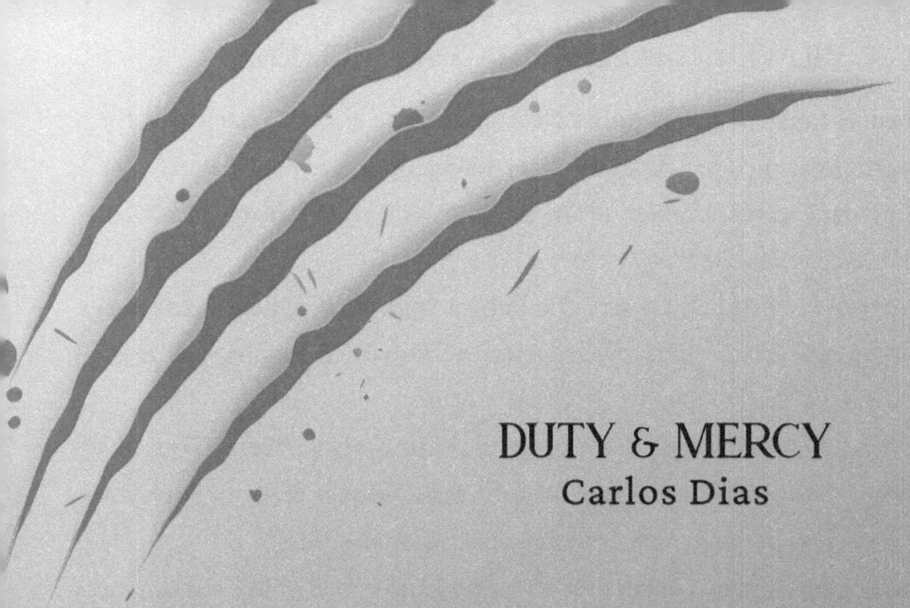

DUTY & MERCY
Carlos Dias

Aeldway was an old town. Decaying. Diseased.

The people on the streets reeked of wet dog and faeces. The glow from the fires in the decrepit stone homesteads was blocked as Raekar passed by them. Everyone came to the windows to witness the Venator's coming.

"Lord Venator, please have mercy. A coin? A coin for the old and the parched? The sickly and the hungry?" a man begged, extending a spindly hand.

Raekar looked down from his horse. The moonlight shone on the beggar's arm, revealing the loose grey skin, the patchy hair that covered it, and the grown putrid nails.

Disgusting, Raekar thought. "You deserve no mercy, filth," he said.

"But, my family… We are victims. We need the money for the cure. We are—"

"You took that curse upon yourself. You should have chosen a clean death."

"I was forced, Lord Venator. I was—"

Raekar dismounted and grabbed the man's torn shirt, lifting him up. He was incredibly light. His breath was warm and carried the powerful

139

stench of rotten meat. His gums were pushed all the way back and the teeth were growing. He was in the later stages of the Lycan Plague.

"You have eaten human flesh, beggar, and you dare to plead for mercy?" Raekar asked.

"No, no! I...I didn't, no sir," the beggar said. Raekar heard his heart beat faster and faster. His eyes darted nervously, revealing yellowish colouration.

"Do not lie to me! Your teeth grow, yet your body weakens. Your lust for power is second only to your foolishness. Did you really believe you would become like *them*? Was it worth another man's life?"

The beggar's eyes went feral. He snapped and growled like the dog he was, showing a tongue that had swollen in his mouth.

"I needed it! I needed it! Cure me, Venator! Cure me!" he yapped. Raekar held the frenzied man back as if he was a child throwing a tantrum.

"Your only cure is death."

Raekar grabbed a silver dagger sheathed on his lower back and stabbed upward, driving it through the beggar's chin and into his head.

The man still moved and squirmed. Raekar twisted the blade. The body went limp.

Aeldway was in a much worse state than Raekar thought. The Hunt must be completed.

Raekar opened the door to the local inn. The smell didn't differ much from the one lingering on the streets. There was just the added pungency of alcohol.

There were Lycan-plagued inside.

The interior of the establishment was dark, with a low ceiling bent like it was about to collapse. There were sixteen patrons in total on the first floor—six of them afflicted—but Raekar heard more from the rooms above.

Lycan Plague. The disease developed when one drank the blood of a werewolf and could then be passed on with a single bite.

The blood would often be passed around in the streets of these smaller or older towns, offered as a remedy for illness or a shortcut to strength. Those who drank it would then offer their bite to others. It could take over a town completely in a matter of months, especially if its people struggled in poverty.

After taking in his surroundings, Raekar sat on a stool by the counter. The others by his side regarded him with either suspicion or awe. Just another night. Raekar had already been fortunate that the place wasn't closed when people heard a Venator was in town.

"Good evenin', Lord Venator. May I get you anythin'?" the innkeeper asked, as a bead of sweat trickled from his bald head down to his cheek.

"Information."

"Of course, Lord Venator. This humble servant of the Hunt will answer with nothin' but the truth." The innkeeper bowed slightly.

"For how long have there been Lycan-plagued walking your streets?" Raekar asked, his eyes meeting the innkeeper's.

"At-At least two months, Lord Venator. Maybe more, I reckon," the innkeeper whispered.

"And your Lord chose to not send word of this?"

"I know nothin' of that, sir. He only told us to be wary and to stay at home during the nights. It was runnin' me out of business, it was."

"Is that why you have taken Lycan-plagued as your patrons?" Raekar asked. The man's armpits were drenched. The question was a mere test of character.

"I—"

"Do not lie to me. I will know."

"Yes. I let them in, Lord, but only because they'd have nowhere else to go. Truly, Lord, I feel for them," the innkeeper said.

He was telling the truth. The man did it out of pity - and out of ignorance. If he knew the danger, he would have never allowed a single one of them in. Still, it would not be worth punishing him for it. Not that night.

"Where in town did the first case of the affliction occur?" Raekar asked without blinking.

"It was three streets over, Lord. Meredith was the first to fall ill."

"Does she still live?"

"No, Lord. She passed not long after."

Raekar glanced over his surroundings once more. A few of the patrons were staring and tried hiding it quickly, but not quickly enough. All of them were nervous, but not *especially* nervous. The smell of the plague could mask any signs of guilt, but Raekar was still confident no one else in the room knew more of that matter.

"Where was Meredith's abode?" Raekar asked.

"It's the house with the beautiful night roses in the front garden. You can't miss it," the innkeeper answered.

"Thank you for your time."

"Of course, Lord. Please, if you need a place to stay, it would be my honour to—"

"No."

Raekar stood up and left the inn.

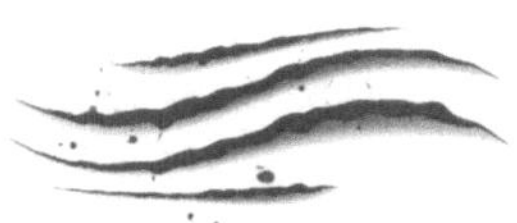

The deeper he walked into town, the worse it became.

Lycan-plagued were everywhere. Even inside their homes, along with their families who didn't recognise the signs yet. Raekar could even hear the sounds of ravenous eating in alleyways.

He'd been taught to feel disgust for them. He couldn't escape those teachings, yet he knew his actions showed a corrupting compassion.

Any one of his brothers sent to a town like this would've killed every single one of its denizens that showed even the faintest hint of the affliction. Or they would burn the whole town to the ground for sinking into this level of heresy and impurity.

The Venator served Queen Kereline, as they served her ancestors since the inception of the kingdom. For centuries they have rooted out ancient evils, exorcised curses and crushed mindless rebellions against the Holy Church of Silverlight.

They were needed. Sorely needed, else the world would turn rabid and feral.

The Lycan Plague was one of their oldest enemies, created by witches and their werewolf guardians. It created servants for them when the Lycan-plagued answered the howl of the werewolf whose blood created them. The *Hyle Sacramentum* it was called.

Raekar couldn't kill an entire town for the heresy of a few. There were still those afflicted that didn't give into the plague's impulses. There were still those that fought back, those worthy of mercy.

He saw night roses with their pale blue petals in front of one of the houses. It had an impeccable garden, but the building itself was cracking with age, leaning to one side.

Someone moved in the window.

Raekar knocked. People rushed about inside, smelling of the plague. He heard them mumbling to each other. They were scared. Everyone was scared of the Venator.

The door pulled open.

"Lord Venator, welcome to our house," an old man said. His eyes were bloodshot, his beard reached almost up to his cheekbones and was long. His teeth, however, were human. Rotten, but still human.

"Are you the family of the one named Meredith?" Raekar asked.

"Aye. That's us," the old man said, opening the door to show his wife.

The signs were much more obvious on her. Fur had started to form in patches on her thin arms, and her back showed a heavy curve. Their mouths trembled, their legs looked unsteady, and their heartbeats were loud. The interior of the house reeked.

"You are afraid," Raekar stated matter-of-factly.

"Forgive us, Lord Venator, but we've heard what happens when you arrive in a plagued town," the woman said.

"I will stay outside if you want me to," Raekar said, taking a step back.

"Nay, please come inside. We know this town don't 'ave long. I'm Wilbur, and this is Anabel," the old man said.

Raekar walked inside and sat on a low stool close to the fire. "Your daughter bit you."

"She did, Lord Venator—"

"Raekar."

"She did, Lord Raekar," Anabel corrected herself before continuing. "On the second week of the illness, while we tried to keep her comfortable through the fever. Then I bit my husband."

"So, she was bitten herself," Raekar said.

"Nay, Lord. She was the first afflicted. I never thought my daughter to be a heretic," Wilbur said.

"If she had truly been the first, the fever would have begun in the first few days, not the second week," Raekar corrected.

Wilbur looked confused. "But we were told that by the guard, that she was caught with the —"

"So, our daughter… Her soul is saved? Oh dear, her soul is saved!" Anabel cried.

"You were saying the guards reported her affliction to you. Where did Meredith spend her days?" Raekar continued, looking to not waste too much time.

"At the Lord Burgauth's manor, working. Worked there for four years. I was mighty proud of her on her first day," Wilbur said.

"Nowhere else?"

"Nay, Lord Raekar. She came straight back home. An honest woman, she was."

Raekar looked at both of them, and smiled. "Your family is strong to resist the urges. Your faith keeps you safe," he said. They both were comforted by that, but there was still hesitation in their hearts. Still…fear.

"Will you burn Aeldway, Lord Raekar?" Anabel asked.

"Your town will be safe, but those with the plague must await their deaths alone once I am done with the Hunt. You surely know what that means."

"Aye. We'll gather who we know, Lord Raekar. The Silverlight will hold us," Wilbur said, grabbing his wife's shoulder.

"Thank you. I must leave." Raekar bowed.

There were good people in this town. Good people whose lives had been shortened by someone else's greed.

The Lord of Aeldway lived outside of town, in a walled off estate.

"I'm not looking forward to dealing with a Lord, Bregan," Raekar said to his horse. Bregan shook his spotted head in agreement. Venator kept close bonds with their mounts and with each other, but were told to always be cold and distant with the people.

The single dirt road climbed uphill until it came upon the gate to the Lord's estate. The wall was but twelve feet in height, and there were men carrying torches walking about.

"Who goes there?" one of them shouted.

Raekar remained silent.

"I think it's one of the Venator," another guard said.

"Right. Brimmed hat, grey cloak. Can't see the silvered blade, though," the first one murmured. They were unaware Raekar could hear them. "You may enter! Open the gate!"

Raekar dismounted and took Bregan by the reins. He slowly walked inside the courtyard, and the guards came down the walls to gawk at him, while some others stopped him.

"Lord Venator, please hold. We will fetch Lord Burgauth immediately," a red cloaked captain said.

None of those men were Lycan-plagued. Raekar watched them carefully, without addressing them. There were twelve of them watching him in that one moment, and more would certainly be waiting inside.

Nobles would often be offended by the presence of a Venator, since it would be telling of their incompetence. It wasn't that uncommon to end up fighting their soldiers, even if it could never be a fair fight.

The door to the manor opened and with it came the smell of the Lycan-plagued. Part of it emanated from the tall lord. His black beard was creeping closer and closer to his eyes, but he maintained a strong physique. Raekar almost second-guessed himself, thinking the man could be a werewolf, but the closer he got, the more evident the plague's scent was.

What concerned Raekar was that more of that smell came from inside the manor.

"Lord Venator. No need in asking you what you have come here to do," Lord Burgauth said. "I will tell you that we will resist. We will not let you murder our entire town under the pretext of a holy purge. The Silverlight can—"

"If you speak heresy, Lord Burgauth, then I will be forced to kill you," Raekar said. All the soldiers placed their hands on their blades, but they were shaking in their boots.

"How dare you speak like that to me! I am the appointed Lord of Aeldway! I will not tolerate threats from a—"

"Lord Burgauth," Raekar paused, and the Lord took a step back. "You are Lycan-plagued, as are a lot of your people. There are some who have already consumed human flesh or are doing so right now on your streets. Why is it that you did not call the Venator sooner?"

"We can handle this situation by ourselves. We do not need your order to tell us that there is no saving our people," Lord Burgauth said.

His eyebrow twitched, his neck strained on the last word, he squeezed his left hand, his heart beat faster. He was lying.

"Lie to me one more time, Lord Burgauth, and I will take your life. A man who lets his people die to save his own hide has no place in the Queen's land," Raekar said.

The Lord bit his lip and frowned. Raekar could tell the man was evaluating the odds of making it out alive were he to challenge one of the Venator. In truth, if Raekar died, then two would be sent in his stead. Those two wouldn't ask any questions.

"What do you want to know, Lord Venator?" Burgauth finally asked.

"A woman named Meredith used to work in your estate. She has died of the plague and infected her family. What did she do?" Raekar asked.

"She…" Burgauth hesitated.

"Remember my words, Lord. I intend to keep them," Raekar placed his hand on his sword.

"She was my daughter's maid," Burgauth blurted out, and his shoulders finally relaxed. The heart beat was slowing. He had given up his charade.

"I must see your daughter. Now."

"Very well, Lord Venator."

The young woman jumped frantically at the sight of people. She rattled her cage and wounded her rotting flesh hitting the bars. Her tangled brown fur got caught in the iron nails and was torn away from her skin.

The cage was in her bedroom. The expensive wardrobes, ornate desk and silver-embroidered curtains were still intact. The canopy bed, however, was kept inside the cage, and so it was splintered and ravaged.

"She has consumed human flesh," Raekar said.

"Yes, Lord Venator. She has," Burgauth admitted. "I gave her that flesh. I was desperate."

"You have worsened her state, all the while committing the highest form of heresy. I trust you know the punishment for you and your daughter." When Raekar turned his head to look at the Lord, his soldiers stepped forward again. They were still unsteady, but they were loyal.

"Like I said, Lord Venator, I was desperate," Burgauth said, approaching the cage. "My sweet Cecilia was very ill with a different affliction. I sent word to all other nearby towns, I sent word to the city and even to the capital. I requested a healer from the Church, or someone that would at least look at her. No one did.

"After years serving in the Queen's army and offering my life to her and the Silverlight, *this* was my reward.

"Priests and bishops preach of a loving goddess, ever vigilant in the night sky. A protector that moves the tides in our favour, or against us if we're unworthy. Was my daughter unworthy? Was I unworthy when I almost died to defend the Queen's land?" Burgauth turned and was face to face with Raekar. Raekar wasn't fazed.

"If you only show your faith when the tide is in your favour, Lord, then it is as worthless as your efforts to save your daughter," Raekar answered. He didn't feel pity for a Lord, much less a heretic Lord. "Lycan Plague can cure all other illnesses, but if one's body was already weak at the time becoming afflicted by it, then the urges will be more difficult to control. Especially if your daughter was the first in this town."

"She was. A witch on the run offered a cure to my daughter's disease in exchange for protection. I would do anything that got me more time with Cecilia, and so I accepted," Burgauth said proudly.

"At the cost of your people's lives."

"Any cost is worth paying. I would've rather her been bitten by the werewolf, but indeed her body was too weak to survive an even more aggressive transformation," Burgauth growled.

"Where is the witch and the werewolf you made the bargain with?" Raekar asked, still unfazed by Burgauth's behaviour, nor by the sound of more soldiers arriving on that floor of the estate.

"What is your name, Lord Venator?"

"Answer my question, Lord Burgauth," Raekar pressed.

"Do you have a family? Or are your brothers and sisters of the order the only family you know?" Lord Burgauth continued, pacing around Raekar.

"Lord Burgauth, answer my question. Now."

"You think you have power over all of us. The Queen and the Church use you to keep us under control. Under their *boot*. The ones you so loyally serve have made our people desperate. *They* are the sinners," Burgauth said. His scent changed. The Lycan Plague emitted an overpowering musk, but it was waning.

"You have condemned your people, Lord Burgauth. The weight of your heresy cannot be shifted away from your soul," Raekar said. The soldiers stepped forward again. The smell of their sweat had become stronger with time. Doubt had crept its way into them.

"No. My people were doomed the day they were born under your false goddess."

Burgauth jumped forward and in one movement, Raekar took out his silver dagger and stabbed the man through the heart. He dropped the body as he spun towards the cage, throwing his blade through the bars and into the Lycan-plagued woman's head.

Two soldiers ran forward, raising their blades, but such a tight space could never allow for them to fully swing their weapons. Raekar moved toward one of them, crouching for an elbow in the stomach followed by one to the back of the head, knocking the man out. The second soldier finally had space for a swing and Raekar allowed it. The blade hit his left arm as he stood. It was a strong swing, emboldened by panic.

Not strong enough.

More soldiers were by the door, witnessing that moment. The one holding the blade dropped it.

"Do any of you know where the witch and the werewolf are?" Raekar asked.

"Will you kill all of us?" a younger soldier dared to ask. His mouth seemed dry with shock.

"None of you are plagued. If you renounce your Lord's heresy, I have no reason to kill you."

They all looked at each other and whispered, hesitating in the hallway. Raekar sensed the conflict between the loyalty to their lord, their faith, and self-preservation.

"We do. We renounce it, Lord Venator," the red cloaked captain said, stepping forward. His grey hair and beard were drenched in sweat.

"Now answer my question. Do not lie. I will know," Raekar said. He rested his hand on his sword, still sheathed at his side.

"Lord Burgauth sent them through the tunnels. I guided them to the entrance myself. They left but a week ago, when the threat of the Venator coming became too pressing," the captain answered.

"Where do they lead?" Raekar asked.

"Into the mountains, Lord Venator. There is refuge in the caves, made for the people of Aeldway should they need to run."

"Thank you, captain. Now leave, soldiers. Help gather the Lycan-plagued that have not consumed flesh. Check their teeth. If they have not yet grown and if the gums have not receded, then they have not feasted," Raekar ordered.

"And what will we do with them after we gather them?"

"You will send them to the caves in a day's time, and that is where they shall live until the plague takes their lives."

"What of those that have eaten flesh?" the younger soldier asked.

"Kill them."

Raekar walked to the body of Lord Burgauth. The hair was growing on his neck, and his muscles were starting to swell. He tried transforming. The man was a werewolf and a recent one, given how slowly he turned. It probably had been part of the bargain.

After taking the keys to the cage, Raekar opened it and retrieved his dagger.

"Captain, take me to the tunnels."

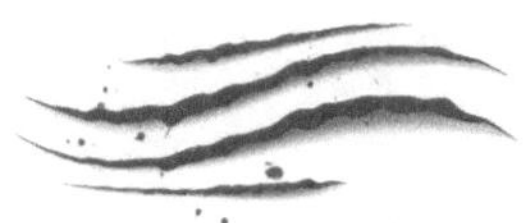

The passages were narrow. Raekar wondered how the townsfolk would be rushed out of Aeldway through here safely. It would take them ages.

The stench of rats and bat droppings was overpowering; there were no sounds beyond the slow trickle of water, and the torch's light did not extend far. The risk of being ambushed was high.

The tunnel opened up into a small cavern. There were unlit torches left on a table, as well as some old rope and minor supplies. Most likely a checkpoint of some kind. By the looks of it, Aeldway hadn't needed to use the passages for a long time.

Raekar looked for any sign of his prey, but there was none there. They would've been careful. For all he knows, they could already be very far from the caverns, on the other side of the mountains.

They had previously evaded another of the Venator, leaving him gravely wounded. It had taken some time until signs of Lycan Plague began showing near where they had last been seen. Then it was just a matter of following the trail.

If they escaped, the Venator feared they would have a small army of Lycan-plagued at their call, judging by the distance they had already travelled. Mindless servants that would only answer to the werewolf's savage commands.

He continued through the dark tunnels.

The passage began to widen, as the stone of its walls appeared to be more heavily worked and cut. There was wooden shoring supporting the ceiling, and the floor seemed to have even been paved a long time ago.

The tunnel led Raekar to a wooden gate. It was reinforced with iron, but it seemed old and rusty. Upon closer inspection, he noticed that it was torn off its hinges. One push and it would be knocked over, possibly announcing his arrival.

Air rushed through in a sudden gust, carrying the stink of werewolf. There was another scent…sweeter, herbal almost, tantalising…tempting.

The witch.

They were preparing the ritual needed for the werewolf to make the call.

"So be it." Raekar kicked the gate down and it fell with a loud crash. It echoed through the caverns and bats fled in response.

He walked into a chamber filled with crates, bedrolls, furs, and leathers. There were some beds set up as well. Raekar didn't smell any food, only the scent of whatever the witch was concocting for the ritual.

There was a door on the far side of the chamber, and one standing open on the right. The scent drifted from the latter. He moved toward it without hesitation.

Beyond the door, there was a long hallway. He walked fast, the scent growing more and more intense, enough to hide any other. The floor was dusty and old, but there were footprints on it. Two pairs. One quite smaller than the other.

The hallway opened into a monstrous cavern. Stalagmites rose beside him, trying to meet the cavern ceiling, which Raekar could not see. From where he stood, the floor seemed as flat as it could be made, paved around the larger natural rocky structures or boulders that couldn't be torn down.

There were iron braziers spread across the space, still holding rotten and moist pieces of wood. It was a hall built for the refuge of a large population. Old and monumental.

And dark.

The smell grew even more. His footsteps were as silent as he could make them, but they still faintly echoed through the cavern. Raekar often spun and extended his torch outward to see if he spotted anything beyond, but it wasn't enough.

It's time.

"Lys'argen," Raekar whispered to the torch. Globules of silver light formed from the edge of the flame and drifted far up into the cavern, then out in all directions.

Raekar continued walking. It was impossible to see the entirety of the cavern from where he stood. There were too many rock formations protruding from the ground, forming a light maze. Too many hiding spots for his enemies, which he was now convinced were present.

As he circled around a particularly tall stalagmite following that sweet scent, he noticed a campfire. Leather satchels and crystals lay strewn across runes drawn in blood.

Raekar approached the camp. The fire had been put out recently, but the scent he was after came from one of the satchels. The runes began to glow bright red, and he stepped on them quickly, smudging them and stopping the enchantment on them.

He heard two pairs of footsteps behind him, noticing two scents to match them. They had been masked until now.

A melodic, yet sarcastic voice creeped from behind him: "Well, Venator. I guess you've found us."

A man and a woman stood before Raekar.

She had long raven hair, deceptive glowing golden eyes, and wore half-plate armour that looked heavy. However, witches often enchanted their armour to be weightless, so they could remain nimble to weave their incantations.

The man was tall and built like a monster. His eyes were a deep red. He wore no armour nor any weapons. He didn't need them. The long spiked brown hair that also grew from his neck was indicative of his lycanthropy. Some werewolves liked to be more overt about their power.

"Come to avenge your brother? Not very wise, considering you'll meet the same fate," the witch said.

"I come to avenge no one. I come only to fulfil my duty to the Queen, the Silverlight, and the people," Raekar answered.

"The people? The people who have been desperate under your Queen's rule? The people who die in your order's murderous purges? You don't fight for the people, you fight for a delusion that has gone on for long enough," the witch said, as her eyes glowed fiercely.

"The people would not die if you did not infect them with your heresy, or your dog's blood," Raekar answered, shifting his gaze towards the werewolf.

"Dog? Aren't you the hypocrite? At least I fight for a cause! You just fight for made up rules you're told you have to follow," the man growled.

"We make the people stronger. We give them the ability to fight back against you," the witch intervened.

"You curse them. Doom them to death—"

"They only die if they never answer my call. One Hyle Sacramentum and death will hesitate to touch them while I live," the werewolf said, stepping forward.

"Yet they will be your servants."

"They will be fighting for their own freedom," the witch said, "Not depending on your Church's healers who never come to their aid!

"Entire cities crumble under the weight of simple diseases. Diseases *I* could fix if I was allowed to practise my magic. Yet the healers are sent to the borders, to protect against a threat that only exists because of your queen's *holy* expansion…because of her greed." She also stepped forward.

"You wield unsightly magic and your pet carries a curse. You may frame it however you like, witch, but the truth remains: you turn people into ravenous beasts that eat each other alive, and for that you deserve to die," Raekar said drawing his sword, the Black Blade.

The wolfen man paced in front of the witch, smiling at the sight of Raekar's weapon. "You're the one who carries the Witch Killer? Aren't you forgetting something, though? Where's your silver, little Venator?" The man's body twitched as his bones cracked and grew. The skin stretched and the muscles swelled, and as his own flesh broke, black hair grew, a wolf's snout sprouting from his face.

"Glad'argen," Raekar whispered to his blade, and as he drew his hand across it, the edge ignited with silver light.

"Weak tricks for a weak man," the werewolf said, jumping forward with the speed of enhanced muscular legs.

Raekar held his blade forward, hoping to counter the werewolf's strike after he committed to it, but a flash of red light in the room told him to move. As he rolled out of the way, the blood left on the encampment tried reaching for him like vines seeking to restrain.

A strong pain pierced Raekar's side, as claws found their way just below his ribs. He was thrown into a jagged boulder, hitting with thunderous impact before falling to his knees.

"Begging for mercy already, scum?" the werewolf spat. He was a big specimen, and his body had many scars, indicating he had survived a good number of fights against the Venator.

Raekar got up. Blood poured out of his wound, but it would heal. He took out one of his daggers and as he threw it at the werewolf, Raekar moved as quickly as he could.

The werewolf extended his hand, and the witch weaved magic behind him, a rune carved on his paws stopping the dagger. Raekar lunged at the werewolf, feinting a strike towards the stomach but instead sliding to the side, slashing the leg. The beast-man cried in pain as the silver-lit sword opened a blistering gash.

Raekar used that momentum to run towards the witch. He was fast, but as his sword was almost to her heart, a rune on the ground flared and Raekar was knocked onto his back, unable to block it with his sword.

The werewolf lifted him up by the throat and then slammed him into the ground as it cracked and sunk. Raekar coughed blood, raising his sword to block the werewolf's claws, swinging it to drive the beast away. He slashed at the beast's palm to disrupt the rune carved there. The werewolf reeled in pain and Raekar used the distraction to get up.

"Why do you fight for the tyrant Queen, Venator? Why will you not fight for the people?" the witch asked.

"This kingdom has known peace under the Queen's rule. Faith in the Silverlight unites our people," Raekar answered, not taking his eyes off of the werewolf.

"I'm also your people! I was born in this kingdom, yet I can barely speak without being called a heretic! My magic is part of who I am, it's my mother's legacy! Yet you say it's not worthy of being seen, nor heard? Under whose authority?" the witch asked, furious.

"The Silverlight is *my* only authority. I am proof of Her mercy," Raekar relaxed into a more confident stance, pointing his silver-glowing black sword to the ground.

"Then let her save you from us." The witch drew sigils and runes in the air around her, as her protector charged Raekar once again.

Raekar slashed his blade in an upward motion, but the werewolf easily dodged. The witch finished her incantation, grasping at the faint red runes that lingered around her, pulling out two whips made of blood red flame. She immediately swung both in Raekar's direction.

At that same moment, the werewolf struck from the side.

Raekar raised the Black Blade to block, as it was the only blade capable of resisting a witch's magic. The claws of the beast went deep into his heart.

It could never be a fair fight.

The Venator sending one of their brothers alone to face a witch and a werewolf…It was a grossly unfair ordeal that was birthed from their overconfidence. Birthed from years of unchallenged success that came at the cost of wiping out entire towns of defenceless Lycan-plagued.

His heart beat once, the muscle contracting around the claws of his enemy.

Raekar wasn't like his brothers.

He threw his cloak away, staring them in the eye as his skin burned. His joints screamed in pain, his muscles rupturing and sewing themselves back together.

He forced his heart to beat once more.

Then again.

And again.

Raekar's hands grew. His whole body grew. His jaw cracked as it extended and his legs regained their strength.

"You… Why would one of us bite a Venator? Why?!" the werewolf shouted. There was fear in his voice…and his heart.

Raekar grabbed the werewolf's arm and pulled it out of his chest, as the wound closed almost immediately. He then crushed the bone under his own grasp and threw the now smaller opponent away, towards the witch.

Silver hair covered Raekar's body. A werewolf born under Her light, *blessed* by Her light. A man who had been granted mercy for fulfilling his duties.

"You proudly wear the very heresy you want to purge, Venator. You are living proof of your order's hypocrisy," the witch said, taking a step back. Her heart skipped a beat. Raekar could hear it.

"I wear this heresy as a burden, a curse. But a curse I shall only keep as long as I serve the Silverlight. The day I am no longer able to fulfil my duty, my life will be forfeit," Raekar said.

With his blade still in his hand, he once again drew his hand across it and its silver glow passed on to the claws on his left hand. He did the same with his right hand, and then placed the blade gently on the ground.

"Do you feel it brother? The hunger? The fury? The Call of the Pack?" the other werewolf asked.

"No. My faith drives all of it away. It does not, however, drive away the smell of fear that comes from both of you." Raekar moved with a speed uncharacteristic of someone his size and cross-slashed downward with both hands at the chest of the smaller werewolf, who tried blocking with his arms. They fell limp on the ground, and the beast-man fell to his knees.

Raekar ran the heretic's head through with his silvered claws, slamming them on each side.

Two flaming whips cracked and hit Raekar's shoulders. There was no pain. A witch couldn't hurt a werewolf, for werewolves were their protectors. It had always been so, even when Raekar received the curse.

"There are more like me, Venator. This doesn't end with my life. There will always be more," the witch said, letting go of her magic.

"Evil will always be a part of our world. The Silverlight is surrounded by darkness and every cycle She is consumed by it. Yet, She dares to be reborn, shining again for all to see.

"So must we all do. May Her light grant you peace in death, witch." Raekar pierced the woman through her heart, lifting her up to look him in the eyes, and then he threw her body away.

He stood in silence as his transformation reverted. He collected his torn clothing and covered himself with his cloak.

The Hunt is over.

FIRE AND FANGS
J.F. Sebastian

SHE IS STANDING alone, head down, under the burning, cascading water as it washes away the grit, her own remaining hyena hair, and the blood she has just shed. There are two men standing guard outside, but being much older than her youthful appearance suggests, they pay her no attention—her body appears too young to attract leering gazes. Comforted by this, she allows herself to kneel on the metallic floor, enveloped in vapor, as water cascades around her like rain on corrugated metal. Her body shudders as violent images of the day's massacre flash through her mind, so she turns up the heat again for the brief respite from the pain it will bring. This time she flinches, for she is back in her more sensitive human form with her hair follicles now bloody and the raw skin of her fingers tender where her sharp claws had been.

A loud banging on the door startles her, pulling her back to the reality outside the shower. "Time to get out. This isn't a spa," a voice asserts.

She's momentarily distracted, pondering what a spa might be.

"Okay," she says.

She takes a deep breath. The putrid smell of rotting flesh fills the air. She suddenly becomes acutely aware of her nakedness and of the grotesque aftermath of her transformation—wet masses of hyena hair, discarded skin, and remnants of gore scattered across the metal drain. With a shiver, she gets out of the shower and grabs her towel, hastily wrapping it around herself.

"I'm ready," she says.

The heavy door unlocks and groans open. As she steps out, she looks at the mess she is leaving behind, feeling the instinctive urge to bury it somewhere. Even after too many years to count, the knowledge that she can't, that she has no choice but to leave behind the proof of her transformation, still makes her feel vulnerable and uncomfortable. Yet she hangs onto that feeling, a small discomfort in comparison to the horrors she committed, the horrors she knows she will be required to commit again. It's a price she's willing to pay, a grim acceptance that accompanies her nightly transformations.

She's crouching in the tall grass outside of a small village that seems to seamlessly merge with the surrounding countryside. Unlike the imposing urban landscapes she knows so well, with their cratered roads, crumbling buildings and smell of death, this settlement feels like an integral part of the natural world. It is different yet somehow so familiar that a warm sensation envelopes her soul as a symphony of nature surrounds her—the steady buzz of insects, the night birds' melodic chirps, and, intermittently, the high-pitched and almost human yip of a hyena. Her soul animals. But, most of all, the air carries the aroma of multiple fires, and beyond that, the tantalizing fragrance of something cooking, something achingly recognizable. Her mouth waters not as a hyena but as a human. It is the salivating mouth of a little girl on her way home after having fetched water for her family, knowing exactly what her mother is preparing for dinner.

Amidst this sensory reverie, a voice pierces her ears, and the collar around her neck tightens, pulling her back to the harsh reality of her captivity and the unseen presence of the one who controls her from somewhere out of sight. She shakes off the haunting memory, unsure if it's even a memory at all, and shifts her focus to the human targets in the village. From this distance, she can discern their exact locations, her mind already mapping out the deadliest route. She begins to walk steadily, her claws ready, aware that she will eliminate every target in that village. Yet, paradoxically, a sense of confusion accompanies her, as if she is returning home, even though centuries have passed since she had a home to return to.

It is another mealtime in the dimly lit confines of her daily life. She is surrounded by the clatter of trays and the distant hum of conversations in yet another military camp. One of countless similar moments she has experienced over decades, centuries, where she sits alone and away from everyone else. She might have hated the isolation once, when the child she looks like matched the child she was inside. But that was a long time ago. Now she enjoys these moments of relative peace, for these are the only moments when she can be something other than a weapon. She also likes it when each day unfolds predictably, blending into the next in the mess halls where she pretends she is part of their armies, or in the enclosed environment of the cells they usually hold her in. Despite some differences in countries or enemies over the years, and no matter how many times she is swapped between squads or armies like a secret weapon, everything mostly remains the same.

She looks up from the stack of meat on her plate and, as she takes a sip of her energy chocolate milk, notices wary glances, fleeting expressions of apprehension that dance across other soldiers' faces. She gets the same looks even when they are clad in full military gear and holding lethal weapons. Even though she has an idea of what she really is, she knows that amid the military personnel, and among humans in general, she's a peculiar anomaly—part of the system, yet kept apart. This is why soldiers maintain a respectful distance from her, their unease palpable. Part of the reason, she has come to understand, is not because of how lethal she is, but because her appearance betrays an agelessness that both intrigues and unsettles those who catch a glimpse of her. To them, she'll never be an orphaned girl but a weapon as well as an enigma, an entity both powerful and unpredictable.

She has seen sympathetic faces before, of course, faces that have come and gone throughout the years of her captivity, while the passage of time never etched into her unchanging features. From time to time, a sympathetic soldier, usually female, occasionally joins her, attempting to breach the barrier that separates them. They talk, share snippets of their lives but, as eager as those friendly faces might be, conversations usually fizzle out for she always has very little to share beyond her memories of a multitude of wars and battlefields and distant memories of a childhood she might, or might not, have experienced.

She looks at her plate again and reflects on the fleeting connections she has made, remembering the names and faces of those who once dared to see beyond the perceived threat. Some of them met untimely ends, their sympathy extinguished in the line of duty. Others witnessed her capabilities firsthand during a mission, their initial warmth replaced by the realization that she was not just a child, but something altogether different. So, in the end, only the routine persists and these occasional attempts at camaraderie fade into the background noise of her existence.

She's halfway through her transformation amid an unfamiliar unit, surrounded by men in uniform speaking a language that feels both distant and vaguely familiar, altered by time and blended with words from other tongues. She is, technically, in a hospital, but the place reeks of death and dust, shattered ceramic tiles, and twisted metal strewn across the floor, walls, and ceilings, like a broken mouth waiting to swallow her. The room her unit is in, a ward that now looks like a morgue where refrigeration has failed, is filled with decaying bodies. With the constant rumbling of the building's walls and the distant echoes of shelling and gunfights, the building might collapse at any second. Yet, strangely, she's indifferent to the threat, wondering how it might feel to be free from the collar or even from the process of thinking and feeling.

Someone's sudden shout jolts her back to the immediate reality. The collar tightens violently around her neck, a burning reminder of the violence of her temporary captors. She instinctively growls at the pain and feels the butt of an automatic rifle hit her at the back of the head as she's hustled forward toward a dark hallway. She turns around to stare at the man who hit her and immediately sees the disgust in his eyes, and in the eyes of those behind him.

"Don't hit me again," she growls in English.

The man lifts his weapon towards her, and his companions imitate him, suddenly reeking of fear. She can feel he wants to press the trigger and kill the animal he sees in front of him, even though she's not even fully transformed.

A weapon is just an object that kills… It shouldn't be allowed to talk, she thinks, a wave of exhaustion washing over her.

She doesn't ask much of her existence but, in that moment, she yearns for the indifference of her previous unit and the isolation of her cell, for indifference and loneliness are far preferable to the disgust she now faces.

The man who struck her abruptly directs his weapon toward a darkened, partially collapsed hallway. In the dim entrance, amidst the debris, she discerns naked feet—the remnants of someone crushed beneath.

"Go and kill them. They are hiding in the dark," the man instructs in broken English.

Stepping forward, she continues her metamorphosis: her skin burns as capillaries expand, and hyena hair emerges. Her jaw and frame then expand and dislocate as her human form changes, yet there is no pain. Instead, she inhales deeply, capturing the essence of war—sweat, gunpowder, blood, decay, and her own primal scent.

The men around her mutter something resembling a prayer, their weapons trembling in fear. She advances, now with clawed hands and feet, and suddenly pauses, sniffing the air again. Amidst the familiar scents, she detects an elusive note of sweetness, of tender flesh and salty tears. She realizes it is the scent of youth, like fresh milk or spring water. Turning toward the men, her transformation incomplete, she declares, her voice now deep and growly. "There are children in there with them. I don't kill children."

A searing pain courses through her neck, and she crumples to the ground. As she looks up, the ominous black eye of a gun stares at her forehead.

"The people in there are terrorists. This is what terrorists do. They use children as human shields."

"I don't kill children," she growls again as the pain becomes unbearable.

"You kill who we tell you to kill!"

"No," she manages to utter through the pain and her clenched fangs.

"Hum, they lied to us; you're as useless as a dog," the man sneers.

He then barks an order, and a succession of metallic clicks echoes. Before she can scream, a cluster of grenades sails into the darkened hallway, swallowed by its obscurity.

She dashes through lightless subterranean tunnels. In the darkness, she discerns endless pale walls stretching straight ahead, vanishing into a hole of blackness even her eyes can't see through. Everything is cold and humid, the slippery walls reminiscent of descending into the very bowels of the Earth. She is getting further and further away from the tunnel's entrance and wonders why the men didn't tell her where the exits would be. She's a war asset and they probably don't want her to try to escape, but the look in their eyes as they saw her true were-hyena form left her wondering if, perhaps, they wished her to end up lost and entombed beneath the hospital's weight. The ground trembles around her as the unrelenting shelling above continues, flattening the city, but she doesn't stop running. Amid the disorienting environment, the only coherent element is the scent of blood wafting from somewhere ahead.

A flash of orange light imprints on the back of her eyes, something that looks like a lingering greenish ghost. She stops running and instead starts walking fast, but cautiously.

Echoing screams fill the air, coming from an abrupt bend in the tunnel. It's followed by another flash, and then a fiery tongue licks the tunnel's opposite wall.

She stops walking and crouches, contemplating the possibility of a flamethrower, a nonsensical choice for an underground space. The echoing screams are replaced by the tantalizing scent of burning meat, prompting an involuntary salivation that makes her feel sick at the thought. For as much as she excels at killing, she never consumes her victims. It is one of the few rules she could give herself. Her captors only care about her eliminating her targets.

Kneeling beside the first charred body, she recognizes the smell as one of the men in her unit. She is confused for a second, however, for she doesn't remember the man going into the tunnel before her. There must be another entrance, or maybe an exit, somewhere up ahead. Despite her focused mindset, a faint glimmer of hope surfaces.

"I guess I don't want to die entombed," she muses.

She checks the next corpse, wishing it could be the one controlling her collar, but those men seldom take the most risks on the battlefield.

As she progresses through more scorched remains, a shiver courses down her spine, the hair on her back involuntarily rising. There is an absence of familiar scents from the burnt materials her mind has catalogued over the years. Whatever, or whoever, killed these men carries a smell of a kind she has never encountered before.

Magic, she thinks, confused by the sun-like aroma of flames burning out of no wood, gas, or gasoline.

Even though she has encountered, fought, and even killed magical beings before—albeit rarely—it's not precisely fear that grips her now, but the revelation of something unknown and potentially perilous.

Rounding the bend where she saw the flames flicker, she enters a large room, stepping into a nightmarish tableau. The vast space resembles a classroom, with broken and charred desks, chairs, and a blackboard, but the normalcy ends there. A small group of men, engulfed in otherworldly flames, writhe and scream in a grotesque imitation of a dance. Some are on fire, others rolling on the floor, their agonized cries weaving into the strange whooshing of the flames. Amidst the surreal inferno, a child, wrapped in ethereal scarves of magical blue and red fire reaching out like tentacles, stands with eyes burning like coal.

As the child spots her, a tongue of fire suddenly extends toward her, seizing her in its fiery grip. But instead of fighting back or trying to escape, she embraces the searing pain, closing her eyes, allowing herself to surrender to the heat.

"Finally," she thinks, vaguely surprised at her acceptance of the end.

Then, just as quickly, the torment ceases, and she opens her eyes in the lingering heat. The boy, now only partially ablaze, gazes at her. He shows no fear, only an unexpected sense of relief.

A distant yell catches her attention, drawing her eyes to a soot-covered man standing in a corner. He clutches a large book adorned with intricate silver and gold patterns while gesturing in the air with his other gnarled, blackened hand. Although she doesn't comprehend the language, the authoritative tone triggers a familiar response within her, for she could recognize an order in any language. The boy, in turn, looks at her with sudden sadness and shakes his head before speaking in anger at the man. The man snarls something in response and, with another gesture, sends the child to the ground in apparent agony.

Acting on instinct, she rushes toward the man. Just as he lifts the book in a futile attempt at self-defense, she lunges, clamping her jaw around his neck.

It's not the broken English in her ear that jolts her back to her senses, but a soft hand on her seared shoulder, as light as a bird or a mouse. She feels strange and almost recoils, because nothing has ever touched her when she is in her hyena form.

"Are they dead, you animal? We saw fire… Have you killed them all?" a gruff voice yells in her earpiece, and she winces as the device around her neck suddenly tightens, eliciting a whine of pain.

The soft hand moves from her shoulder to the device; a sudden flash of heat, sparks flying, and the collar melts off her neck, burning her a little. Looking up, she sees a dirty, shaggy boy with dark hair—a normal-looking boy, but with coal-like fire at the back of his dark eyes…just like she's always been a normal-looking girl but with too much hair on her back.

Getting up, she's suddenly ashamed of her beastly appearance, so she immediately kneels in front of him, touching her collarless neck.

"How…how did you do that?" she asks, rubbing her skin for the first time in a long time.

The boy looks at her with a smile, cupping his hands. A little blue flame flickers into existence, almost like a hummingbird, illuminating his face in the darkness.

"Thank you. Thank you for…freeing me," she says with relief, pointing at the melted device.

The boy shrugs, then points at the dead man still holding his book.

"Oh," she says. "He was controlling you with this book?"

But the boy doesn't respond. After a short, awkward silence where they both smile, the boy cocks his head and asks, "What is your name?"

"People call me Alem. I don't think it's my whole name, I just…don't remember. And you?"

The boy just stares at her, looking confused.

"Oh, I'm sorry!" she exclaims. She then clears her throat, places her right hand on her heart, and says, "My name is Alem. What's your name?"

The boy cups his hands together. "My name is…" he starts, before conjuring a tiny dancing flame and theatrically adding, "Naar."

"Naar? That means 'fire,' right? Is it because you can control fire?" she asks, pointing at the bodies around them. She knows he doesn't understand her, but she can't help but probe, trying to communicate with this child who is so different yet so much like her.

"No. I *am* fire," the boy replies proudly, each word accented by a tongue not used to pronouncing the language.

"Where are you from?" she asks. But the boy remains silent, looking suddenly frail, and she feels a deep-seated need to take care of him, to hug him and tell him things will be okay for him. For them.

"What do we do now?" she murmurs, mostly to herself. She pauses, her gaze sweeping around. There is as much death in the tunnels as there is outside, but at least outside offers a possibility of escape and, perhaps, safety. "Hey, Naar, do you know how to get out of these tunnels?"

There's a blank look on the boy's face; his understanding of her words is limited.

"All I know is that anywhere is better than here," Alem continues. "I think we should just…leave. And try to find our place in this world. We don't know each other, but I need your help, and I think you need mine." She pauses for a while, smiles at the boy, then continues, her hands mimicking walking, then pointing towards what she hopes he'll interpret as an exit. "Do you understand 'help'? I need your help to get *out* of these tunnels?" she says, her movements punctuating her urgency.

Naar nods, looking serious, then comes next to her and puts his dirty hand in her clawed, bloody one. Alem doesn't remember the last time anyone took her by the hand, let alone in her hyena form. Something burns the back of her eyes and she shakes her head, ignoring it for the moment.

"Okay. Let's go, I guess?" Alem says, gently squeezing the boy's hand.

Naar squeezes back twice, and his body begins to illuminate the darkness. Wrapped in his warm glowing aura, they enter the dark tunnels, walking together towards the slightly less dark obscurity ahead of them.

MOTH(ER)
Chase Anderson

MY FIRST MEMORY was of her room, white and bathed in light. I sat on the floor, trying to help Mother with the laundry, folding towels much larger than me. The walls were clean, the hardwood floor shone. A breeze carrying birdsong filtered through the forest into the open space.

Mother had studied color science at college, where she met Father. She taught me how glass prisms hung in the windows made the dancing rainbows on the wall. The clear light held all the colors within, she said. It bounced from surfaces to your eyes to show you how something truly looked. I didn't understand, but I liked how all the towels were blue, like the sky, like our eyes.

"You look just like me," she said, "when I was your age." Sometimes she would pull out photos of her brothers and sisters, children lined up on a bench. I'd never met these people. Which face was ours? I pointed to a person and asked if that was her.

"No, dear, this is me."

I searched her face hard for similarities but found none. The picture was from a really, really long time ago. People changed. Maybe I'd be able to tell when I was older.

I stopped thinking about faces and listened to the soft birdsong instead.

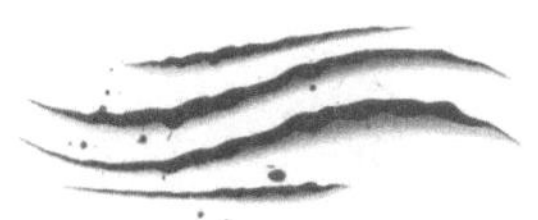

They tried to teach me at preschool, but the teachers weren't as good as Mother. She'd already taught me all about color and light, so my fingerpaints never turned into a brown, muddy mess. Miss Teacher told us that pink was a color, but I blurted out, "No, it's not, it's a hue." I was put in time-out because she wouldn't accept I knew more than her.

"Preschool is just to learn how to get along with other kids," Mother said. "Or for kids with bad mothers who work all day."

I had a good mother but bad teachers, I told her, so they never taught me how to make friends.I waited for Mother to tell me how, since she knew so much. She looked down at me from her seat on the bed. There was a white wicker chest between us, which always creaked when I touched it.

"You're supposed to figure that out yourself," she finally said. "I can't do everything for you." She kept talking, and my gaze shifted to the prisms in the window. A coating of dust blocked the light from getting out, or maybe in. There weren't any rainbows on the walls. I walked over to fix that.

"What are you doing?" Mother snapped. "I'm talking to you." She huffed. "Maybe this is why you don't have friends. You don't listen."

She had to be right. If Mother got frustrated with me, the kids who didn't know me surely did, too. They wouldn't give me a chance if I didn't try harder. I'd show her I was smart, just like her, and could figure things out on my own.

Miss Teacher pulled me aside. I flinched, ready to be scolded again. "You're going to be a big sister," she said. But she had been wrong about things before, so maybe she was wrong about this, too. I asked how she knew. She smiled. "Grown-ups know these things."

I was unconvinced.

Mother and Father never said anything about it, so I knew Miss Teacher was wrong. A few months later, she mentioned it again.

"I am?" It had been so long, I'd forgot the previous conversation.

She laughed. Not a real laugh, but the kind people force to pretend to be feeling something else. "When your mom goes to the hospital to have the baby, we can make her a card to celebrate."

Mother and Father said nothing when I got home. Miss Teacher was wrong again.

One day, Father picked me up.

"Where's Mother?" I asked.

"She's in the hospital. For a little vacation."

Grown-ups said things like that to mean something else so kids wouldn't know what they were talking about. They wanted to surprise me with the baby! That was why they'd kept it a secret.

When Mother came home, she went straight to her room and shut the door. I waited in my room, listening for her to come out, to tell me the surprise, but she didn't. I crept to her door and opened it.

She was lying in bed, a big quilt on top of her. It was dusty from hanging on the wall, the bright oranges dulled to yellow, the white expanses grayed and fuzzy.

"Are you sick?" I asked. People went to the hospital or stayed in bed when they were sick.

"It's nothing," she said. It was dim, with the blinds drawn and the curtains askew. I knew she was lying, but I had no idea what was wrong. She didn't look sick, she didn't take medicine.

The next day at preschool, I asked Miss Teacher if we could make a "get well soon" card. Mother would like that.

Miss Teacher got down to my level and looked me right in the face. "This isn't something a card can make better," she said. I really wanted her to be wrong, but something told me this was the one time she was right. It gave me a bad feeling in my stomach, like butterflies trying to escape.

Mother made my lunches and drove me to elementary school. That's what good mothers do, she said. Sometimes she helped me with my spelling. Remembering the order of the letters was hard.

"FRIday ENDS my week with FRIENDS," she said.

Friday didn't mean that for me. I didn't have friends. But if I said that, I'd be arguing, and then she'd be around me longer, and I didn't want that.

Her hair was short now and she looked lumpy in the sweatshirts and sweatpants she wore. There were always big beige band-aids on the backs of her hands.

Whenever I was around Mother too long, my head would get dizzy and I'd feel like I wasn't really there. I didn't like that feeling, so I tried to stay away from her. But she was my mother, a good mother, so why did being around her feel bad?

I asked a teacher. She got very serious.

"Is your mother hurting you?"

Where had that come from? She never hit me, she never would. I told the teacher that.

"Oh, so you're uncomfortable around me?" Mother asked a few days later. I didn't know how she found out.

"No," I lied, even though it was a really bad one. There was no way I could make up a story to have her think something else. But what else could I say? The real answer would hurt her feelings and make her mad at me.

"Well, that's fine," she said. "Sometimes I don't really like being around you." The corners of her mouth kept moving, even when she stopped talking. I wanted to run away, but that would make things worse.

She left first, going to her room and all the things in it so she wouldn't need to come out, except for dinner.

"Don't upset your mother," Father told me when he tucked me into bed.

"I won't." Another lie. So many things I did upset her. Or even things I didn't do. I couldn't trust what I thought I knew. Things always turned out wrong when I did.

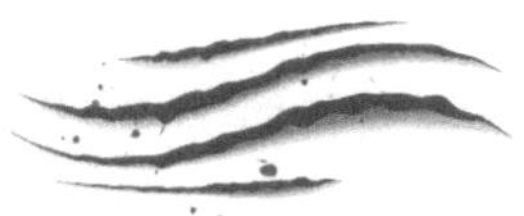

In middle school, she stopped making me lunch, but she still drove me to school, since that was what good mothers did. I knew that wasn't true, though. The other kids had divorced parents, or only their mother, or they took the bus, and they were always happy around their mothers.

I met their moms: some wore sloppy clothes or had short hair or messy houses or no jobs, just like mine. Why did those things in *my* mother make me feel bad?

There was something wrong with me. The kids in the books I read solved their problems by trying hard. I tried and tried, but it never worked.

So I stopped trying at all.

Can you explain why the sky is blue? the test question asked.

Yes, but I don't want to, I wrote.

Why did this character feel this way?

I don't care.

What happened in the year…?

Stuff.

There *was* something wrong with me. Everyone said so. They took me out of class, they made me take a bunch of tests for babies. Which shape is a triangle? Which face is smiling? Draw a house, a dog, you, your family. They made me use crayons. I thought about using complementary colors, how I couldn't blend the wax into new hues, but why bother? This was a punishment.

The man running the tests took my paper and looked at it for too long. Somehow, I got it wrong. Maybe I really was stupid and my lying fooled everyone. He asked me who each person was. Me, the shorter one, Father with the black hair, Mother with the yellow hair.

"And what are these?" He pointed to the two lines rising from the top of her head.

They were… I didn't know what to call them. I would see them sometimes, but not always. Obviously, I shouldn't have drawn them. "I think I colored too fast," I said. I couldn't tell if he believed me.

"And what about these?"

I'd drawn big blobs on either side of her stick figure. That sense of being far away came again. I said the first thing that crawled out of my mouth.

"Butterfly wings. I saw a big butterfly outside today."

"I need you to draw reality," the man said. "Not what's in your imagination."

"Okay."

He handed me another piece of paper and I drew exactly what he wanted so this would all go away.

"… Did you hear me?"

"Could you say it again? The TV is loud."

A lot of things were making noise: the air conditioner, scraggly animals in cages, the rustling of papers under my feet as I shifted my weight. I didn't want to look at them, but I didn't want to look at Mother, either. Her face had gotten blobbier, fuzzier, her eyes darker. Bandages spread to her fingers, bare at each joint and making her hands look chunky and segmented.

"I said…"

She was saying words, but it was nothing—white noise, swallowed up by the lumpy webs clinging to the walls. Every time I was here, there came that dizziness, that sense of things not being real. Shapes in the corner of my vision squirmed. Father never said anything about it, but then again, he barely went into her room anymore.

"Did you hear me?"

"Yes." I hoped she wouldn't ask me to repeat it, but I tried to guess what would be the right answer.

"Good, finally." She rearranged herself on the mattress. Puffs of dust floated into the air. I turn to leave and rushed out, but in my haste I knocked a box over, objects crashing into each other. Dust and must filled my lungs and I coughed, my eyes watering. How could she stand this?

I scuttled for the door. The hallway was a mess of cobwebs and cramped space, but at least the walls were still white. I leaned back and stared at the ceiling light, willing my body back under control, through my eyes, not some ghost over my shoulder.

There was a moth in the light, struggling, crawling over its desiccated brethren. How did he even get in there? Did he not see the bodies? I thought to set him free, but I was too short and there was no room for a ladder or even a chair. It's just a moth, I told myself. It can't comprehend the situation it's in. Maybe it'll just fall asleep and never wake up. That's better than being chewed up by some creature.

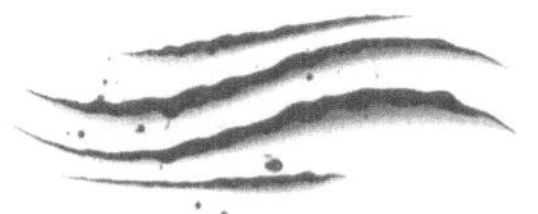

I knew that things weren't normal. Other parents left the house, they had guests over and knew their children's friends. They let them go out and have fun. I'd tried telling people before about what things were like at home, but no one believed me. I couldn't go out because I'm grounded, everyone's house was messy, I was exaggerating.

Of course no one believed me. I've lied countless times, for little things that don't matter, for big things. Remember in third grade when I lied to the principal? I always lied about studying. Everyone said that: my classmates, the aides, Mother. I was the accumulation of every mistake I'd ever made, and no one would let me forget it.

But college… That was a fresh start. No one would know me, I'd have a dorm room, it wouldn't come pre-loaded with stuff I wasn't allowed to throw away.

Mother said she'd take me to visit, but she didn't leave her room, not even to eat dinner, so I wasn't disappointed when she didn't. Father took me to a college that specialized in color science. The campus was open and bathed in the light of the spring sun.

"It snows a lot, though!" the tour guide said. "It gets cold!"

Insects didn't do well in the cold. That meant they wouldn't be squirming on your clothes or in your books. They wouldn't find their way into your room.

But it was an expensive school and all our money went to Mother, for doctors to fix her hands, for more things to fill her room, things that got trampled underfoot and chewed full of holes. And that, somehow, was my fault.

All my effort went into studying. After school, I used the small freedoms I had to spin into greater tales of success. Everyone embellished their college application essays, so it was okay.

And it wasn't like anyone would believe the truth.

"Show me the letter." Her arm reaches out, fingers unfurling in a series of clicks. I can't tell if I'm seeing dirt or tiny hairs. They waggle at me, waiting.

I hand it over. She reads, eyes unmoving. A moth lands on the back of the page and flutters, trying to find a grip. There is no way I should feel it from where I stand, but the micro-current shakes the hanging threads, worms undulating at the disturbance. I can feel their eyes on me, scolding me for daring to disturb their peace.

"Why didn't you get a full scholarship?" is all she can say.

"They save those for the athletes." And the really smart kids, I leave unsaid; you can't fib your way to better grades.

"But it's so far away, I won't be able to visit you whenever I want."

"It's the best school for color science." Lying has gotten easier with time, and she no longer bothers to learn about my life. The only things that she cares about stay in that room.

"Aww, you want to be just like me!"

In this room, it's difficult to think in words. There's too much movement. Creatures reach for me through the bars of their cages, moths fly by, worms threaten to drop on me. The bulb and the window, both layered in dust, warp the light into a false hue that your brain thinks is orange. But, under all that, it's still white.

A decade and a half ago I sat on that floor. It was clean. The room was full of light. I remember tiny details—the crystal prisms, the rainbows on the wall. Mother smiling and upright, not hunched over by the weight of her wings. Her hair was long and flowing, not twitching antennae that sensed disturbances in the air. Her hands were soft, warm, with pliable skin and fingerprints. The hands of a human. Of a mother.

How could such wretchedness share the same space as something that had been so pure, so happy? Maybe that was a lie, too, something I had made up to convince myself that I'd once had a Mother and not… this. This thing that grasps me and chews me full of holes and makes my skin crawl. This thing that no one would believe even if I told them.

"Did you hear me?"

"That's right," I lie. "I want to be just like you."

KINDERTRANSPORT
Elana Gomel

Her elbows on the windowsill, Debbie stared into the brown and gray landscape of fens and mudflats. The ruins of the factory stood out against the purple horizon, its chimney curving like a claw.

In the kitchen below, Mother moved around with the quick decisiveness of a predator, her body bumping into the counters as if it were much bigger than it actually was.

Debbie's brother Franz crashed through the door in a bubble of giggles. She lifted him up, tickling his plump chin, and held him close, waiting for the noises below to subside. The door banged as her mother went out, and she relaxed.

Franz thrust his pudgy hand into his overall pocket and tried to wriggle out. She grabbed his hand and forced the fingers open. Mauve seedpods scattered on the floor.

"Bad, Franzie, bad!"

She knew where he had gotten the pods. Recently, while spying on their mother, she had seen her put on her raincoat and trudge through the fens toward the abandoned factory. She came back with a bulging sack. Next day, Debbie's tea tasted bitter and tangy. She volunteered to give Franz his afternoon snack and poured his tea into the sink together with her own. Even contemplated getting rid of the seedpods that were stored under the flour bags in the pantry, but this would've revealed to the adults that she was on to their plans.

The front door opened again. She tensed, but it was neither of her parents. Instead, a familiar voice brought a wave of heat to her face. She rushed down, dragging Franz with her. Prince stood in the hallway, the sulfur light of the setting sun seeping in together with the wet-fur scent of the coming rain.

"Hi," she said timidly, her heart in her throat. His name was actually Prince—his aged parents' folly—but to Debbie, there was nothing ridiculous about it.

"Let's go!" he said.

"Where?"

"For a walk."

They strolled together in silence, Franz tagging behind.

"Marge wasn't in school today," Prince said.

Debbie hoped the dusk masked her expression. Marge had sparkling blue eyes and long curly hair, and Prince had recently spent a lot of time chatting with her during the recess.

"Maybe she's sick," she said neutrally.

"Her mother says she is." The word *mother* was reshaped into a curse by the venom in his voice. He stopped under a solitary streetlight that shed sickly radiance into the rain and faced her.

"She'll never come back. They ate her."

Under the blanket, Debbie clicked on her flashlight. She'd found the book in a pile in the school library, where water-warped volumes were left to dry out before being used for kindling. The book was old, dealing with the very beginning of the Troubles. Many words were hard, like pebbles drawn from the deep well of time.

Pictures helped her make sense of the story. One in particular fascinated her. In this picture, a child was being led into a shelter by an armed soldier. Dog shapes slinked and growled beyond the reach of the soldier's antique rifle. The child's arms were lifted in supplication, and the soldier looked tense.

As Debbie learned from the text, this child and many others were killed. The big soldier, despite his heavy rifle and round helmet, failed to protect them. The dogs got them.

But the book indicated that some children were saved, taken from the predators and sent away to a sanctuary. Much of the book dealt with their lives in the safe place, but Debbie skipped over that part because it described a world that had vanished so long ago it did not even evoke nostalgia. What she found endlessly fascinating was the notion of children escaping the dogs by relocating to a new place.

The book called this escape "Kindertransport."

The flashlight flickered and went out. Below in the kitchen, her parents mumbled, their voices blending into a stealthy animal noise. In his bedroom beyond the thin partition, Franz cried out. She tensed, but he calmed down, lulled back to sleep by the gentle fall of rain that splashed onto the mossy hummocks and brown ponds of the fens.

But as Debbie slipped into indistinct dreams, she heard a distant howl.

Marge died. Of pneumonia, so they said, but nobody at school believed it. They had a closed-casket funeral, and her parents' faces were the color of wet clay as they stood by the graveside. Marge's classmates, huddling at a distance, eyed them fearfully. Debbie stood by Prince. Now that Marge was dead, she was prepared to pity her.

"They killed her," she whispered to him, just to confirm they were in on the secret together.

"Hush!" Mr. Shaw scowled at her. His lugubrious face suddenly appeared to change, his narrow jaw longer than any human jaw had the right to be.

While the crowd dispersed, Prince whispered: "Gym, after dark."

In the fitful murk of the gym, Debbie counted seven children. Prince was speaking when she slipped in.

"They're pretending nothing's happening. It means most of them are already changing."

"They show nothing!" This from a younger girl named Nina with straight straw-blond hair.

"Are you daft? They show nothing until it's too late! Until you wake up and their teeth are in your throat!" The speaker was Buddy, Prince's sidekick.

"I saw a dog by the creek," said Martin, a serious, dark-eyed boy who had been mercilessly bullied in the lower grades until Prince took him under his wing.

"There are no dogs left!"

"No, it was one of them," Debbie said. "They drink poison and give it to us, so we will become like them."

"My Gram told me the real dogs were killed because everyone thought they spread the infection, but then it turned out they did not," said Veronica, a mousy older girl. "It was people who infected dogs, not the other way round!"

"Infected how?" the boy named Stefan asked.

"I don't know. But this is what they are. They're human beings at daytime, dogs at night. And they'll kill and eat us if we let them!"

They all fell silent, contemplating the beastly muzzles under the familiar faces of their parents and grandparents.

"Don't you know what happened in Coal Creek?" Prince asked rhetorically.

Coal Creek was the nearest township just beyond the fens where the marshy ground rose up in green folds crowned with abandoned houses. Their parents never talked about what had happened, but the children had figured it out: Coal Creek was destroyed when its adult inhabitants turned against each other and tore each other to shreds with their newly sprouted fangs and claws.

The children of Coal Creek were devoured by their parents.

And then the army came and killed the monster-dogs.

"Marge," Prince tossed into the silence as his final argument.

Debbie swallowed. Marge's name could still work her magic. And to offset this magic, she spoke out.

"We can do something," she said. "We can escape."

And she told them about the Kindertransport.

She was at her desk during the recess, making a list, when Nina came over. Debbie looked up, frowning. Now that Marge was dead, Nina was the prettiest girl in school. Her parents were well-off and bought her custom-made clothes. She was even wearing some spicy perfume.

"What are you doing?" Nina asked.

"Making a list. Stuff that we need. Clothes, raincoats. Tins."

"We don't need much food. We only need to get to Swanton, where the army is."

"What if Swanton is overrun too?"

Nina shrugged. Her hair was amazing—almost white, straight, and glossy.

Debbie went back to her list, but Nina still lingered, as if deliberating whether to say something more. Debbie sighed. "Look, you don't have to come."

"No, I want to. Something's going on, that's for sure. My folks are getting weird. And Marge… I spoke with Alice, her cousin, and she told me Marge's face was all puffed-up and swollen the week before… When she was at home, nobody was allowed to see her. And then…"

"She died," Debbie finished for her. "They killed her."

"I saw her parents today. They look…kinda normal."

"Have you seen them at night?"

"Have you seen yours?" Nina countered.

Debbie had had enough. Jumping to her feet, she angrily retorted, "I think you should stay here!"

Unfortunately, Nina did come, while Franz was supposed to be left behind! This was what Prince decreed, arguing that a toddler would slow them down. But Debbie said no.

She could hardly believe she challenged him like that. But it was inconceivable she would go without her little brother. She pointed out the place in the book where the Kindertransport children's ages were mentioned, some as young as Franz. By being the book's keeper, she had become the voice of history.

The book confirmed that yes, it could be done because it had been done before. Children leaving their parents behind, saving themselves, escaping the slinking dog-shapes. And so, Prince gave in.

They left the house at midnight when their parents were in bed, mingled snores coming from the half-opened doorway of the master bedroom. As they tiptoed past it, Debbie remembered how she had insisted on the door being left ajar as a child, when her parents had been her protection against the monsters lurking in the dark.

But they were the Kindertransport now. And the snoring creatures in the dark room *were* the monsters.

Franz was good as gold, trotting obediently by his sister's side, until he started lagging behind and she had to carry him. The rest waited for them by the largest rill in the sodden landscape of the fens.

The plan was to reach the abandoned factory compound tonight and hunker down while a search, if any, was mounted the next day. Then strike out toward the big town of Swanton, where the army was quartered. They would ask the soldiers for protection, just as the Kindertransport children had.

They plowed silently through the soaked vegetation, trailed by the rotten smell of peat. Buddy slipped in a puddle with a splash and Prince cursed him out.

In the tangle of shadows to Debbie's right, something stirred. Tall reeds swayed, moonlight dropping through them like a handful of coins.

A thin voice shrieked.

The children scattered.

Debbie ran, but the weight of the sleeping toddler in her arms slowed her down. Franz woke up and started bawling. She slipped in the mud and landed on her back, Franz shocked into silence on top of her.

The bone-white moon was eclipsed by a long muzzle filled with crooked canines that seemed too big for the unexpected delicacy of the monster's flat, narrow head. The head, perched on the snake-like neck, dipped toward her.

The moon shook off the clouds and she could see the creature more clearly: the worm-pale body with heavy haunches and long clawed forearms; the mangy, colorless fur; the tiny, rounded ears; the bloodshot eyes with tired blue irises. It smelled strongly of spice.

Debbie stopped breathing.

Her fingers dug into Franz's arms. The toddler let out an indignant scream. The clawed paw nudged him, and Debbie rolled over, trying to shield him with her body. With a deep sniff, the monster cocked its head. Its nose was black and wet but shaped like a human nose.

Then, it seemed to lose interest.

It rose up, walking on two legs. Its long forelimbs grazing the ground as it shuffled away. Its small tail jerked convulsively on its bony backside.

Debbie sat in the mud, clutching Franz, who was quietly chuckling to himself as if amused by the entire incident. Eventually, she dragged herself to her feet.

She spotted the rest of the group huddled around something long and dark on the ground.

There was a stain wrapped around Martin's throat like a long scarf. Debbie covered Franz's eyes, but he shook her hand off.

"Prince?" Buddy whispered.

Shadows obscured Prince's face and Debbie was glad of it. His defeated, slouching stance told her all she needed to know. She spoke before she knew she would.

"We have to leave him here," she said.

She expected protests, but they followed her silently. She hugged Franz tighter and tighter, never having felt so alone in her life.

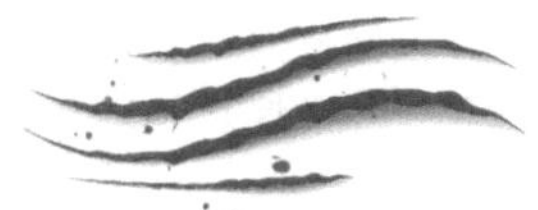

The drizzle started again around dawn, just as they reached the factory. It had been abandoned only five years ago but already its rusty machinery and cavernous buildings had acquired the patina of age. It was cold and smelled of rust and rot.

Debbie finally managed to have a fire going in the fireplace in what used to be the office. She was feeding it with old paperwork. The other children were just a scattering of damp blanket cocoons among the broken furniture that nobody had the strength to move away. She had arranged a nest for Franz in the footwell of a desk.

She haphazardly picked out words and phrases on the mimeographed copies she was throwing into the fire. "Psychotic lycanthropy." "Canine pseudo morphosis." "Chimerical mosaicism." "Dogs."

The last word leaped at her through the thicket of strange phrases that hemmed it in like a cage.

A shadow fell upon the page. Prince. In the pale dawn light, he looked sickly and diminished.

"You need to sleep," she said, avoiding his eyes. "You'll have to lead us to Swanton tomorrow."

He smiled crookedly. "Me? I thought you've taken over." She started protesting, but he waved her off. "It's okay, Deb. You have the book. What are you looking at?"

Glad of the change of subject, she showed him the papers. "It's a record. They wrote down how many people in the factory went on medical leave."

He shrugged, uninterested, and she missed her chance to tell him that the people were on leave, not for themselves but because they had to take care of a sick child at home.

She missed it because the door rattled.

It was the inner door connecting the office with the factory proper. It was latched, but they had not bothered to reinforce it, having focused their fear on the door to the outside which they had barricaded with chairs.

The door rattled again—a strangely gentle, almost apologetic sound, as if an office worker who had come in too late was asking to be let in.

The cold seemed to soak Debbie's limbs, gluing them to the floor. The fire guttered and dipped.

Prince stepped reluctantly toward the door, casting a glance at her over his shoulder. Later on, she tried many times to parse the meaning of that glance. Was it concern? A challenge? A cry for help?

The door was metal with a large rust patch shaped like an ameba. Prince was dragging a desk toward it, and the screech of it woke the others. Their heads popped up from the blanket cocoons like hatching moths: Buddy's jowls; Veronica's messy locks; and sleek white-blond hair miraculously un-mussed by sleep.

The rest of them were still gathering their wits when the white-blond head rose on a long neck, a slinky body launching itself at Prince.

The next couple of minutes edited themselves out of Debbie's memory. She could only recall staring at the red splatters that added new tentacles to the rust amoeba on the vibrating door.

Nina crouched over the corpse, growling. Her changeover had not gone as far as that of the thing on the marsh.

She was still recognizably herself, but her body looked like a melted-down candle. Her jaw had grown into a shallow muzzle fringed with a white beard and her blond hair had become a solid, shiny mat capping her lopsided skull. She still wore her clothes, but they filled out in the wrong places. Her body had grown strange protuberances on her back, stomach, and thighs. Her hands seemed raw, unfinished. She dipped her head toward Prince's body and jerked it up again, trailing something long and wet.

The smacking sound she produced was shockingly loud, but even louder was a scrambling sound close to Debbie. Franz, woken by the commotion, crawled from his nest, and toddled toward the bloodied creature that lifted her head and sniffed deeply.

"Franzie!"

Trying to catch him, Debbie careened into a chair and crashed to the floor, cutting her forehead on a protruding piece of metal. When she got to her feet, Franz was enveloped in the creature's dripping embrace. She groped for something heavy to strike with…until she realized what she was seeing.

Nina was not eating Franz.

She was feeding him.

Holding him in the crook of her arm like Debbie used to do when Franz had been a baby, she dipped her other paw in the pool of blood and lifted it awkwardly to the child's face, letting him lick her fingers clean. He turned his smeared face toward Debbie and smiled.

And then the rattle of the office door resumed. Only now it was less a rattle and more a deliberate knocking, as if whoever had been waiting behind it was now losing patience.

Debbie lunged forward and flipped the latch. A dog trotted in.

He was a big creature, yellow-brown, with a strong muscular body and a long bushy tail. He cocked his large head. There was a darker strip along his back and across his muzzle that made him look as if he was wearing a harness.

The dog wrinkled his muzzle, baring his large glistening canines. And then he spoke. The pronunciation was so bad that Debbie only understood that it was speech but not what it meant. He had to repeat it twice.

"Don't worry. You're safe."

The dog's name was Nicholas Rathbone. He had been five years old when his father, the chief accountant at the factory, had brought him to work because he was afraid to leave him at home.

Home had been Coal Creek.

His father was on the phone with some army bigwig, pleading for something, but the phone connection was so bad neither could hear the other. Eventually it was lost—forever. But then it did not matter because the army was already in Coal Creek, rounding up the children.

Nicholas and three other dogs had led the children to a storage shed. It was cluttered with chaotic piles of junk: peeling enamel pots, torn blankets, and sodden books. She wondered why the dogs bothered to collect objects they had no use for. But among the detritus of the past, she found several scratchy horse-blankets that were now the children's only protection from the cold. The dogs did not like fire. Before they left the office, Nicholas had lifted his leg at the fireplace and peed upon the embers.

They locked the creature that had been Nina in another shed. She went obediently. Now Debbie wanted to know what would happen to her.

Nicholas wrinkled his muzzle. "She is too old," he said reluctantly. Debbie was astonished at the correctness of his grammar. Despite the hardship of shaping human words with a canine jaw, he took no shortcuts.

"Old?" This came from Veronica.

Debbie was glad that somebody else took over the interrogation. She was too drained to be a leader again. All she cared about now was not letting Franz out of her sight.

"You are all too old," he said. "You can start the changeover, but you won't finish. Like the one hunting in the marshes now. But she is not good at it. She scares away ducks and wild geese. We tried to teach her, but she ran away. She's one of yours."

"One of ours," repeated Debbie uncomprehendingly.

Then she remembered the blue eyes of the creature that had killed Martin. The sealed coffin, probably filled with rocks. The stony faces of Marge's parents.

The army had come on the day five-year-old Nicholas was seated in the corner of his father's office, folding scrap paper into boats. He heard shouts and people running. His father told him to hide in the closet and not come out until he was back.

He never came back.

Nicholas stayed in the closet for twenty-four hours, listening to the screams and loud popping sounds. When he finally crawled out, propelled by hunger, the factory was empty. Only the bloodstains on the concrete floor indicated where the bodies had lain. He did not lick the bloodstains, not then.

The craving came later.

"Are you telling me that the army killed the people in Coal Creek?" Veronica sounded indignant. "You're lying!"

The dog looked at her with his amber-colored eyes and Veronica turned away. Debbie hesitated. But she had to know.

She pulled the Kindertransport book out of her rucksack and

opened it on the much-thumbed picture of a child escorted away from the snarling dogs by a soldier. Nicholas looked at it for so long that she thought he had lost the capacity to understand pictures. She did not expect him to be able to read at all. But he could do both.

"It's an old book," he finally said, "from before the Troubles. I think the soldier wants to kill the child."

"Kill him?" Debbie cried in disbelief.

But looking at the familiar picture, she could suddenly see it anew, like one of those trick drawings in which a duck becomes a rabbit. She could see the fear in the child's eyes, the helplessness in his tiny arms raised into the air, the anger masquerading as brisk efficiency on the soldier's face. She could see, suddenly and with piercing clarity, that the rifle pointed at the child.

Not at the dogs.

"He is probably one of us," Nicholas said. "And see, our people are here. But maybe they are afraid to help the child. Maybe there are more soldiers keeping them at bay. They will shoot them, too. They would like to shoot us, but they are afraid to come out here. They still don't know why their poison stopped working. Why we were cured."

"Cured of what?"

"Of humanity."

Nicholas had gone away. Debbie suspected he was as uncomfortable in their company as they were in his. His very presence gave her an itchy, shivery feeling, as if fur pushed from underneath her skin.

"It can't be!" Stefan cried. "We're human beings, not animals!"

"He says there are no human beings left," Debbie reminded him.

Buddy muttered something incomprehensible. He sat apart from the others, his meaty fists resting on his tattered blanket.

"Not here, at any rate," Veronica said, and the others nodded in agreement. "We must look for them."

"Where?" Debbie countered. "Not in Swanton, if what he says is true. The army will kill us. Where else would you go?"

There were other cities but so remote as to appear legendary. Perhaps they *were* legendary.

The others regarded her warily. Suddenly, she felt suffocated by their presence. She did not know where she was going until she found herself back in the office, staring at the black amoeba of blood and rust on the door.

Somebody was standing behind her.

"Nicholas?"

It was not Nicholas. Another dog, much like him, but bigger and darker.

"We took the body away. We let the girl out and she is hungry. She doesn't understand that we don't eat our own." The dog's speech was clearer than Nicholas'.

"Who are you?" Debbie asked.

"Amanda Smith."

A she, then.

"What are you going to do with him?"

"Bury him."

Debbie nodded. They sat on the floor together as the night fell.

"They made poison here," Amanda said. "Stuff to keep us imprisoned in their bodies. They released it into the town water."

"Did it work?"

"For a while. If we don't change before puberty, we remain in human bodies. But the poison was losing potency, so kids started changing, and the army came to take them away."

"And your parents…"

"They tried to resist, to keep us. And were shot. I was also shot. I was seven. I crawled into the marshes. Survived. Changed over."

Outside, it rained again.

Hesitantly, Debbie stretched her hand, touched Amanda's wet fur. "Why?" she asked.

"The dog growled low in her throat. "Nobody knows. I think, men in the old times, they tried to make dogs smarter. But it got out of hand, infected them too, and blended us all together."

"So, what are we? Humans? Dogs?"

"We are what we are. They have no right to make us into something else."

Debbie was soaking wet when she made it back into the factory from the marshes. In the predawn light, she could see the faint outlines of the buildings against the gray sky.

And the huddle of animal bodies around a small figure.

"Franzie!" Debbie caught him in her arms, pressed her face into his silky hair.

The dogs surrounded them in a silent ring. They were looking at Debbie. There were five of them. She thought Nicholas and Amanda were among them, but she was not sure. They all looked like huge, threatening beasts to her.

"I can't leave him with you," she said. "He is so little. He needs me!"

"The poison is no longer made here," Nicholas said, nodding to some seedpods nearby. "But it's in the groundwater. This plant soaks it up."

"I was eating it too," she said defensively.

"It has no effect on you. Not after puberty. You are already locked up in this body, and you'll never be yourself. But your brother…it may delay his changeover, but it won't stop it. Then he'll be like the girls in the marsh."

"What will happen to them?" she asked.

"They can't hunt," another dog said. "Not properly. They will starve, or the soldiers will kill them."

They left the next morning. Debbie did not look back as they trudged wearily through the raw drizzle toward the town. She did not want to see Franz' face as he stood in the courtyard, surrounded by the dogs, staring toward her retreating back. Or worse, not staring.

"So, what are we going to do now?" Buddy asked. "Tell our parents?"

"We will come back," Stefan said. "My dad has a gun at home."

"To kill Nicholas and Amanda?" Debbie yelled. "Are you nuts?"

"To kill the dogs."

Debbie stopped, backing off from the remaining Kindertransport. There was a demarcating strip of dirt between them now. Them on the one side, her alone on the other.

They had refused to accept what the dogs had told them. No matter the fur under their skin and the nameless hunger in their dreams, they would never see themselves as anything but men. Men with guns, killing the monsters that were themselves.

She could not go back to her desperate parents, feeding their children poison to keep them in acceptable bodies. Nor could she stay with the dogs who would resent and fear her. She was neither one nor the other. There was no place for her.

The Kindertransport whispered among themselves. She was being cast out. Her fingers dug into the cloth-bag with her meager possessions, and she felt the reassuring hardness of the book inside.

She read it all wrong. But she had created a story that moved others to follow her into the unknown. And if she did it once, she could do it again.

"We don't need guns," she said, and the familiar sense of power flooded her as her words rang strong and true. "I have a better way. We can still find our folk—people like us. We can find a sanctuary. I will lead you. I will save you. We are the Kindertransport."

THE FATE IN YOUR FLESH
Aggie Novak

I FELL IN LOVE with the curve of your entrails. I wasn't supposed to—you'd travelled far and spent much so I could divine your future match. Your parents watched closely as I sliced through the layers of you: epidermis, dermis, subcutaneous tissue, muscle. Matters of marriage—compatibility, fertility, love—revealed themselves to me most clearly in the intestines, so that's where I first delved. I trailed a finger—disinfected by my strongest magics, never worry—from appendix to cecum. That was when I knew your love would be strong. I traced the greater curvature of your stomach, from fundus to pyloric sphincter. That was when I knew your love would not be very long. I caressed the arc of your duodenum as it looped behind your transverse colon then became the jejunum. That was when I knew your love would be me.

Your parents, I knew, would never, could never approve of such an outcome. Pythoness, Priestess and Diviner of Fates I may be, but the position did not come with jewels, or lands, or marriage. Without my title, I was nothing, but you—you were everything. I wanted to blame the full moon, the powerful alignment of constellations—Muraenid and Capreolin glowing bright in the eastern sky—or the rousing magics of Lurralde's *Gaua ko Ehito*. Even safe in my tents, deep in my own workings, the festivities called to me. I wanted to blame those things, but I could not. In this, I was not wrong. Knowing, as I did, of the predicament we were now in, I kept my revelations from my face.

A glance at your ileum, the shape of your gallbladder, the tilt of your pancreas, the size of your uterus, told me there were many suitable suitors I could suggest for you. Men who came with deep coffers and political alliances. Women with large estates and untold beauty. People with fame, status, resources, and the ability to give you children or bear them for you. People better than me, people who could make you happy and support you through long years. But that was not the fate I read in your flesh. Besides, I am a covetous creature, and right then, exposed to the depths of you, I had never wanted anything more.

"The procedure is complete," I informed your parents. "Please, if you would await me in Elysium while I finish."

Elysium was my waiting room, a paradise of burning oils carefully curated to put minds at ease, sweeten moods, and deepen generosity. Everything designed to evoke love and eternity, and to fill my purse. I breathed in and ran my fingers through my sleek curls, then licked the slick coconut oil from my fingers. I breathed out, laying an intoxicating enchantment that would keep your parents busy for some time.

Licking my finger once more, I ran it down your neat incision, sealing you up. Such magic, however much I wished otherwise, required a toll from you, a sacrifice of the body. I concealed the scar in the crease of your belly button and kissed away its sting, feeling the pain against my tongue to spare you.

When I rose from your navel, you watched me with dark eyes, deep and wonderful and knowing. You didn't appear happy, nor did you appear sad. You appeared certain.

"You," you said.

I offered you my hand, silver-and-gold-nailed, silky with lotion, sizzling with magic. You took it. Your hand was smaller than mine, with thick fingers and calluses that told me despite your status, you worked with your hands. A hobbyist sculptor, perhaps, or gardener. There was no spark, no shock, but we fit.

"We must run."

You didn't argue. You kept pace with me as I led you through the curtains and draping fabrics of my tent.

But you did offer a warning. "My parents won't let me go easily."

"I know."

As we pushed to the outside world, I drew on the magic of my home to aid us. I paid the toll for us both, a fiery line of pain like a brand across each cheek. By the time we tumbled out into the thrumming streets of Lurralde, we were simply another pair of cavorters, indistinguishable from the other revellers of *Gaua ko Ehito*.

You were transformed, sharp features and blunt hairstyle softened under the rounded nose and long, sleek-furred ears of a hare. Elegant antlers curved upwards from between the ears, ends tapering into points. A pink silk ribbon, tied into a perfect bow at the back of your head, held the mask in place. I was the predator to your prey: an autumn-coated vixen with a snow-white chin and matching wings sprouting from the cloak around my shoulders. Two more additions to the evening's endless menagerie.

We danced through the streets, unable to do anything else, twirling together and with nameless others, but never letting our grip on each other go. The merry streets had a power of their own, and it was all I could do not to lose you, lose us both, to their rhythm. Slowly, so slowly as if by accident, I guided us to the edge of Lurralde, where the fairy lights twinkled out, the cobblestones gave way to dirt, and instead of brick and stone, straight-trunked trees loomed overhead. The sucking tides of Lurralde lessened here, the gentle tug of a stream no longer strong enough to pull us under.

But our passions still ran high, yours especially, untrained as you were, and you drew me to you, skin to skin, curve to curve. And the power of the *Gaua*, the power of you, was such that I could not find it within myself to resist.

You were not shy as our bodies moved together. Fate did not speak to you as it did to me, but I was Pythoness and you trusted in what I knew. And I, of course, was not shy. I, who already knew you as intimately as it was possible to know someone, though our interactions had been few.

Masked as we were, we exchanged no kisses, no pressing of mouths to flesh. But much was expressed through burning gaze and hot skin, through firm grip and raking nails. Our bodies entwined as easily as our fates.

When we rested, a tangled nest of limbs, sweat, and warm breath, finished but not sated—never sated—you trailed your fingertips over me. Over the peaks of my nipples and the dip between my breasts, learning the shape of me as I knew the shape of you.

"We should go," I said, reluctant to break our touch but aware that sooner or later, they would hunt for us—for you—beyond the streets of Lurralde.

"Wait." Your hand was twisted into my hair, tugging gently at my curls. "I would look upon your face."

Before I could stop you—before I could spring away, move your hand or scream a warning—you pulled at the green bow holding my mask in place, unravelling it.

As the fox's visage slipped from me, so too did the protections. We were exposed. Sensing the magnitude of your mistake, seeing the horror written on my face, feeling the tension seizing my muscles, you helped return my mask, retied the bow.

Without a word, we got up, hand in hand, and ran. The forest swallowed us, and it felt like safety, but I knew it was not. As we ran, I sang. Uneven ground smoothed before us. Branches curved away; roots tucked in. An unnatural wind urged us on, filling our lungs and lightening our feet. And I bore the price. Whips of pain lashed at my soles and my calves. I ran all the harder, as if that could help me escape it.

A hound's braying reverberated through the night, and I knew my efforts were not enough. Once the blood beasts had our scent, there was no magic in the world that would allow us to outrun them.

Your breaths in my ear, heavy and even, turned to sobs.

"Is there nothing you can do?" you choked out, strangled by exhaustion and fear.

I stopped, yanking you to a stumbling halt beside me. The time for running had ended, and our options were few.

"You have a choice," I told you.

I did not attempt to keep the sorrow from my voice nor the heaviness from my tone, for it would be a sorrowful and heavy decision to make. You squeezed my hand.

The first choice wasn't a real one, but I offered it anyway. "We could keep running until they catch us. Likely, you will be spared, unless their bloodlust is too great." You shook your head. "You could turn me in. Blame this misadventure on me." I smiled, though without joy. "There are plenty of worthy matches another Pythoness could divine within you."

"Or?"

"Or…" I paused, hesitant to commit, to utter the words that would confirm I had no other way out. "Or I could change us. So the blood beasts can't find us. So no one can."

"But?"

"But it will be permanent, there will be no going back."

You gripped me tighter still. "Would we be together?"

"Yes."

"Do it."

I nodded. "If it is what you wish, I choose it, too. Just know," I raised a hand to your cheek, caressed your velvet skin, "I cannot pay the price of this transformation for you. We each must pay it alone. The pain will be great."

"Do it."

You did not look brave. You looked tired and so afraid. But you did look certain.

The need to hide behind the masks had passed, so I lifted mine, then yours, and kissed you. At first, I was tender, soft lips to soft lips. You deserved that much. One loving kiss. Then I bit hard, deep into the tissue of your lip. I licked up the blood, swallowed it down.

Just as I could open them, peek inside them and read their secrets, I could also remake bodies. So, I summoned every bit of power I possessed, and did not let you go.

The agony was total and complete. Every nerve in my body shrieked—nerves I had seen in the bodies of those whom I divined but that I had never thought to feel within myself, from the length of the vagal nerve to the minuscule trochlear nerve. Every bone screamed as if snapped. Calcaneus, talus, cuboid, navicular, cuneiforms, metatarsals. It grew until I could no longer separate, no longer remember the names for the parts that hurt. I thought we still held hands—I could not have relaxed those muscles even if I wished to.

Losing consciousness would have been sweet relief, but this was not the sort of magic given to mercies. I did not know how long it went on, but eventually, it did end, as all things must.

You twitched next to me, the weight of you still there, and I felt relief that you still lived. I knew that you were good and that we should move from this place. Hounds, humans. Footsteps, voices. Insects, rodents, water, wind. Everything in the forest spoke, and I was certain I could hear it all.

I unfurled my wings and blinked my eyes open. The night was bright, all in sharp contrasts. You, with your sweet brown fur, twitching nose, and fluffy tuft of a tail, looked like prey. But I knew those antlers, wicked-sharp and steel-strong. You smelled like home.

I nudged you with a russet paw, and you sprang to your hind legs with instinctive agility. Your heart fluttered wildly, a tiny frantic drum. I rubbed my nose with a paw and watched you, waiting. You tilted your head and blinked. Your amber eyes were bright and intelligent. And certain. You hopped forward in a graceful bound, then looked back, waiting for me to follow.

I tucked my wings tight against my flanks, then, by your side, I ran.

THE BETTER TO SEE YOU WITH

John Kuyat

Don't open your *eyes,* he thought. And kept thinking. *For the love of God, don't open them.*

But he heard it. He really heard it this time. The lock clamping back. The unmistakable unbolting of his front door, the squeak of its opening. And footsteps. Small and light but real paddings accented by creaks in the floorboards like every terrible thing ever known. They sang. They shrieked. *I'm here, Charles. I'm walking the hallway.* Soft paddings getting close. They were so loud now, the footsteps. And his heart, trip-hammering.

The door of his room now, opening. This door doesn't squeak. First, it yawns, and then it cackles in a horrible accelerando. The hastening of rhythm. *Taaah te-te-te-te-tah.* The patters are in the room with him now. They echo off the walls. The floor is ceramic. It catches it all. Her feet; they clip and clap like a skeleton's knuckles rapping the lid of a casket. *No! It's nothing like that.* But it is like that. It's exactly like that. *One…two, three, four, five.* The two through five counts are softer than the one. They are the reverberations. Her shoes play full measures of this grave music as she walks.

And she is right by him now, he senses. Leaning over him. Right in front of his face.

Don't open your eyes!

Then, her voice comes, low. "But what beautiful eyes you have, Charles," she says. In a whisper, calling him by name. How does she know his name? Her voice makes his skin wriggle. At the nape of his neck, where worms might dig and begin to break down a body. "The better to see me with," she continues. She deploys it in this manner with a syntax that is a demented poetry.

Don't open your eyes!

"And what a nasty little mind you have, Charles. The better to—"

His eyes snap open. Almost without volition. Her pale face is there, grinning wide under the scarlet hood. It looks fragile, like fine china, but her teeth are big and foreboding. Much too big for that small brittle face. It's dizzying. His breath catches. He coughs up a yelp, clutches his chest, and blacks out.

Charles Perry woke hours later. A cold sweat sprinkled his arms, his forehead. It soaked through the pits of his oversized cotton tee— already yellowed from compounds of prior sweat—and dripped from his shoulder-length black hair, which had glommed onto his back. He resented his hair and purposefully neglected its wash and upkeep as a way to punish it. The result was a knotted, grease-laden gnarl of seagrass that would catch fire if he so much as thought of striking a match. His scalp suffered too. Dehydrated and itchy, it presented a playing ground for flame.

Under the scalp, his brain sprang begrudgingly alive and into a fit of migraine. A myopic pain that centered like a sniper on the crease of his brow and popped straight through to the back of his skull. He sat up and held his head tight with both hands. Keeping it in place. It was the drink, of course. The drink and the ridiculous program he'd watched that evening. A *Twilight Zone* installment. In the episode, a woman was being haunted by her adolescent self and by a nightmare that snuck up on her from the depths of memory. What a silly thing to put himself through.

It was two fifteen in the morning. About what time had he passed out? He'd shut the television off around eleven or eleven thirty. So, midnight, perhaps? Out for two hours. He'd accomplished *some* feat of sleep then. A silver lining.

The moon was another one. A big bright jewel from the window, casting its alien blue half-light across the entire room. A room, which wasn't a bedroom, though it was where he slept. The room, by most, would be considered a bathroom. But after several weeks of sleeping in the tub—a claw-footed vessel he insulated with a duvet and pillows for comfort—he found himself referring to it in this way: as his bedroom.

He liked the bathroom. The cool tiles and porcelain bath. It chilled his head, assuaged the relentless aching of his brain. He even wrestled the rickety RCA Victor in here to get loaded and watch his thrillers. Add to that, the window in this room commandeered the most moonlight. The moon was a security blanket. A nightlight for all the world. It did well to keep the monsters at bay, or most of them, anyway. Late night was scary enough. Thank God for the moon.

These days, though, the cold and the moon could do very little to quiet the pain screaming in his head. It worsened by the hour. It raged like a bull.

There was a finger of whiskey left in a tumbler on the floor by the tub. He'd been sipping it while watching the tube, hoping to numb the dark thoughts. The bourbon did nothing to quiet those, either. Still, he finished the glass. The acidity of the drink sliced through the headache for a moment. It distracted his body with a new pain, an abdominal one, so immense he immediately retched, dispelling a whiskey-bile atrocity onto the floor. It hit with an absurd *splat!*—a comical cartoon sound—on the Listerine-colored tile. That alone made him retch again.

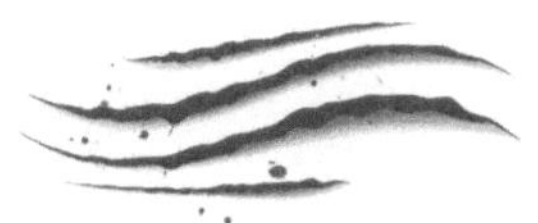

The pain was total. His stomach, his head. He could barely see the road in front of him. His brain was a kettlebell, weighting his skull down like sandbags on a hot-air balloon. It lolled to the left side of his neck as he drove to the hospital. His back was pressed far into the leather bucket seat. So far back that the seat cushion nuzzled up against his shoulders and trap muscles. His arms were extended, locked at the joints beneath the elbows. It was how Frankenstein's monster would operate a vehicle if forced to.

There was a gastrointestinal sickness. It stormed inside him and threatened to manifest in a horrendous expulsion from the car window, which was partially wound down. Because the air outside was cool. That helped. The moon was bright, and the night still. Silver linings. The radio was on, playing softly. A twangy, doleful song, which was eerily soothing with tightly wound harmonies in the chorus. The singer was rattling on about some fairytale.

The solace was brief before the fire burned in his head again, scorching a forest of brain cells and blurring his vision. Making him see things that weren't there. Hear things that were…like a humming. The radio oscillated between stations and static. *Don't look behind you.* A child's song, the hum coming through the stereo. *Eyes on the road. Don't look behind you.* He spun the knobs, frantic. The thin red tuning pointer mocked him, roving over the numbers like a snake's eye. He mashed the power button with the index knuckle on his right hand enough times to erode small bits of skin from it. Nothing worked. The hum persisted, graduating to a melody, a whistle. Something recognizable. Old notes sewn into the soul, stitched with a bloody hand.

"Who's afraid of the big bad wolf…"

The radio was broadcasting only static now, the white noise of afterthought.

Instead, the song now came from the backseat of the Corolla as it jumbled down the freeway.

Don't look behind you.

"*The big bad wolf…*"

Don't.

"*The big bad wolf.*"

He didn't want to, but his dark gray eyes rolled up to the rearview like slow-moving magnets. In the mirror, he saw her again. The little girl. The white face and scarlet hood. Smiling, singing, giggling. And he felt himself freeze over as the steering wheel whizzed beneath his fingertips, the tires abandoned the pavement, and the car tumbled from the highway into oblivion.

"Charles Perry." He delivered his name between short, heavy breaths to the woman working the emergency room's front desk. The three-mile walk from his totaled car—smashed into a pine somewhere off-road— exacerbated the illness and his exhaustion.

"Fill out this form please, Mr. Perry," the receptionist said, handing him a clipboard with a thin sheet of paper on it, which in one instant levitated and in another fell like a bad turn of magic. The tall, rawboned man stood in front of her, hunched over, clutching his side and sweating profusely. His face was sallow and his eyes bagged. His dark hair was ludicrous and wet. The receptionist's eyes darted up to meet his. She was an unassuming woman. Young, with fair skin and light blue eyes. Her chestnut hair was done in bangs, and she wore a red chiffon blouse with a Peter Pan collar. She stood up now and revealed herself to be considerably short.

"Oh my! I'll see about getting someone right away, Mr.…Mr. Perry. Just if you wouldn't mind having a seat here while I do." She moved past the front desk, through a set of double doors, and disappeared down one of the hospital's long corridors. Charles suspected Hell would start with a walk down one of those. Not a highway.

He dropped defeatedly into a chair and remained in the waiting room. A room empty save the company of the magnificently dreadful overhead lights and an elderly woman in the corner. In this moment, his heart ached for the natural light of the moon. Ached with every other inch of his body.

Minutes drooled by. The receptionist did not return. The clock ticked. The lights buzzed. He nodded off.

Something thumped. Had been thumping, perhaps, because he'd been asleep and dreaming the sound. In the dream, the sound was a boiler in an old house. Not his house, a stranger's house. How had he gotten here? That boiler was awfully loud. He hoped the pipes wouldn't burst in this terribly strange house; or cottage, more like. A cane lay against a wall in the cottage. No. A heavy cane was crossing the linoleum floor of the waiting room. The old woman from the corner, thumping her cane with each step, employing it as a climber would a grappling hook. She was before him now. He jumped back in his seat, startled.

"Hello," he said. She didn't reply. Her eyes blinked. They were little black insectile beads—almost buttons—pitted deep in her doughy face and outlined by purpling death rings. Her white hair looked like it needed a drink of water. She slouched forward, her chest over her cane, which she bore tightly in both knotty, veiny hands. Her face was closer now, beaming with a wildness and with teeth that did not impose on the rest of the face but were small, gray, and flat and missing in several places. Altogether, it was a differently horrid thing.

"What do you want?" Charles said. This time slightly louder, becoming impatient, while shifting as far back in his chair as he could. A form of claustrophobia was settling in. "I'm sorry ma'am, but what do you—"

In an instant, her right hand abandoned its place atop the cane. It fell on him like a talon, finding purchase on his forearm. Her nails, long and dirty, spiked his skin, threatening to breach it. His head swelled in excruciation. The very worst of pain. His vision dissipated. A final thought haunted him, and it begged him not to open his eyes.

But, of course, he did. And at first, it was all mahogany. A vast ocean of dusty floorboards in front of him. For miles with a far-reaching latitude that ended at a bedpost. Had he collapsed?

But no, this wasn't the hospital. It was a strange house with a tincture of familiarity.

Bang!

There it was: the familiarity. It was the pipes, and he knew he'd been here. When?

Bang-bang!

The next two bursts coming in close succession of one another. It was a conversation they were having. The kitchen to the basement to the washroom. Human and intelligent. It was a real language. Announcing arrivals, departures, the weather conditions against the cedar shakes. Whatever the rooms of a little cottage would discuss amongst themselves.

Then came the pain again. The most omnipresent communicator. It surged in his stomach, and he acquiesced to it, bending into the fetal position. His hands to his face, his knees tight to his chest. No. Not those ligaments. Foreign things instead. Tufts of hair over where only skin should be. Deep black, gray in some parts. Thick black nails, uncut and sharp, where dull, translucent ones should be. Surely, a hallucination. He tried to rise to his feet but couldn't. He was paralyzed. He was… grounded to his seat by the strength of the old woman's grip on his arm. His human arm. He huffed a sigh of relief.

"Ma'am, let go." No response. "Ma'am, please let go!" He jerked hard and finally freed his forearm, though her nails dug shallow and bitter tracks down it, leaving an unsolicited souvenir. "Jesus. What's your problem?"

She stifled a cough, or it was the beginning of a laugh. She was laughing, and it was a guttural noise emerging from the belly like a bat from hell and swelling until she was fully whooping with the violent din.

This was a mistake. He needed to leave and now. He was rushing for the door, adrenaline momentarily overriding a stomachful of hurt. He was jogging, craning his neck for a split second to see the old woman still heaving with manic laughter. He pushed open the door, and his momentum carried him into a fall as he hit the cold earth outside.

And toppled into daylight. How long had he been waiting in the ER? It couldn't have been more than fifteen, twenty minutes, right? But the sun was striking with the strength of a summer's day, and all around him was green. Forestry unfolding forever, and he among it. On the ground again and unable to move. Crippled by the pain, which ripped through his stomach. He screamed, but what he actually produced was not that. It was a howl. Then, a cry, but really a dog's whimper when it's been wounded. *Help!* he tried to say but didn't. It was a bark, sharp. It hurt his own ears, which were sensitive, picking up the tiny drone of a far-off yellow jacket and a brook's trickle two acres through the bramble.

He longed not to hear those things. Somewhere was the more awful sound of a hunter cutting through deerskin. There were scents to match the noises. The pollen: a stinging, prickly aroma. The groundwater, which smelled alive with its mud rock and mist. And then—there was the stag's blood. Metallic. Freshly oxidized, but somehow equally fermented and old. He covered his nose, which was a snout with hands that were paws. What infernal dream was this with layers and scenes like a Dante supposition?

The migraine reintroduced itself, as did the abdominal pain. With all his energy, he worked to move. There was something weighing him down, truly, and it wasn't the old woman's clutch. And then there was the creak of rusty hinges. A door, and more footsteps. These steps were many, and the ground they traversed was dusty on a dirt path leading to and from a cottage home. There were two sets of legs in front of his eyes now. Young legs and old ones, and two sets of hands that dug their fingers into his hide. Further into his muscle. They wrapped his bones. The fibulae, the radii. And dragged him.

Into the cottage. With the clang and bang of boiler and pipes, the cane in the corner, mahogany floorboards. He'd been here before.

"Are you beginning to remember?" the young one said. She clapped her hands and jumped in place. A flash of red fabric swam about her ankles as she did. "I think he's starting to remember, Grandma," she shouted now, ecstatic. "What a nasty little mind you have. The better to remember with. Do you remember now?"

And finally, he did.

It was a late afternoon in spring. A time when all the soundmakers in Forest Grimm had settled warmly into their routines. The yellow-jackets were in siesta, so there was no buzz. The common grackles were picking up the catbirds' break in song with their rusty cicada warble.

And the wolf was in the bramble, splitting the occasional twig with a pop that pierced like resin busting in firewood. He did not slink today. There was no motivation nor stealth in his step, and, though he felt a hunger coming on, he reminded himself not once had he ever failed to trap a meal. Opportunity would come, as it always did. He much preferred this line of thinking to letting instinct overrule. For he was multidimensional and complex. He wasn't some shark. He had talents and interests besides the hunt.

He weighed these thoughts while prodding up the plant-cluttered hillside, which led out of the bramble and onto a footpath. On the trail, he took brief inventory of the burs thumbing a ride on his shag, plopped to the ground, and began rolling over the well-trodden soft earth, removing the tiny urchins. At mid-romp, however, his ears stiffened, and like submarine sonars, honed in on a peculiar trickle of laughter discordant with the forest's regularly-scheduled programming. A noise that sounded a lot like opportunity.

At once, the wolf stopped his dematting. He clumsily regained his footing, tripping slightly as he scrambled back onto all fours, and gracefully, finally, he began to slink. He moved slowly. Paw to paw. His haunches shifted. Left to right, and right to left like a tailfin. Patiently, he waited for the next chirrup of laughter or until he hooked a smell. Seconds later, both things happened. The disembodied voice giggled. The wolf's head locked onto the noise. The prey was on the path and only a quarter mile north. As for the smell, it was human.

After a thousand feet, his slink hurried to a trot. Because the taste of *her* was in the air. His tongue hung foolishly out of his mouth, draped over the right side of his jaw and swinging like a wad of melted chewing gum while he jogged. When a fleck of cardinal red crested the dirt trail, his trot became a run. The movements were irrepressible—not that he wanted to repress them—because he was lapping at it now, the taste, with his long, pink tongue, trying to lick the mirage. The vision of his incisors sinking into her. He sprinted.

A hundred feet ahead. Fifty. *Faster!* The muscles in his hind legs tightened. Ten feet now. His back paws braced against the ground. They pushed hard. Gravel and scraplettes of earth jettisoned from his pads. He thrust forward, soaring, stretching his arms out for the kill.

The red form spun around, unveiling the prey—the source of forest merriment and human smell—to be a young girl. Her brows were raised on high-alert. Underneath, her clean blue irises bulged from the lifeless whites of her eyes. Her face too was flush with nightmare, which is to say, it was inexplicably colorless. Her mouth was a horrid black O.

But the wolf never landed the attack. A searing, mid-forehead pain interrupted the pursuit. It clanged through his skull and shook the bone. He crumpled to the ground, whimpering. A set of ashy, blood-spotted legs stood in front of him, blocking his view of the prey. He saw and heard as the weapon, a wooden cane, bounced off the dirt in front of his snout. *Plunk-lunk-lunk-lunk.* The blunt force of the blow yielded a full-blown concussion, making his eyelids heavy.

And then…darkness.

Wearily, his eyes fluttered between worlds. In one, there was blackness and serenity. In the other, a box. No, something rounder. More concave than a box. And cool. In the box world, a sadistic, wiry hand unhinged his jaw from his muzzle. Callous fingers pressed a tiny pellet to his tongue. The crudeness of the hand's skin repulsed his tastebuds. He gagged.

The pellet was an opiate administered prior to the surgery. The operation was amateur at best with imprecise, damning cuts made through his stomach and performed in the tub. Not a drop of blood defiled the precious mahogany. For a time unknown, the wolf felt those in-and-out cramps. They ebbed and flowed. Until at last, they ceased, and there was a great weight of something, implausibly heavy like a boulder, being dropped inside of him. Then, with more deftness than was present during the incision, hands, both rough and smooth, old and young, stitched him back up.

Yes, he remembered now. How quickly it all fell apart. First the hunt, and then this. Paralysis. Forever tethered to the cottage floor by the heavy stone. The only movement now came in sleep. Dreaming, he imagined himself a rawboned man on two legs, but even then his two legs ran. From the little girl. Because she would come for him. She would never let him forget. And if he opened his eyes (*Don't open them!*), then he would remember. And he would look on, frozen, as the crone and the girl lived their lives before him.

A HORSE WALKS INTO A BAR
AM Sutter

Hell was an emergency room on a Sunday night.

Terri paused at the sliding ER doors, turning to look at his friends crowded in the small sedan. Dave waved once from the driver's seat, and then he jerked the car forward, tearing out of the hospital parking lot to leave Terri alone at the ER in a town he didn't know.

Terri's fading buzz did nothing for the pulsing pain spiraling up and down his arm. It felt like his wrist was swelling, threatening to tear through his skin. While he waited to see if his friends would loop back around to come in with him, he gingerly cradled his arm. He lost the blue car to the dark, despite the intense glow of the full moon; when it became obvious they'd gone back to the rental house and its terrible horse farm without him, he finally turned and stared at the glass doors. He hoped at least his friends would get revenge on the horse that kicked him when he had stumbled into the pasture to take a leak. Maybe they could nudge it with the car. Hard.

Beyond the doors, the ER was surprisingly quiet, the empty waiting room bright from the fluorescent lights. Terri paused at the front desk, trying to ignore the cheap, peeling laminate of the desk, and waited for the man behind it to look up. The man continued typing on his computer, ignoring his surroundings until Terri coughed.

Terri winced as muscles tensed in his back and sent radiating spasms down to his fingertips. He swore he could feel the ends of his bones grind together. The man wiped a hand across his nose, snorting back congestion, and Terri fought to swallow his disgust.

"What're you checking in for?" he asked Terri.

"I think my arm might be broken." The limb in question pulsed in time with his words, but the man seemed uninterested.

The man brought his hand down to type on an old computer, something glistening on the back of his palm. He glanced up at the clock, studied the slowly ticking hands, and then turned back to the monitor. "It couldn't wait till tomorrow?"

Gaping, Terri wondered where the hell his friends had left him.

"No, it couldn't," he said.

"Up to you, then." The man sniffed to clear his nose once again and handed Terri a clipboard with forms. "Fill these out and give 'em back when you're done."

Terri grabbed the papers with the fingers that still worked and attempted to stomp away from the desk, but every footfall clicked his bones together, forcing him to soften his steps. He sat down in a plastic chair, its legs stained gray from the scuff marks of shoes, and glanced over at the only other person in the waiting room.

The blonde woman sat hunched over a worn copy of *Dracula*, one hand spreading the pages and the other wrapped protectively around her stomach. Foot tapping, she looked up from the book and seemed surprised by his presence. She quickly slid her gaze away to stare at the wall clock above the front desk. The timepiece was the only decoration in the waiting area, aside from a large, generic print of horses stampeding through an open field. God, why was this town obsessed with this animal? He scrawled in the blanks of the medical history sheets and pushed himself up, grunting against the pain in his arm. When he approached the front counter, the man glanced up from the computer, and the blue light of the screen made his eyes look hollow.

"How long is this going to take?" Terri asked as he handed back the forms.

The man squinted at Terri's tangled handwriting but said nothing, only glancing up at the clock again.

"Can I at least get something for my arm?"

Sighing, the man picked up the phone and muttered something into the receiver, glaring up at Terri and gesturing for him to go sit back down. Terri rubbed his shoulder, hoping somehow to relieve the ache without going near the fracture, and stumbled back to his seat. The woman with the book studied him as he sat down, but he ignored her in favor of hanging his head and bending over his knees. He thought about pulling out his phone, but a spasm of muscles in his arm vetoed the idea. Instead, he considered the rust climbing the sides of the vending machine and the balls of dust and hair resting in the shadowed corners of the waiting room. The filth made him nauseous; he thought emergency rooms were supposed to be clean.

Someone cleared their throat, and Terri looked up. A different woman stared at him, arms crossed over the front of her white coat.

"Yes?" he asked, his dropping blood alcohol sharpening his tongue. She must be the emergency room doctor. God, she probably could tell he was buzzed.

"Let's give you something so you stop complaining about the wait, okay?"

A brief, sharp pain stabbed his good arm, but it barely registered above the constant, aching throb in his hand. Deep bruises had formed along the creases of his wrist, and the skin pulled tight, turning red as the swelling took hold. He glanced up at the doctor, who clicked the needle back into a cover. He thought he saw a drop of old blood on her finger, but that was improbable. She wouldn't walk around with…fluid on her hand, would she? Now that he thought about it, she hadn't even cleaned his skin before the shot. He didn't think this was how hospitals usually ran.

"Now, appreciate the fact that you have to sit here. A longer wait means you're not dying," she said. Terri thought doctors were supposed to have compassion. Didn't she appreciate that his arm *hurt* and that he had a hangover growing as they spoke?

He dropped his head again to cradle his temple in his good hand and tried to swallow back the pain. Out of the corner of his eye, he watched the doctor stop to speak to the man at the front desk. Her tone was lazy, unhurried. Terri clenched fingers against the headache, trying to tamp down his anger. No wonder everything was so slow if the medical staff pissed around like this all the time.

The woman next to him kept glancing up from her book, staring at the doctor's back and then the old wall clock. He wasn't sure what she kept looking at—maybe the doctor's ass, which he couldn't help but notice even through the blocky, unisex fit of her coat. Or maybe it was the ugly brown stain on the trim of the white coat. It dyed the cuffs of the sleeves and the hem that fell along the doctor's thighs. He hoped she'd take off the dirty garment before seeing him.

When the doctor disappeared down the hallway, the woman stood up, closed her book, and walked to the entranceway. She forced an unhurried, casual pace, but Terri saw the lines etched into her face, the worry that carved wrinkles along her eyes and downturned mouth.

"Checking out?" the man at the front desk asked her.

"It's getting late," she answered. Although Terri didn't get her explanation, the man seemed to, instead looking at the clock and nodding. She didn't stop, just kept walking until the doors parted before her and she stepped out into the night.

Her sudden flight uncoiled an unexplainable fear deep in Terri's gut, but whatever the doctor had given him started to take hold. He felt heavy, dizzy. He didn't know why it unsettled him so much; maybe it was just the oddness of everything. Still, perhaps he should catch a cab and drive the hour back to the city to find a real hospital.

"Mr. Harkford?"

Half-standing, facing the glass exit doors, he looked over to where a nurse stood, a clipboard in hand and eyes repeatedly glancing up at the clock. She tapped a pen against her thigh. Terri didn't like the way she jittered, standing alone in the lobby with just him and the buzzing overhead lights.

"Yes?" he answered.

"The doctor will see you."

He shifted between the balls of his feet, looking over his shoulder at the exit. Unease warred with the pain that broke through the medication with startling, sharp spasms.

"Let's go, then," she said, eyes once again flicking to the clock. For people so focused on time, they sure had kept him waiting.

Not bothering to see if he followed, the nurse took off down the hall, her clogs squeaking against the tile. Terri trailed after her, holding his arm stiffly against his side and trying to breathe through the shockwave each step sent through burning nerve-endings. She led him into a small exam room off of a side hallway, where she took his blood pressure and medical history, then left him to scrape a shoe down the metal exam table while he sat and waited.

He wondered if Dave had made it back with the others safely. The bones shifted in his arm as he fought to get comfortable on the table, interrupting his thoughts. For a brief moment, childish anger welled up, and he entertained the idea of the car wrapped around the fucking horse that had kicked him — of a smoking engine and a quiet cabin, of muscled, hooved legs tangled in all the wrong angles. Terri startled when someone knocked on the door. It opened a moment later to reveal the doctor from earlier. She smiled widely as she entered the room, and though the clock chimed in the lobby with the hour change, only she alone in the hospital didn't seem to notice the time.

"I'm Dr. Mehl," she said and sat down on the stool by the counter. The wheels groaned in rusted protest as she pushed it across the floor, staring at his paperwork instead of where she was going. While she was distracted, he dragged his gaze up her rumpled, stained clothes, past the collar of her scrubs that followed the dip of her collarbones, and really studied her for the first time.

The doctor looked too young and too pretty to be practicing. He immediately felt uncomfortable, painfully aware of the way he must smell — like beer, weed, and sweat. Then she pulled off a soiled glove with her teeth. Terri swallowed back the queasiness, attraction dying quickly, as the doctor tossed the glove into the wastebasket. She glanced up at him and the downward turn of his lips.

"Now, why the long face?" Dr. Mehl asked. "Equinthropy?" She laughed at her own joke and ran a hand through her long, strawberry blonde hair. It looked like pieces of animal lard were caught in the strands.

"I don't get it," Terri said and blinked. The meds soured his stomach, and he felt as if he couldn't quite grasp what was happening. Reality seemed delayed, cutting in and out with every flicker of the fluorescent lights.

Dr. Mehl frowned, as if disappointed by his stupidity. "It's a joke. You know…" She circled a hand in the air. "Because a long face means you're sad. And horses have long faces— Jeez, you've never heard that one before?"

"No, I know the joke. I just don't get why you're making it." Terri was angry at this point. Of course he would get the worst clinician. She probably coasted through med school on her looks and now was stuck with the worst shift. Who else would work a Sunday night?

"It's a full moon; I thought I was being clever," she protested.

"Can you just help me?" He shook his wrist for emphasis and immediately winced at the jolt of pain that broke through the nauseous haze of the drugs.

"Let's get you signed up for some X-rays," she said with a smile. Her lips were pink, moist, and he caught himself staring. In her wide grin, there was food stuck between her canine and incisor.

A knock on the door made them both look up. The nurse from before slid herself halfway into the room.

"Dr. Mehl, don't you think you should go on break?" the nurse asked. "It's getting late."

The doctor rolled her eyes. "This'll be quick," she assured. "Just going to get the request in, and then you'll be rid of me."

The nurse looked unsure but didn't say anything; she simply disappeared from the narrow opening of the cracked door. Dr. Mehl watched the other woman leave before turning back to Terri.

"Why don't you wait here? I'll have the radiology nurse come get you once the request is in." She reached over to pat his good arm, and heat warred with the revulsion in his stomach. Her touch was soft, but there seemed to be dried blood in the beds of her fingernails. Had she washed her hands after she took off those disgusting gloves? He couldn't remember.

She left the room a moment later, closing the door behind her and leaving him in silence. He reached into his back pocket but found it empty. His phone was probably somewhere on Dave's backseat as his friends swerved drunkenly down the highway. At a loss and bored, he let his gaze fall to study the floor.

The grout of the tile was stained yellow-brown—from blood, dirt, or piss, Terri couldn't tell. Didn't want to be able to tell. He'd never been in a hospital so dirty before, but he supposed he hadn't been to an emergency room before, either. Maybe this was just how things were. The pain meds continued to wreak havoc, making his gut churn and his brain feel too light for his skull.

A muted clatter and yelp of pain carried through the thick exam door. Terri glanced up, his focus brought back by the sudden noise.

"Dr. Mehl," he heard, though it was garbled, desperate. *"I think you should go to the breakroom."*

"I think you should—lock the door and lie down."

There was the sound of a struggle. He thought he heard a scream, a muffled wail of lost hope, before it was cut off by a wet, gurgling noise, like the sound of meat fed through a grinder. Anxiety tried to push through the fog squeezing his brain. It forced him to his feet, and he stumbled to the door to put his ear against the cool wood. Things remained quiet through the barrier; he finally opened the door and stepped out into the empty corridor.

He paused in the hallway, the lights bathing the tile and white walls with a harsh yellow glow. The brightness made the shadows in the corners cut sharp and lit up all the stains splattered across the cheap paint. An odd noise crept in low from the lobby: a crunching, grinding sound, like leather snapping. It was maddening, building and digging through the air like the screeching of a dying bird. Lulled by the calm of the drugs, Terri followed it, stopping short as he rounded the corner.

In the lobby, chairs lay strewn across the waiting area. The front desk seat spun on its side, abandoned. Blood congealed on the ground in thick, rubbery clots that curled around themselves like sleeping children. And there, in the corner of the lobby by a broken vending machine, crouched the source of the sound.

Something hunched over the mangled corpse of the nurse, peeling off strips of skin like a tanner ripping out a weak ligament. The figure crouched on all fours, and something wasn't quite right with the hands. Fingers had fused together, forming fleshy imitations of hooves. And the head—Terri backed up, kept backing up until he reached the exam room. It hadn't seen him, had it?

Just the drugs, he told himself. *Just the drugs mixing with the booze. You should have told them you'd been drinking.* Except, he'd never had a trip this bad.

He heard a noise near the bend in the hallway and slammed the exam room door shut. There was no lock on the door, but he couldn't bring himself to venture out in search of another hiding place. Pulling the table to block it was difficult when his one good hand slipped on the paper draped across it and caused it to tear. There was movement outside the door and heavy breathing. Hand hovering over the table, he held onto his own sharp inhale. Maybe whoever it was would walk by, continue on down the hall and leave him to come down on his own. He'd open the door when everything made sense again.

"Mr. Harkford?"

The doorknob clattered as someone on the other side turned it. Their words mashed together, slurring like someone was drunk and had trouble moving a loose mouth. It made Terri think of a smile too wide, a long jaw hinged too far up.

"Mr. Harkford, you need to open the door, or I'm going to have to call security."

It sounded like the doctor. Almost. He thought about dragging the table away and opening the door before he got in trouble. But her words slurred worse the more she talked, like she couldn't master the sounds that required lips.

Something hit the door hard. It cracked into the exam table and then ricocheted shut again. The noise caused his heart to stutter, and he threw himself against the blockade, desperate to keep it in place. Another slam: this time the door seemed to buckle and bend. The wood groaned. Terri dug his feet against slick tile as the table slid a few inches. He looked around the windowless room, but there was nowhere to go.

The door bulged against the table again, a violent movement that rammed the metal into his broken wrist. A graying curtain of pain enveloped him, and he stumbled back, landing hard on his ass. The sound of shrieking metal cleared his vision when the thick legs of the exam table screeched against the floor. The table was forced back just enough to let the door open a crack.

Something shoved its head and upper body through the opening.

The ripped and stained white coat hung over shoulders it no longer fit, and red hair hung in greasy strands, the ends tangled with what looked like ground pork. Skin stretched over a long, long skull and tore apart where it pulled too thin, revealing wet, glistening bone. A horse's skull, blood caked across flat teeth where they'd ground strips of skin like hay. Terri stared into a large, horizontal pupil and remembered the doctor's joke earlier.

Oh, he thought as the horse's head turned its frozen smile to him. Those teeth gnashed together, shredding deep red muscle between stained ivory, chattering that they were still hungry.

Oh, was all he could fathom as the thing that had been the doctor pushed the door open wider, pulling melted fingers after that long, long grin.

Why the long face?

MIDNIGHT RUN
J. Weintraub

SHE HAD TO run despite the lateness of the hour and the frost in the air. All night she'd watched those thin, icy fingers creeping up the windowpanes, forming their silvery, lacy webs as the frames shivered slightly in the wind, and she almost resisted the compulsion to run. But the glacial cold would also keep others inside, and on such nights, especially this night, she needed to be alone, even though venturing into those empty streets could expose her to the threat that'd been terrorizing the city for the past two years.

Yet this last concern meant little to her, since she'd lived with a constant sense of fatality from the moment Eric had died, anyway. He had always insisted he'd never intended to infect her, that it had been an accident, that he would never do such a thing, but now that he was gone—and she began to consider their time together more dispassionately—she no longer believed him.

They'd fallen in love almost from the day she had arrived at the research station in western Kenya, and from the very beginning, Eric had identified a certain affinity between them. How often, she asked herself, had he declared they were one and the same, body and soul? He even tried to convince her to share his passionate belief in the animistic religions they were supposed to be studying, but that was a line she refused to cross.

"You'll see," Eric promised as he lay dying in front of her. "We're one and the same, and who we are transcends everything we know. Even this small world of ours. You'll see."

But all she saw was that what had led to his death would surely lead to hers, and for that, she would never forgive him.

Once she had returned home, her anger and passion regularly erupted into a furious rage she could not control, and especially at those times, she needed to be alone. Often, when the pressure became unbearable, she was obliged to run, running deep into the night and into the early morning hours, returning with the rising of the sun, weary and depleted but relatively at peace with herself.

She'd always loved running. "You run like a girl! You run like a girl!" her brothers used to yell after her when she was very young, and perhaps that was the incentive she'd needed to train long and hard enough to qualify for two state championships in the middle distances. A torn Achilles tendon prevented her from competing in college, but although she could never regain the speed she had as a teenager, once her leg healed, she continued to run whenever she could. In fact, she'd even registered for a local marathon and began intense training for distance and endurance when she'd won that coveted research grant to study religions in Africa. The marathon and her doctoral dissertation would then have to wait for her return.

And now, with her return, both were very unlikely to happen.

She never enjoyed running in the cold, though she'd become accustomed to it, and her gear, piled on the window seat covering the radiator, lay awaiting her. As she slipped into her several pairs of fleecy sweats, she realized that the additional layers would not only provide sufficient warmth, but in flattening the contours of her body and concealing her gender, they would provide an extra touch of safety.

It'd become dangerous—more dangerous than usual—for a woman to venture outside alone into the city at night. After the third murder, the papers had noticed, and by now the count had reached ten. Most of the victims had been walking the streets for professional reasons, but there was also a middle-aged housewife on her way to an all-night pharmacy to pick up a prescription for her disabled husband. A student ornithologist, in search of a rare owl, had been found in the wooded bird sanctuary, and in the past two months, a pair of young career women were added to the list—one a lawyer, the other an investment banker, both of whom could find the time to jog only at night or in the pre-dawn hours. The first had been found in a dry creek bed crossing through Northern Park at the other end of the city, and the second in a ravine bordering the reservoir.

The ski mask she slipped over her hair and face would contribute to her anonymous appearance. This she covered with a woolen cap, and over the cap, pressing it tightly against her temples, the hood of her sweatshirt. Still, she felt she had little to fear, since she was unlikely to encounter anyone on her nocturnal runs, even in warmer weather. The route she preferred to follow wound through a stretch of parkland largely abandoned by the municipal authorities and commercial interests. She would enter through a gate, which never seemed to be locked, and immediately turn onto a side trail, bordered with dense shrubbery and lined with maples and elms whose branches arched low overhead. The path would lead her through a pair of underpasses, bringing her to the edge of an artificial lake that had been used for recreational boating. A pair of wooden docks—from which paddleboats and canoes had once been launched—had partially collapsed into the stagnant waters, complementing the remnants of a small bankrupt amusement park at the other side of the lake, its booths and sheds decaying along a short midway.

The green surrounding the lake had turned largely into a swampy bog, but the path she would follow rose to higher and drier ground and then sharply descended into a long tunnel beneath the observatory through which a tram, connecting the park to the center of the city, used to run. From the tunnel she would cross over to another tree-lined path—this one edged primarily with poplars—that would bring her back to the gate, where she would begin again, adding further laps around the park until she was exhausted and the turmoil howling inside her had largely been silenced.

This night, as soon as she stepped over her building's threshold, the difference between the dry heat of the foyer and the glacial chill of the fresh air sent an uncontrollable shudder throughout her body. But it also invigorated her, and the shivering was quickly followed by a steady animal energy that took her from a tentative jog to a pace far too rapid for the start of a long workout.

After only five minutes, she was inside the park, and she slowed considerably as she headed down her usual path, where the shadows seemed to welcome her. Although this night she was surprised by the brightness of the moonlight filtering through the linked branches and dead foliage overhead. Settling into her pace, she was comforted by the sharp crunch of the dried leaves that accompanied her every step.

But upon entering the first underpass, which ran beneath a wide boulevard that cut through the park, the crackling beneath her feet seemed to have doubled, as if they were casting a shadow of sound. Was this simply the pounding of her running resonating against the walls of the enclosed space, or had someone followed her inside? *Followed?* she thought, questioning herself. And *how paranoid is that?*, and although she never expected to encounter anyone on a wintry night such as this, she was occasionally accompanied by a scattering of others, running and walking in both directions, in all seasons.

As she exited from the shaft, the echoing behind her diminished, but it had not faded entirely. Someone was behind her and gaining on her fast. She thought for a moment about disrupting her workout to look back over her shoulder, if only to give the other person a sense of her awareness, but the woolen cap and the hood over it blocked her peripheral vision, and to look around she would have to come to a complete halt, something she was reluctant to do.

Just prior to reaching the second underpass, she slackened her pace, as if inviting the other runner to pass her before they entered the darkness and narrowness of the tunnel. But he—and now she was sure he was a man—also slowed, although he was now close enough for her to hear that he was breathing heavily as if he'd been struggling to overtake her. Once inside the cavernous space, which extended beneath a row of boathouses, she increased her speed. He did, too. But he failed to close the short distance between them and she emerged back into the moonlight that sent pillars of illumination through the archway of entangled branches above her.

Maybe I should slow down again, she thought. *Let him pass me and be done with this silliness. He can't even know I'm a woman.*

And then in the fraction of the second, between the concussion at the back of her head that coursed through her nervous system like a bone-shattering electric shock, and her momentary loss of consciousness, she heard her brothers yelling after her, "You run like a girl! You run like a girl!"

She didn't recall tumbling to the earth, but she must have instinctively braced her fall with her shoulder, since the soreness there was the first sensation she felt upon awakening. Flat on her back, she tried to prop herself up on her elbows, but her vision blurred and her head spun and she probably would have fallen back anyway, even if the crushing weight pressing down on both of her shoulder hadn't forced her down to the ground. When the rear of her head rebounded against the surface, she again almost lost consciousness.

"Don't fall asleep," he said, as the pressure from one of his knees turned the soreness in her shoulder into a sharp pain. "I want you to be awake for everything, and tonight, I can take my time, since it doesn't look like we'll be disturbed." He pulled off her woolen cap, and as he leaned forward, his shifting weight almost suffocated her.

"And, of course, we can't have this, can we?" he said, gripping the hem of her ski mask in both hands. "It gives me such pleasure, you know, to see the fear in a face."

He ripped the mask off her head.

Instantly, he leaned back.

"What have we here? The bearded lady in the circus? Something from a freak show?" And then he realized what he had stirring beneath him, regaining full consciousness, and that the twisted rope coiled in his pocket—intended eventually to garrote his victim—would be far from sufficient to protect him. For her part, she regretted he could not see the look of fear—that he said gave him so much pleasure—in his own face.

After finishing her lap around the park, she ended her run with a sweet taste in her mouth and only one additional regret. The blood on her sweats did not bother her, since those stains would disappear completely after several wash and spin-dry cycles. But she was truly sorry that the sharpness of her claws had ruined another fine pair of leather gloves.

THE SALT CIRCLE
Warren Benedetto

"I JUST DON'T WANT you to get hurt," Linda said, wiping her nose with a soggy, crumpled tissue. "I'm worried about you."

I extended my eye stalks toward her, giving her what I hoped was a look of indignation. I couldn't believe she tried to spin it like it was my fault. "If you didn't want me to get hurt, maybe you shouldn't have been so quick to deploy the chemical weapons."

She waved her tissue dismissively. "It's just a little salt."

My eye stalks retracted reflexively, reacting to the mere mention of the word. "Right. And Vietnam was 'just a little napalm.'" I slid off the seat of the chair, down the leg, and onto the cold tile floor, traveling on a thin layer of slime toward the phone on the wall.

"Where are you going?" Linda asked.

"To call my boss."

"To tell him what?"

"Well, I guess I'm not going to work today, am I? Unless you plan on sweeping up this mess." I jabbed one of my eye stalks at the wide circle of salt she had poured on the kitchen floor around me. "Now I've gotta get someone else to handle the Rosenberg account."

"You were going to go like that?" Linda cocked a skeptical eyebrow and motioned to my limbless body.

I hesitated, caught in a lie. "Maybe." Avoiding Linda's glare, I slithered up the wall to the phone and jabbed at the speakerphone button with one of the short feelers on the bottom of my face. A loud dial tone filled the kitchen.

Linda watched me struggle to negotiate the dial pad for a few moments before asking, "Do you want me to dial that for you?"

"If you wouldn't mind."

She stood with a beleaguered sigh and lumbered across the kitchen. Suddenly, her bare foot slipped in the trail of clear slime I had left on the floor, sending her reeling backward. Her head hit the edge of the counter with a sickening crack, then smashed onto the tile with a dull, wet thud. A dark pool of blood began spreading under her cheek. Her eyes stared at the baseboard under the dishwasher, wide and unseeing.

"Linda?" My voice was barely a whisper. "Babe?"

With a quick poke of my feeler, I turned off the speakerphone, ending the incessant drone of the dial tone. The silence was suffocating. A cold wave of fear rippled along my mottled flesh. Air whistled in and out of my breathing pore as I struggled to contain my panic.

I called her name again, louder this time. "Linda!" No response.

With a grunt, I peeled myself off the wall and flipped end-over-end onto the kitchen floor, landing on my back with a *splat*. Then I rolled over and wriggled toward Linda, undulating along the floor as fast as my slug body could take me. Which, admittedly, wasn't very fast. It didn't matter, though. There was no saving her. She was dead.

If I had been in my normal human body, I would have wept over my wife's lifeless corpse. But in my current form, the best I could do was allow my eye stalks to droop in a grim facsimile of grief. I couldn't let myself cry—the salt from the tears would melt my face off.

Once my initial shock subsided, I looked around the kitchen to assess my situation. The salt circle Linda had poured on the floor was intended to keep me from leaving the house and potentially alerting the neighbors to my unusual condition. What is my condition, you ask? It's sort of like…you know how, when the moon is full, a person turns into a werewolf? Well, it's like that, except instead of a werewolf, I turn into a slug. And instead of a full moon, it's triggered by 8:00 a.m. morning meetings.

I highly doubted anybody in the neighborhood would recognize me in slug form, but Linda was adamant that my affliction should remain a secret. She didn't want to raise any suspicions with the Homeowner's Association or, more importantly, the Garden Club. They had a particular aversion to any invasive species that might threaten their precious tomato plants.

The salt circle was a devious trap. Any contact with the salt would send me into writhing paroxysms of agony—it was like being burned alive by a million scorching cinders—so I was stuck inside the circle until I reverted into human form. The problem was, I had no idea how long that would take. Sometimes, it was only a few hours before I awoke naked and covered in slime somewhere in our house. Other times, I stayed transformed for days, subsisting on a bland diet of spring mix and kale until my limbs and head regrew enough for me to make a ham sandwich.

My options for getting rid of the salt were limited. I had no arms, so I couldn't properly operate a broom. Theoretically, I could summon the Roomba from the living room via the mobile app on Linda's smartphone, but there was no guarantee the robot vacuum would effectively sweep up the salt—it was just as likely to smear it around the kitchen, turning the whole room into a toxic wasteland. I could try to do something dramatic, like dropping from the table on top of the Roomba and riding it out of the kitchen like a hovercraft, but that plan was fraught with peril. If I misjudged the drop, I could be sucked under the thing and sliced into sushi by the vacuum's whirling brushes.

I cleared my thoughts and tried to go back to basics. What would I do in this situation if I *wasn't* a slug? I'd dial 911, of course. And then…what, exactly? The paramedics' emergency training probably didn't explain how to handle a call from a talking gastropod. Best case, they'd pick me up and fling me into the garden. Worst case, they'd drop me into the garbage disposal. Or worst-worst case, they'd pour salt on me themselves, just to see me squirm.

I looked at Linda's body again. Her mouth hung open, a thin trail of drool leaking from the corner of her lips and onto the floor. The way the saliva glistened in the early morning light reminded me of my own slime trail. Then it hit me. *Yes! That's it!* I could dial 911, then—in the time it took for the ambulance to arrive—I could slither down the wall, across the kitchen floor, and into Linda's mouth. After the paramedics forced their way into the house, they would put Linda on a stretcher and would carry her out to the ambulance, with me along for the ride like a stowaway in the wheel well of a passenger jet. Once outside, I could squirm out of her mouth and drop to the grass, where I would wait until I returned to human form. It was a perfect plan. Absolutely foolproof.

Or so I thought.

The first part of the plan went flawlessly. I crawled back up the wall to the phone, activated the speaker, then clumsily dialed 911 with my feelers. Once the operator answered, I explained that my wife had fallen in the kitchen and had hit her head on the counter. "I think she might be dead," I said. I told the operator our address. She said help was on the way.

After ending the call, I dropped back to the floor and squirmed over to Linda's body, avoiding the pool of blood that congealed around her head like a grisly halo. I paused to give her a small peck on the bottom lip, then slipped into the moist darkness of her mouth. The inside of her cheek was velvety warm under my belly. The air within was malodorous—I could smell the remnants of a hard-boiled egg still stuck in the ridges of her molars and the gaps between her teeth—but it was tolerable enough under the circumstances. I curled into a small loop, rested my head on my tail, and waited for the ambulance to arrive.

Within a few minutes, the doorbell rang, followed by loud pounding and muffled calls from outside. When nobody answered, the first responders circled the house looking for an alternate entrance. Hurried footsteps shuffled up the sidewalk to the house's side door, which opened into the kitchen just a few feet from Linda's body. "She's in there!" someone shouted. More knocking, more shouting. Finally, glass shattered and tinkled to the floor as one of the paramedics smashed out a window panel in the kitchen door and reached through to turn the doorknob.

I felt a wave of relief as the paramedics entered the room. My plan was working; I was almost free of the salt circle. All I had to do was wait for them to load Linda onto a stretcher and carry her out of the house.

Unfortunately, that's not what happened.

I probably should have anticipated that they'd try CPR. It was obvious, in retrospect—they wouldn't want Linda's brain to be deprived of oxygen for any longer than necessary. And what's the first step of CPR? That's right: mouth-to-mouth resuscitation.

First, a paramedic rolled Linda onto her back and tilted her chin up toward the ceiling. The inside of her cheek sagged a bit, creating a wide pocket of space next to her back teeth. I rolled into the gap, narrowly avoiding a pair of gloved fingers as they adjusted my wife's tongue to clear her airway.

The next thing I knew, a hot wind that stank of coffee and stale cigarettes blasted over me. I closed my breathing pore as much as I could, but I was too late to avoid getting a lungful of the paramedic's rank air as he breathed into Linda's mouth. The temperature cooled momentarily while he drew away to apply chest compressions. Each pump of his hands on Linda's breastbone rocked her body like a miniature earthquake. Short blasts of sulfurous, egg-tinged air escaped from her lungs with each successive compression, further fouling the atmosphere in her mouth. Then the paramedic's fetid breath returned. This cycle repeated itself several times before the guy asked, "Anything?"

"Still no pulse," a different voice responded.

"All right. Charge the defib."

Horror rippled down the length of my body as I realized what he meant: *defib* was short for *defibrillator.* They were going to shock my wife back to life, to jumpstart her stalled heart with a jolt of electricity. And I was *inside of her body.*

A high-pitched whine filled the room: the sound of the defibrillator charging. I tried to call out, to beg them to stop, but I couldn't produce a sound. Instead, I heard the paramedic speak the word I feared was coming.

"Clear!"

My nerve endings exploded with white-hot pain as the electricity from the defibrillator surged through Linda's body and into mine. Every muscle seized, causing my long, soft form to go as straight and rigid as a finger. I made a noise that sounded like "Hnnnngg!"

"Still no pulse. Hit her again."

"All right. Clear!"

"Hnnnngg!" Intense pain. Searing heat. Blinding light. I writhed and twisted in Linda's mouth, trying to stretch myself toward the narrow seam of brightness between her lips. I had to get out before the paramedics shocked her again.

"Jesus fuck! What the hell is that?" I heard the clatter of the defibrillator paddles dropping on the floor.

"What?"

"In her mouth! It looks like—"

"Is that a hand?"

A hand? I thought, momentarily confused. I rotated my eye stalks to look down the length of my body. Sure enough, a small, perfectly formed human hand protruded from my side. I watched in horror as it grew larger, extending further from my body, giving way to a wrist, then a forearm. The hand breached Linda's lips, forcing her mouth open and reaching out into the kitchen as it continued to grow: elbow…bicep… shoulder. At the same time, another hand materialized from the other side, forced outward by the rapidly growing arm emerging from my mantle. It, too, stretched out of Linda's mouth.

I squinted against the sudden brightness of the sunlight flooding in through my wife's now-gaping maw. I could only imagine what it looked like from the paramedics' point of view: a giant slug with human arms crawling from a dead woman's mouth like some kind of obscene oral birth.

My transition back to human form happened quickly, triggered and accelerated by the shock of the defibrillator. The girth of my body rapidly increased, dislocating Linda's jaw and causing it to open wider than should've been humanly possible. I could feel her teeth pressing into my flesh, threatening to puncture my fragile skin.

As my face emerged from Linda's mouth, I was able to see the paramedics for the first time. One was a muscular young man in his early twenties. The tag on his shirt identified him as Charlie. The other was an older man in his mid-forties named Frank. Frank knelt next to Linda's body—he was the one doing mouth-to-mouth and wielding the defibrillator paddles. Charlie squatted nearby with the main defibrillator pack in his hands.

My eye stalks slowly retracted until my eyeballs were seated in the sockets of my hardening skull, perched over a partially formed human nose and a writhing slug mouth. At the sight of my malformed head— half slug, half human—Charlie's face turned the color of old newspaper. He made a strangled gagging sound, then dropped the defib pack and bolted out the kitchen door.

"Whaaaat the fuck?" Frank exclaimed. He backpedaled away from me, his boots slipping in the blood from Linda's head and smearing it in big, bold streaks on the tile. Then he reached up, grabbed the edge of the counter to pull himself to his feet, and followed Charlie out the door.

With the paramedics gone, I dragged my flaccid body out of Linda's mouth, slipping onto the floor just as my legs grew back. The return to human form was relatively quick; the transition to full human size took longer. At first, I looked like a tiny homunculus—a perfectly formed human the size of a small squirrel and the color of caramel candy. From there, my body grew proportionally until it was back to its original size: about five-foot-nine, two hundred pounds or so. The slime dried, returning my skin to its original texture and color. Within a few minutes, I was myself again. I was naked. I was cold. But I was me.

I stood up on shaky legs and looked down at my wife's body. Her mouth was torn wide open, her lower jaw sagging almost to her collarbone. Her eyes stared vacantly up at me. The defibrillator was on the floor next to the body, along with a large duffel bag full of medical supplies that the paramedics had left behind. The salt circle was broken, a spray of tiny white crystals scattered across the floor from where the paramedics had entered and exited.

Still numb with shock and exhaustion, I wandered absently over to the utility closet and pulled out a broom, then swept the salt into a dustpan and dumped it into the trash. I felt terrible about what happened to Linda. She didn't deserve such an undignified death. Yes, I was frustrated about the salt circle, but deep down I knew she was only trying to protect me. She loved me unconditionally, regardless of how I looked or whether I had bones.

Sirens wailed in the distance, their volume rising as they drew closer. The paramedics had called the cops, an understandable reaction after what they had seen. I went into the bedroom and slipped on a pair of pants, then returned to the kitchen to wait for the police. Not surprisingly, they arrested me under suspicion for the murder of my wife. After photographing and fingerprinting me, they locked me in the county jail pending my arraignment, which was scheduled for 8:00 a.m. the next morning.

They never understood how I escaped. There was no sign of forced exit, no evidence of foul play. The only thing they found was a thin trail of slime leading between the bars, out through the front door, and into the grass outside.

TIME FOR A CHANGE
Mark Towse

COLD WHITE LIGHT sweeps across the house, sucking out any comfort in its path. Crunching gravel has my aching fingers clamping even tighter around the mantle.

This is a bad idea.

Back in relative darkness again, the flickering candle on the patio fights for survival. The car door slams. A silhouette. Footsteps.

Inhale. Exhale. I could hide. Maybe if—

I promise you, Bec, this is the only way you'll be free of him.

Olivia's voice settles me a little, but I feel nowhere close to as brave as when in her presence. "Without closure," she told me, "I'll never be able to move forward; I'll always be running."

And God knows I've tried everything else.

His familiar rhythmic rap of the door sets my skin on fire. All my rehearsed words start tumbling like kicked over alphabet blocks. As I walk to the door, I feel like I'm going into battle without arms.

I'll be there with you, Bec; remember that. I won't leave your side. None of us will.

There he is: the love of my life.

He smiles his once-powerful smile and raises the bouquet. Never been a flower kind of girl, but I'll take them over a broken jaw any day of the week. My trembling fingers lock around the door handle, the metal feeling colder than ice.

"Hi, Paul."

"Rebecca, you look amazing."

I stand my ground as he leans in towards me, blue eyes all childlike and hopeful. Familiar spicy aftershave wafts in with the gentle breeze, tainting the smell of cooking food and causing my stomach to churn. Still, I allow his lips to find my cheek. Warm breath sends a shudder down my spine. I refuse to move, reaching my hand out and imagining Olivia's fingers coiling around mine. *I won't leave your side.*

He pulls away and offers the flowers. "I missed you," he says, his eyes even more alive with expectation.

People always struggled to understand why I kept letting him back in. They used to look at me as though I was stupid, not quite all there. And, Christ, they only knew the half of it—the marks I couldn't cover with high-top dresses, scarves, and long sleeves. I thought this man was the love of my life. We were happy once, as content as can be with such an absurd existence. To this day, I can't pinpoint when the darkness consumed him, but as the saying goes, love is blind.

"Wine?"

"Sure," he says, closing the door behind him. "A beautiful night."

"It is. I thought we could eat on the patio."

He eyes the table outside and takes the glass of red. "Stunning place, but a bit off the beaten track. Drove past it twice. Whose is it, anyway?"

"It belongs to a friend, a proper country girl." Olivia runs it as a safe place for abuse victims, *Shady Pines Retreat.* Quite often, she'll just let people have it for a few days, a chance to embed themselves in nature.

"Can I give you a hand with anything?"

"No, sit down. It'll be ready in a few minutes."

"What a view." He folds his arms, surveying the wooded area at the back. "Smells amazing out here. I mean, the food also, but the air's so fresh and invigorating."

I call this eggshell mode, usually lasting a couple of days after an event but inevitably giving way to darkness. That's how I used to think of it—that there was a demon inside of him, and I was the only one who could cast the evil out—a tumultuous life spent walking a tightrope between love and fear.

"It is beautiful," I agree. The place is already beginning to feel like a second home. "The pine, the wildflowers, the faint smell of smoke. The simple things, eh?"

"The ones we lose sight of," he says as he pulls a chair out. "How have you been?"

I begin slicing the lamb, my appetite returning. How have I been? How have I been? My bones are fixing, but the scars will remain forever. "Getting there."

"I was surprised." He inhales again, a city boy all his life. "When I got the invitation, I mean."

"Dinner's nearly ready. Help yourself to more wine." But I notice his glass is already replenished. He's *tried* giving up alcohol before, even booked an AA meeting once after a particularly nasty *episode*. Just another offering to temporarily appease.

"I didn't see another house for miles," he says. "Don't you get scared out here all alone?"

"It's the safest I've felt in years."

The chorus of crickets fails to disguise his sigh, but he says nothing as he lifts his glass to his lips.

"I hope it's good," I say, carrying his plate through. "Don't usually go to the trouble with it just being me, usually a sandwich or microwave meal."

"Looks great."

I feel his eyes on me as I put the plate down. "There's more if you're hungry." The candle's flame flickers as the gentle breeze blows across, bringing more of his scent and an image of our old bedroom: the extended crack in the ceiling, the sheer purple curtains. I grasp the back of my chair for support, waiting for the dizziness to pass.

"So what am I doing here, Bec?"

"What do you mean?" I retreat towards the kitchen counter, full of doubt once again.

"You haven't replied to my texts for weeks, and then out of the blue, I get an invite for dinner."

Gripping the plate to stop my trembling, I make my way back to the table. *This is the only way you'll be free of him.* "Let's eat before it gets cold."

He smiles and nods. "It's really good to see you."

To anyone who didn't know our history, I imagine we'd look like lovers at the beginning of our relationship—gentle classical music playing in the background as we dine and drink wine under the light of a glorious full moon. We talk about our jobs and our friends, mutual and new. We smile. We chew. We open another bottle, letting nature's perfume wrap around us. The night has all the awkwardness and superficiality of a first date, but ours takes place on a thin sheet of ice that could crack at any moment.

"I think about you every day," he says, reaching for my hand.

I recoil and pray for strength. "Shall we have dessert?"

"That depends on what's on offer?"

"Baked Alaska. I'll go and—"

"Sit down!" The shadow passes across, the demon leaving just as quickly, softness returning to his face. "Please."

I think this marks the juncture at which small talk ends.

"Why am I here, Bec?"

"So I can move on. So we can both move on."

He says nothing, but from the corner of my eye, I see the napkin crumple under his grip. No going back now, though. "We share a history, Paul, a portion of time that has come to an end. Let's close that book and move on to the next."

"What if I don't want to?"

"You just don't have that kind of power over me anymore." I clasp my hands together. "I'm doing this regardless, and I was hoping tonight you would finally agree to let me go. I know you follow me. I know it's you on the other end of the phone." I swallow hard, watching the napkin unfurl as he consumes the dregs in his glass. "It is, isn't it?"

"Doesn't it prove how much I love you, though? My heart is breaking, Bec, can't you see that?" He fills his glass again. "I'm nothing without you."

Stay strong, Bec; we are with you. "Your heart might be breaking, but mine is just mending." I lift my gaze from the table to his blue eyes. "Some of my bones, too."

His face twitches, a familiar sign he's on the defensive, his offense never far behind. Leaning back with hands clasped behind his neck, eyes towards the stars, he exhales. "My parents have been married for over forty years. They never gave up on each other."

"How many times did I take you back? How many?"

"Had their fair share of wars but came out better from it."

"War?" I lean in towards him, crossing into no-man's-land. "Every couple argues, Paul." I feel the hair prickling on my neck and arms. The air feels charged, like just before a storm. I can almost see the thundercloud forming around him. "But no marriage should end in broken bones and blood."

"And I can't apologize enough for that, Bec," he says, all sincerity sifted out by gritted teeth. He leans towards me, hands knitting together, wedding ring on show. "But I've done my time. Had a chance to reflect on my actions, and I—"

"You're what?" I'm taking charge and it feels fantastic, reciprocating his advance until our heads are only inches apart. "A different person? A man of God?"

His eyes widen, his nostrils flare. "I'm not the guy you used to know."

He gives me the puppy dog eyes, but I see his knuckles turning white. Always the same lines, same routine.

"I can't even remember the guy I first met," I say, thinking back to what Olivia told me, releasing my words with as much dispassion as possible. "He's buried under mounds of tainted soil."

"Why am I really here?"

"I told you already."

"I don't believe you." He settles back in the chair. "You still love me, don't you?"

I look deep into his eyes, beyond the innocence of the blue. "No."

"You're lying." Lines carving their way across his temple, he gently shakes his head. "There's still a way back, Bec; I know it." As he lunges forward again, reaching for my hand, the breeze wraps around us, extinguishing the candle and bringing smells of damp tree trunks, moss, and carrion. I try to break free from his grasp, but his fingers coil around my knuckles like a giant's.

"Tell me there's still a way, Bec."

"Let go of me."

"Not until you tell me we can be good again." He momentarily releases his grip, sliding his hand to my wrist and yanking me towards him. "Please, Bec. One more chance. One last chance."

We're here with you.

"No."

I feel his elevated pulse on my skin, his grip tightening. Air is heavy, polluted with his aftershave and the smell of rotting meat. "You always were a fucking tease," he says, his sky-blue eyes now loaded with the promise of a storm to end all storms.

"Let fucking go of me, Paul!"

He clamps down harder, his warm smile at the door a fleeting memory, replaced with the demon's leer. "That perfume you know I like, the music, the low-cut dress, eating under the stars—all for what, Bec? Some twisted joke? A way of hurting me?"

I hear rustling leaves. And breathing, heavy and excitable.

"Look at me when I'm talking to you!" He pulls me in, wrapping his other hand around the back of my head. "This is not how it ends!" Glasses tumble, plates clatter as he rakes against my softness, his lips devouring mine, his tongue hungrily searching within.

As I revert to well-practiced numbness, orbs like glowing embers light up the woods around us, moving in time with the music and creating an almost magical display. A fairy-tale romance to the outsider. He comes up for air, resting his forehead against mine. "I love you so much, Bec. We can start again; I'll show you." His left hand wraps around my waist, his right slides up my low-cut dress, something I could never wear for so many reasons when we were together. "One more chance."

More ember-like globes appear as he applies his lips to mine with sickening intensity. I hear blood whooshing in my ears. Scenes of violence in my mind melt into the vivid imagery behind my *beloved's* shoulder, each branch visible with impossible clarity, the grass beneath dancing to the breeze.

There's fear, but only of the unknown.

Placing my palms on his back, I bring him into me. He lets out a groan as his tongue gets busier still, his hands squeezing my breasts. There's a crackle, what I think at first to be the forest carpet, but my skin begins to prickle and my body flares with pain. More snapping fills my ears, accompanied by explosive pain that has me instinctively grinding our rib cages together. He lets out a muffled rasp as I push my lips harder against his, my sharpness continuing to explore his back. Eyes wide, face red, he flails against me, but there's no give at all.

The first time is always the hardest.

Every hair on my body stirs as the breeze blows across once more, bringing too many scents to decipher. He continues struggling, trying to force my head back with his hands and sucking air through his nostrils, his tongue finally retreating like a wounded animal.

As though someone bends my spine like a piece of plastic, pain detonates across my back. I can hear every bone expanding, snapping, buckling. My skin smoulders with intensity as Paul continues offering dampened moans, his eyes widening further still as they stare into mine. His lips form a scream as my claws pierce his flesh, but I steal it from him, just as he stole mine for all those years. Refusing to let go, I dig them in further still, listening as blood pumps violently around a shredded body that now feels puny within my clutches. Fire rages within, skin stretching to accommodate elongated bones. My jaw dislocates, contorts, enlarges as new teeth cut through the rawness, bringing unimaginable agony. Instinctively, I clamp down, feeling his body trembling violently against mine as blood spills down our chins, pure fear in his eyes now.

I'm ravenous again.

But as I bear down, ready to dine, I catch sight of my reflection within the blue, and I release him, recoiling until my back is against the brick. *Embrace it. It's a beautiful thing.* The hair, the eyes, the ears, though. Olivia, I'm scared! *A miracle of nature. We are blessed.* Her voice in my head is like water on my skin, extinguishing the flames until, once again, only magic surrounds me, the heightened sounds of the forest and the ever-approaching golden orbs.

With a hand across his shredded lips and blood spilling through his fingers, Paul lets out a garbled cry. In return, I offer a howl of my own, nearly a decade's worth of screams rolled into one.

He begins a delayed retreat, eyes not leaving mine. I see the knowledge in them, though, and can taste his fear now, far more potent than that rancid aftershave. Behind us, eyes like headlights continue to close in. As a chorus of howls return mine, his leg buckles, sending him crumpling to the concrete tiles.

The night didn't quite go as planned, did it, darling?

Olivia said doubt would creep up on me from time to time, but since seeing him through the glass of the door, the pathetically hopeful look spread across his face and the puny offering grasped in his right hand, I have no regrets. Finally, I'll be free of him, no longer scared to look over my shoulder or answer my phone.

One bite, and it can all be different.

Olivia's first to pounce, launching towards him with a growl, her teeth clamping around his neck, prompting a blood-curdling scream and multiple streams of red that look magnificent against the backdrop of the moon. Writhing and moaning, trying to pry her jaws away, Paul's terror-filled eyes fix on mine, perhaps hoping for a last-minute reprieve.

But this dog has had its day.

I can smell the blood, stronger than before, a coppery bitterness that usually turns my stomach but now only serves to heighten my hunger. He's just prey. Others begin emerging from the darkness, ready for the feast, teeth bared, snouts frothy with saliva.

The only way.

A series of watery gurgles emerge from his throat as they puncture and rip at his flesh. They tug at his body like a rag doll, dragging him this way and that until the twitching finally ceases and the light dims behind his eyes.

She was right.

Moving in, I feel free, empowered, about to feed on someone who ate away at me for most of my adult life. And when we've finished eating, picking the meat from his bones, we'll share a glass of wine and toast to new beginnings—a stronger, unified, dependable pack.

We howl in unison, the women of Shady Pines Retreat.

WOLVES AT THE FAIR
Mir Rainbird

THE MUSIC OF the Ferris wheel was slower than it should be and the mechanism caught unpredictably. The effect made the skin between Colleen's shoulder blades crawl. At least the music stopped when the ride wasn't in operation.

Colleen kicked bare heels against the wooden barrier, watching locals pass by. She always looked, hoping to spot someone like her. Although how would she know?

One of her cousins caught her eye and scowled. He detoured from his patrol to stand in front of her. "Don't you have any work to do, Colin?" he demanded.

As if he and his brothers walking around glaring at people was hard work. Colleen kept her eyes down and gestured at the space around them, empty of customers.

They made less and less on the rides every year. No mystery: everyone knew how scarce replacement parts had become now that no one manufactured more. Who wanted to risk their life on a creaky old coaster? The only ride with anyone on it tonight was the Merry-Go-Round that featured animals hand-carved by their grandmother.

"Maybe you'd get some traffic if you flashed your boobs," Bobby sneered. "Oh, right, you don't got any."

Colleen wore a loose pink dress that ended above her knees, her wavy hair in two little pigtails. Big Bill didn't mind her dressing like this when a cute girl might attract paying customers. When there weren't customers… he minded. So his sons minded, too.

"The cake stand is doing good," she deflected. "And your mom has a line at the psychic tent."

"People are probably asking about the wolves."

Bobby and Colleen turned towards the unfamiliar voice.

"Wolves?" asked Bobby. Colleen couldn't have spoken. She stared at the young man's face, which was the most interesting thing she'd seen all year. She lowered her eyes. This meant she now stared at his muscular chest, bare under the homemade leather coat. Below that were worn jeans. They fit nicely. Colleen ended up staring at his scuffed boots, face burning.

"There've been wolves in the woods hereabouts, so they say."

Colleen had seen a wolf once, when the fair traveled to the west coast for the winter. She had been frightened, but the animal had been beautiful.

"These wolves done anything?" Bobby wanted to know.

"Eating livestock, seducing maidens, the usual. How about this ride?"

Her cousin's puzzled expression smoothed away. "It's a token—a token each." He glanced over the man's shoulder to where two more young men—no, one was a woman, a tall, lean woman with short black hair—had come up behind him.

The man rattled the wooden tokens in his hand, but didn't hold them out. "Two to a chair, huh? Kirby and Hale have each other, but I'd be all alone. Unless you want to keep me company, miss?"

"I-I have to run the ride," Colleen stammered.

"I can do it," Bobby said, quick to make a sale. "Four chits. You just shout when you're ready to get off."

Colleen shot her cousin a glare as he opened the gate. He smirked. Her cousins found it hilarious when men tried to grope her. They wouldn't let her get beat too badly, though, if the man reacted poorly to what he found under her skirt.

The tall pair, who looked alike enough to be brother and sister, settled in first. Colleen sat in the chair behind theirs. The man's knee was warm against hers. He didn't try to touch her anywhere else, yet.

The music jerked to a discordant start as the wheel started to turn. It drowned out the shouting and laughter below, making it seem as if the riders were alone up here in the dark.

"I'm Rex. What's your name?"

"Colleen." She kept her face turned away, although he turned his toward her.

"Colleen. You've traveled a lot?"

"I suppose. I was born into the fair."

"How many traveling fairs like this are there?"

That was an unexpected question. "A few, I guess? There are circuses and carnivals and such, as well."

"Those are different? Which would be most likely to have a freakshow? Or something with wild animals?"

"A freakshow?" *What on earth?* "I don't know, maybe a circus? They have more animal acts."

"Do you like those? Animal acts?"

"No. I don't like freakshows, either." She had been to one once and never forgot the stink of the dark tent and the hopeless, hating faces of the prisoners in their filthy cages. "But I like animals. Why do you want to know about freakshows?"

His voice lost its relaxed drawl for the first time. "I'm looking for one. For someone who was taken."

"I'm sorry," Colleen whispered. "I wish I could help, but I don't really know much. I've only ever lived here, and we don't have any freaks."

The one freakshow she'd seen had been failing. People saw enough oddities for free, these days. The fair had purchased a mangy juggling ape from them. It had died years ago.

"Do you know how to find them? The other shows?"

"No. One of the older folks might know. Why'd you think to ask me?"

"I thought you might tell the truth," he said. "Because you want me."

"What?" Colleen's face burned. "I-I don't even know you."

He put his arm behind her, resting it on the back of the chair. He didn't touch her, but she felt the warmth of him through the thin material of her dress.

He leaned closer and whispered, "I know how it feels to want to take your skin off, Colleen."

Her head snapped around.

He kissed her.

His fingers on her cheek were butterfly light. She could have pulled away; instead, she kissed him back, brushing her tongue against soft lips and then over sharp, even teeth.

When her heart pounded so hard that she had to stop, she told him, "I'll ask around. Come back tomorrow."

"Thank you."

Colleen hesitated. "I would have anyway, if you asked. You didn't have to kiss me."

"Why would I not want to kiss you?"

Colleen frowned down at her lap. Rex took one of her hands and held it until the chair came to rest on the earth, music ending with an agonized squawk.

Bobby's older brother Billy waited with him. They watched with narrowed eyes as Colleen let herself out and moved to the next chair to unlatch it for Kirby and Hale. She didn't glance back at Rex or at her cousins.

"Thank you," Kirby said as she stepped out. She didn't smile, but her low voice sounded friendly.

"Thanks," Hale echoed. He gave her a quick smile: there, gone.

"Thank you, Colleen." Rex's knuckles brushed the back of her hand as he passed her. Kirby and Hale fell in behind him as he walked away.

Colleen took a deep breath and went to face her cousins.

It wasn't too bad, now. There were people all around, and they were supposed to be working. Bobby hissed, "Pervert," and pinched her thigh. Billy glared down at her and said, "Think we got nothing better to do than save your scrawny ass from a beating? Lucky that rube wasn't friskier."

Colleen didn't bother pointing out that they wouldn't have been any happier if she hadn't let Rex kiss her. When she tried objecting to unwanted touches from fair-goers, they yelled at her for not being nice to customers. Unhappy people didn't spend as much. Billy had told her a couple years ago, "If you don't like 'em grabbing your ass, stop pretending to be a girl."

When Colleen argued that different men felt her up when she was dressed as a boy, his face had twisted in disgust. Disgust aimed at her.

She'd given up defending herself a long time ago.

It was hard to ask questions that night. Bobby and Billy were busy telling everyone about Colleen "slutting it up" and watching for her reaction. Her parents pretended not to hear.

When dinner was served, there was a male rush on the food. Colleen took a bowl of soup to Great-Aunt Posy and knelt next to the old woman. "Auntie P," she asked, "How do we know which shows are going where, so's we don't end up in the same towns at the same time?"

"Is that really what you want to know, dear?" Aunt Posy had worked the psychic tent before her niece, Alma, who was Big Bill's wife, took it over. Alma was a better performer and good at telling people what they wanted to hear, but she wasn't psychic. Posy was, at least once in a while. She'd mostly retired because being psychic tired her out something awful.

"If someone wanted to find a particular exhibit at a particular show, but they didn't know which, how would they go about it?"

"That sounds mighty difficult, Col. Back when I was a girl, we had technology that let us get information from all over the world. We could even talk to people far away." Posy's voice turned sad. After a moment, she said, "If the person looking had something belonging to the one they were looking for, or they were related, they could ask a diviner. I never had the gift, but my sister does."

Aunt Posy had a sister? That was news to Colleen.

"How would they find her?"

"Polypheemia…" Posy said very slowly. Her eyes drifted shut. "She's a long ways to the southeast of here." Her eyes opened. "Would you fetch me some water, dear?"

Colleen made her way through the jostling elbows of her cousins and brothers to the water bucket. She was shoved enough on the way back that half the water ended up on her dress, but she didn't care.

"Thank you, dear. You should go out and refill the bucket," Posy told her.

It hadn't been empty, but Colleen nodded and said, "Yes, Auntie." She was glad enough to get away from the hot, crowded tent and the disapproving stares.

At the well, she drew up a bucketful and poured it into the filter, sitting on the low wall as she waited for the water to drip through.

"Colleen."

She jumped and might have fallen backward into the well if a strong arm hadn't suddenly wrapped itself around her.

"Rex! What are you doing here?"

"I thought you might come outside." He said it casually, like it was nothing to hang around in the dark, waiting Who-knew-how long, on the chance he might see her.

Her heart thumped even though she told it he was here for her information, not for *her*.

"My aunt said if you have something from the person, you could maybe find them by divination," she blurted, wondering if he would think that was crazy. Most magic was as fake as Aunt Alma's fortune-telling.

But he nodded like that made sense, so she went on. "She said her sister is a diviner and she's somewhere far to the southeast. I never met her."

"Would you like to?" Rex asked.

"What'd I tell you, boys?" Billy's loud voice broke the spell of the darkness. "I knew Colin snuck off to rub up on his new trick. Guess he ain't found your sausage yet, huh, Col?"

Bobby and Parker grinned nastily. Their youngest brother looked uncomfortable.

"How 'bout it, stranger? You a boy-lover? Huh?"

"Stop it, Billy!" Colleen said. "You want to get the whole town down on us? You know what'll happen if you hurt a local."

"Funny thing." Billy smirked. "I asked around while you were busy sucking this pervert's face and no one knew him at all. He ain't from around here, and he don't seem to have any business here—except with you, Colin."

"He's just looking for a missing friend," Colleen said quickly. "He's not doing any harm. Just forget him, okay? Let's go back inside."

Billy nudged Bobby. "We'll go back inside—when we've taught this faggot a lesson." His grin faded. "Looks like you need some teaching, too, Colin."

Rex made a growling noise in his throat and stepped around Colleen so that he stood between her and her cousins. Colleen took a deep breath and prepared to fight her cousins, something that had never gone in her favor.

Billy's face twisted as he swung a meaty fist. He had fifty pounds on Rex, but Rex caught his wrist and stopped the blow dead. He looked at the red-faced Billy for a minute, eyes narrow, then released his wrist with a shove that sent him stumbling back into his brothers.

"Go back inside while you can still walk," Rex suggested.

"Get him!" Billy shouted.

His brothers didn't go anywhere. The two younger boys were jerked off their feet, Hale's hands over their mouths. Kirby had Bobby on his knees, arms twisted behind his back. Rex kicked Billy's feet out from under him and stepped on his neck.

"Don't hurt them!" Colleen cried, catching his arm. Rex turned to look at her, and she met his eyes for the first time.

"Haven't they hurt you, Colleen?" he asked gently.

"Yes. But they're my family. Please."

He touched her cheek. "We could be your family, if you wanted us. Come with us, Colleen."

"Come where?" she breathed.

"First to find my brother. Hale and Kirby are our cousins," he added. "Once we've freed him, we'll find a place for ourselves. A home. Or we can keep traveling. Whichever you like. Just say you'll come with me, Colleen."

Colleen had traveled her entire life without going anywhere outside the fair. The same tents, the same repetitive daily chores, the same people who wanted her to be someone else.

"I'll go with you and help you find your brother. You don't have to… to…" Her voice fell away under his warm, steady gaze.

"I want to," he told her. His fingers moved to her lips.

"Tie them up," Rex directed his cousins. "Use their clothes. Take that one's coat and boots."

"Are you leaving them tied up here?" Colleen asked worriedly. "What about wild animals? Those wolves you were talking about?"

Hale laughed.

Rex smiled. "Don't worry about that. The wolves are already here."

"There's nothing dangerous nearby," Kirby said. "And someone will come out to look for them soon."

Rex finished gagging Billy with his shirt and helped Colleen into Parker's coat and boots. "Once we're away from here, we'll teach you how to shed your skin."

"You mean that for real, don't you?" Colleen shivered. "Will I be able to put it back on later?"

Rex drew her into his warm arms. "You can't put back on shed skin," he told her. "But you can grow a new one."

She took his hand and followed him into the woods. When they left the lights of the fair behind, they ran.

TOGETHER BOUND
UNTO PERDITION
Matt McHugh

EVEN THOUGH I do not deserve such comfort, I am grateful to awaken and find myself in my own bed.

It is greatly preferable to waking in the stable or under the henhouse or in the woods—exposed to the morning chill—with only the angle of tree shadows hinting at the direction home. That was my experience, for the many years I lived alone, upon reverting to the body of a man from the shape of a nightmare. Now, with someone to leave my cabin door ajar so the scent may summon me even if unaware, I return to myself each time with a surreal sense of normality.

I don't know why it happens. Months, even years, have passed without incident. Then, for reasons never wholly clear—sometimes an illness or injury, sometimes a stirring so slight I barely recognize its beginnings—the torment recurs. Mostly, but not always, in the night. I recall only the start, the spasms and seizures that precede blackout; afterward, I can only surmise what atrocities I committed. It is an affliction I am too weak to control, and long ago came to accept it as punishment for sins that must be too monstrous to name.

That was before Aleka. Orphaned by tragedy, she has seen the worst of what I am, and the chance to earn her forgiveness each new day is the knife edge I walk towards a needle's eye of redemption.

She has laid out a clean, unshredded dressing gown for me. I put it on and step around the partition separating my bed from the rest of the cabin. Aleka stokes the embers in the iron stove to a blaze, a pot of milled oats bubbling on the griddle.

"Are you hungry, Erza?" she asks.

The only thing certain from the night before is that I ate well. But I sit at the table and allow her to serve me. She sets a bowl at my place, honey drizzled over the surface like the pattern of bridal lace. I would, of course, prefer bacon, but I thank her and take a spoonful.

"I haven't gone to the well yet," she says. "This will have to do."

She puts half a cup of beer on the table.

"I thought this was gone," I say.

"Nay. There is a little left. Perhaps today we can afford a new cask."

I do not say, *What have I done to deserve you?* but I have thought it every day for the past five years. Aleka is now sixteen, perhaps seventeen, and it's well-nigh time for her to consider a husband. I have noticed her drawing the boys' eyes at the market or harvest festivals, but she only edges closer to me when she senses them staring. I try to feel disappointment at that, but I know I'm lying to myself. I have become very adept at that skill.

She goes outside and returns with a basket of eggs she holds up proudly. "Very good batch today," she says. "When you're ready, we should milk the goats and bring it all to town."

The goats produce well, too. Nearly a pail a half. My livestock does better under Aleka's care than ever by mine alone. She has a way with beasts.

By mid-morning, we are on our way. It's only a mile to the village but slow-going as I pull the cart over the rutted road. When we arrive, the square is bustling with tinkers and traders hawking their wares, squabbling over barter terms. Aleka leads me straight to the brewer's stall. William, the brewer's son, stands by the kegs, and his eyes light up when he sees her.

In short order, she negotiates a purchase: a small barrel of ale for only a few eggs. That boy will certainly get whipped for such a lopsided deal. By the way William trembles as Aleka sets eggs into his open palms, he will likely consider his licks an acceptable price for the brush of her fingers.

As we stroll through the square, we pass a knot of gossiping women. I tip my hat and several nod politely, but once we are a few paces beyond, I hear a low, venomous whisper:

"Whore-child!"

Aleka tightens her grip on my arm. We continue and I say nothing. There is nothing to be said.

Soon, we start back toward my cabin. It is nearly noon and the sun is warm overhead, but I can sense the approach of Autumn in a breeze that rustles leaves just beginning to turn gold at the tips. I summon the courage to speak my mind.

"The brewer's son seems to have taken quite a shine to you," I say.

Aleka stops. She takes my chin in her fingers, angles my head to face her piercing eyes.

"You take care of me," she says with steely anger. "You owe me that."

I say nothing. There is nothing to be said.

The full harvest is still a few weeks away, but there is nonetheless plenty of work to be done before Winter draws near. Late in the afternoon, Aleka and I are troweling mud into chinks in the cabin's log walls when I hear bootsteps on the gravel path. The constable has come to pay us a visit.

"Ezra," he says, nodding to me, then without looking, to Aleka, "Child."

"What can I get ye?" I ask, wiping the grit from my hands.

"Naught," he says. "I've come to tell folks in the woodlands that there was a wolf spotted last night."

"That so?"

"Aye. The Van Helders lost three sheep. One eaten, two just torn up, all vicious. Mean-spirited beast. You had best keep your livestock indoors. Better to endure the smell than the loss."

"Sound advice, and thanks," I reply. "Sure you won't take anything? I have some coffee, ground fresh, I could make."

"Obliged for the offer, Ezra, but I haven't time. Still a good distance to walk, and I must reach home before dark. You stay safe, my friend."

"God be with you, Constable."

"Aye. And you."

He turns to go when Aleka runs suddenly to him and hugs her arms around his neck. "Thank you, sir, for bringing us a warning," says she.

The constable steps back, startled. His eyes squint and his lips strain to form a smile. "It's my duty, ma'am. God be with you." He continues along the path, his departure quicker than his arrival.

I stare at Aleka, amazed by such a peculiar action. When he's well beyond earshot, she says, "I know that man."

She holds out her hand and dangles a handkerchief.

"From his pocket," she says.

I falter, bewildered, before finally managing to ask, "Why?"

"Come inside and I'll tell you."

In the cabin, she stokes the fire with an iron and brews a mix of my favorite spiced tea.

"Sit," she says.

At the table, she brings me a cup and drops a chip of sugar into it before my eyes.

"Drink."

As I take a sip, burning pain sears my hand. I cry out and stumble to the floor, upsetting my chair. Aleka stands over me with a hot poker brandished like a sword. The glow from the tip sets her eyes afire.

"What are you doing?" I demand, cradling my injured hand.

"I know pain can bring it on." She presses the constable's handkerchief to my face. "Smell it."

I push aside the handkerchief. The poker pushes to the side of my neck. Agony!

"You will heal," she says. "You always do. Now, smell it!"

She smothers me with the handkerchief. I can't help but breathe it in. As I do, I see the constable like a wisp of colored smoke glowing in blackness. The wisp stretches, drifting from my cabin gate, down the path, and winding into the trees.

Already, I feel it. The itching on every inch of my skin. My arms and legs, bending as if stretched on the rack. My tongue, my teeth, swelling, not my own. A mouthful of vomit I know I cannot expel.

"Why?" The gurgling sound I make is the last piece of me that will be human tonight.

Aleka opens the cabin door to the dying twilight outside.

"Because there's work to be done," she says.

When I wake in bed, Aleka is making breakfast. Bacon.

I get up and stagger forward, only a blanket pulled around me. Aleka sets a full plate at my place and I sit. The aroma of salt and sizzling fat is all but heavenly, yet I can only stare at the offering, consumed by the question lingering from last night.

"Why?" I once more ask.

Aleka sits across from me. "What they say of my mother is true. She did what she had to so that we could survive. I was a child, and I saw no shame in it. But the women—the Christian women—who wouldn't spare us a loaf of bread, shamed her. The men who came with their paltry copper coins to bargain for what they wanted, even they showed nothing but contempt. Their cruelty drove from her all remnants of kindness, and she had nowhere to aim her rage except upon me."

She reaches over the table, takes both my hands in hers.

"Some men…what they most desire is to hurt a woman. To see her cower, to hear her beg. The constable—I will never forget his stinking, unshaven face—is such a man. My mother, weak as she was, still protected me from him. And for that, she was shown no mercy. Such a man merits no mercy."

"You sent me after him," I say.

"Yes."

"It's wrong," is all I can say. "No matter the cause, wrath is sinful. Don't you understand, child?"

Her face goes fierce. Her voice remains calm. "I am not your child."

A dagger through the heart could not have pained me more.

"That is true. I had a child once, or rather a wife that was with child." Despite the span of time, the memory is all but unspeakable. "Forgive me. In my grief, I sometimes dare to think of you as mine."

Her grip softens on my hands.

"I was twelve years old," Aleka begins. "My mother was drunken, raving—as was not uncommon—and beating me with a strap for spilling a bowl of stew, when there was a bone-chilling cry outside our door. We both knew what it meant: a wild animal had come for the only goat we had. My mother took a knife and—brave and foolish from whiskey—ran out to the pen. I followed.

"The greatest creature I have ever seen awaited us. Large as a colt but fanged and clawed like a bear. Fur white as ice and a maw stained with blood. Eyes burning like embers. My mother had no chance to even scream before you tore out her throat.

"I ran inside, tried to hold the door, but you shattered the hinges like dry leaves. I prayed as I had never before or since for a miracle. And it was granted. You lay down and slept. I watched you shrivel, shed your fur, and awaken as a man. I was not afraid, for I knew then what you truly are: deliverance."

Aleka kneels beside me, embracing me.

"I never loved my mother. As a woman now, I understand and I pity her. But, as a girl, I wanted only to be free of her, free of the brutality leveled upon her which she, in turn, passed on to me. She rests, but not in peace. You have the power to grant her peace."

"No," I whisper. "Please, no."

"I know the men who hurt her," she says. "I will never forget them, not a one. They will pay what they owe."

"I won't do it."

Aleka stands, tall and terrifying. "Then cut your throat!" she shrieks. "Say the word, and I'll do it for you."

Once more she kneels, takes my hand and kisses the spot she burned not a day before.

"Or live. Live and deliver judgment. Don't you see? This is why God gave you such terrible, beautiful strength. You have no need to atone for what you are. You are an angel of justice."

She takes my chin in her fingers, turns my face to behold her eyes, gentle and pleading.

I am undone, unwilling to separate right from wrong if the cost is her love. God help me, I ask the question. "These men. Where do I find them?"

"In the place all men go who wish to hide their sins. Church."

I don't recall the last time I was in a church. In my childhood, surely, with my parents. That was before I came of age, before my father confined me to an empty barn each night, bound with strong ropes that, in the morning, he was as likely as not to find shredded like cobwebs. By day, he brought me to physicians who covered me with leeches and priests who doused me with consecrated water that left me nothing but wet. At night, my parents barred their doors and windows and prayed I would be content with only sheep and goats. After a few years, I found the resolve to travel as far as I could and never again burden them with my presence.

Today I find myself crowded among townsfolk I consider neighbors, in the local chapel for a wholly plausible reason: the constable's funeral. I hear the weeping of his wife and sons and listen to scriptures that I once knew well.

Blessed are they that mourn: for they shall be comforted.

Blessed are they that hunger and thirst for righteousness: they shall be filled.

Blessed is the man that takes not the counsel of the ungodly, nor sits among the scornful.

Aleka is beside me, and I feel the eyes of many single her out, but she stands tall and sings the litanies without reluctance. As the congregation bends over their hymnals, she tugs at my sleeve and points out members.

There. The tinsmith.

And there. Farmer Jennings.

And there, just in the row before us: Broad Thomas, the brewer.

After the service, she approaches them in turn, tears streaming down her face, and proclaims how deeply she feels the loss of a good and righteous man. One by one, she takes their hands and wipes them with handkerchiefs she never once uses to daub her eyes. I notice each handkerchief is a different strip of colored cloth.

Back at our cabin, for two days she prepares no meals and denies me so much as a crust of bread. On the third night, she takes me out by the woodpile and orders me to strip and kneel. She binds the first handkerchief, a length of light blue fabric, across my face and whips my naked back over and over until I know nothing but the pain and the scent.

The news of the tinsmith's death travels quickly the next day. The ravenous creature, no longer content with livestock, broke down the door of his shop and mauled him in his bed. Every able-bodied man is enjoined to the coalition, a hunting party that will not rest until the beast is killed. When they come to me, I say I am weak and cowardly, with no stomach for chasing predators. It is a deception with truth in every word.

For a week, we wait out each night as gangs prowl the woodland paths with lanterns, wielding muskets and pitchforks. Aleka shows me exceptional kindness, serving me fine, fat meals and mugs of ale. We play cards by candlelight and she sings ballads with her sweet, silvery voice until my head is so heavy she must help me to bed. Gradually, the patrols diminish until not a one passes our cabin for days. On the following night, she gives me a strip of yellow cloth. I hold it to my nostrils as she rips my skin with a fork.

After the scattered pieces of Farmer Jennings are discovered, a meeting in the town chapel is convened with urgency.

"It is the Beast, the Devil made manifest!" the pastor thunders from the pulpit. "A product of witchcraft, summoned to test our faith. But we will not falter! We will not rest until this abomination is reduced to ash!"

The sanctuary resounds with *Amens!* and *Huzzahs!* Outside, the village is being transformed into a fortress. Split rails and heavy barrels barricade the alleyways. Wood for bonfires is stacked at every intersection, and parties are organized like a small army for the night-long watch. A self-appointed marshal asks me for what hour I wish to volunteer. When I say "None," he scowls in disgust at my timidity. All around, makeshift ramparts and knots of armed sentries enclose the heart of the town within a ring of impenetrability, and I know no mortal creature would likely survive an attempt to breach such a perimeter. The silent fury I see twisting Aleka's face tells me she knows it as well.

She starts to lead me away when the brewer's son blocks our path.

"Forgive me, miss," says William. "But I worry for you, alone in the woods. I fear for your safety."

"Fear for your own," she replies. "If you are wise, you'll run from this place and never look back."

She tries to step around him, but he takes her arm. "Please. We have space in our storeroom. Until the danger passes, you can shelter there. You and your father—"

"Don't speak of my father!" she shrieks. Heads turn to the commotion. "You believe yourselves safe? Fenced in like animals. The slaughter will come and none will be spared! This town—all of you—are damned!"

She whirls about, flailing as she rants. There is pity in the eyes of the crowd as they mistake her rage for terror.

"Enough," I say. "Stop."

I grip her wrists and try to restrain her. She rakes her nails over my hand, leaving claw mark wounds. A rush comes upon me, too quickly for me to avert. I strike her across the face.

Aleka is stilled and the audience stares, aghast. She gives me a look that shames me to my core. Without a word, she abandons me and latches on to young William's sleeve. He conducts her toward the brewer's shack.

I push through a gap in the blockade and head alone toward my cabin. Soon, each step I take grows heavier, each stride half the distance of the last. I watch the sunset dissolve among the trees as the last of my resolve ebbs away. I turn back. It is dark, the nightwatch fires in the town square blazing, as I approach the guarded border. A group of club-wielding boys relaxes when they recognize only a single common man seeking shelter. Sawhorses and sharpened posts are pulled aside to let me pass.

When I knock on the brewer's door, Broad Thomas greets me with the barest grunt, then leads me to a stout shed beside his rear porch. Aleka is within, sitting among casks and crates by the meager light of a few candles. She does not so much as glance at me, yet I hang my head as I find a stool to take my place by her side.

We sit in silence until the tale I have denied a voice for years at last forces its way past my lips.

"This curse," I say, "it has haunted me since I passed beyond boyhood. For what offense to God I or my forefathers committed, I do not know. To prevent harm, I chose a life alone. Then I met Ruth. She mistook my isolation as loneliness, my reticence as modesty, and reached out to me with tenderness. In my heartsick folly, I accepted her hand. For a time, I thought the love of a wife, the promise of a family, had freed me. Until, untimely on a winter night, Ruth's water broke. Her labor went awry, and her screams drove me to terror. I failed to remain my better self. In the morning, I woke to find Ruth half devoured, and the son I would never know spilled from her womb."

I do not weep. There are not tears enough in the ocean for such a thing.

"That was my doing—but my true sin came when I buried what remained of them in the woods and returned home to scour the blood."

In the shadows I see them as if fresh, the crimes I labored to hide.

"When I found you, spared from my depravity, I saw a glimmer of hope. I believed if I could become a decent man, if I cared for an orphan I created, I could somehow atone. But you were right when you said I have no need to. Demons can't atone. For that is what I am: a thing spawned only to dispense death—and now to deliver an innocent child from the grip of misfortune into the jaws of madness."

I find the strength to look up. Where I expect horror, I see in her face only compassion and, perhaps for the first time, love.

"There is only one task left, and the opportunity is at hand," she says. "After, we can both be free." She stands, takes up a quartering knife from a workbench. "I will be your deliverance. This is my promise to you."

She bolts the shed door, then finds a coil of leather strap and begins to bind my arms and legs.

"This won't hold me," I say.

"I'm trusting that it won't," she replies.

Aleka produces the last handkerchief: a square of pallid linen. With the knife, she slices into her palm and swabs the wound with the cloth, then smears it over my lips. She steps back and swipes the blade across my brow.

I can barely see from the flow that runs into my eyes. The stink of the brewer and the taste of her blood mix with my own until each breath leaves me all but drowning. Yet, I feel nothing. Grief at last has purged me of savagery where years of enforced goodness failed.

"I won't change," I say. A statement of fact as much as an expression of resolve.

She cuts me again. "Do it! Do what you were born to do!"

"No."

She screams with unbridled fury, begins toppling racks and tearing down shelves, wrecking the storeroom. Through the chaos, there comes a new sound: someone outside pounding on the door. The breaking voice of the brewer's boy calls Aleka's name, followed by the bellow of Broad Thomas himself.

"Girl! Girl, are you alright?"

"Help me!" she cries. "He means to murder me!"

Blows rattle the cabin door, heavy strikes from an ax crack the wood. At last, I feel it. My limbs grow slender and the bindings loosen. The teeth and claws I sprout make short work of the straps, and I strip them away with full awareness of my actions. For the first time, the beast and I are one. Aleka continues to call for help, but with no malice, no fear in her eyes.

The door gives way. I turn to see William push inside, ax in hand. Beyond him, the fat figure of Broad Thomas raises a musket and the flash from the muzzle is the last thing I recall.

I awaken in chains, bound by collars to an iron ring embedded in the floor of a dark cellar. I can feel a musket ball lodged in my ribs, but the wound is healed over without a scar. A sliver of window near the ceiling tells me of the passing of day and night, but no one comes to me. After three days, a cluster of strong men with clubs and pistols enter and drag me into the blinding sunlight. I am marched to the town square, toward a column surrounded by kindling. I am bound, naked, to the post with heavy rope.

Once my eyes adjust, I see the townsfolk encircling me. Some hold crosses or Bibles or other totems. Some raise their hands in prayer. Some shout curses. Amidst the crowd, I behold Aleka standing by the brewer's son; beside them is the hulking shape of his father. Aleka raises one finger from her bandaged hand and points to Broad Thomas.

I look upon the good people of town and imagine who will survive. Which ones—by choice or chance—will I leave alive?

And if Aleka is among them, will she keep her promise to become my deliverance?

Of course, she can only deliver me to perdition.

What a fool I was to ever dream otherwise.

As the torches are brought forth, I wonder what the flames will feel like. Will they be a foretaste of what is to come? Or not even a wisp of the inferno that awaits me? Regardless, I know today is not the day I will find out. I will not descend to Hell today.

On this day, I will raise it.

ABOUT THE AUTHORS

Chase Anderson – Moth{er}

Chase is a weird,queer, digital storyteller who writes weird, queer stories. Formally trained in the world of Unicode, digital presses, and HTML5, he blends art and technology to tell stories filled with magic and monsters. Find his writing and more at chasej.xyz.

Devan Barlow – How Afraid

Devan Barlow is the author of the *Curses & Curtains* series, and the collection *Foolish Hopes and Spilled Entrails: Retellings*. Find her short fiction and poetry in various anthologies and magazines. She reads voraciously, and is usually hanging out with her dog. devanbarlow.com

Warren Benedetto – The Salt Circle

Warren Benedetto writes dark fiction about horrible people, horrible places, and horrible things. He is an award-winning author who has published over 260 stories. For more information, visit warrenbenedetto. com and follow @warrenbenedetto on Twitter and Instagram.

Octavia Cade – The Marzipan Dog

Octavia Cade is a speculative fiction writer from New Zealand. She attended Clarion West 2016 and is the 2025 Robert Burns Fellow at the University of Otago. Her most recent book, *You Are My Sunshine and Other Stories*, was published in 2023 by Stelliform Press. You can find her at ojcade.com.

Carlos Dias – Duty & Mercy

C. Dias has an MsC in Micro and Nanotechnology Engineering and decided to do nothing with it, because writing fantasy sounded like a better career choice. He lives in Portugal with his wife and dog Meco, who are both very proud of his debut novel, Evergaze, even though the dog did say it after being coerced with a treat. He spends his days hammering at his next adult dark fantasy novel, and his nights spooking his players with his Dungeons and Dragons campaigns. linktr.ee/unpopularonion

Elana Gomel – Kindertransport

Elana Gomel is an academic and an award-winning writer of dark fantasy and science fiction. She is the author of seven academic books, eight novels, and numerous short stories and novellas. Her latest books are the dark fantasy novel *Nine Levels* (2024) and *The Palgrave Handbook of Global Fantasy* (2023). She currently resides in California and can be found at linktr.ee/elanagomel.

Hannah Rebekah Graves – Entry of the Gladiators

Hannah is an AuDHD ball of nerves and chaos. Her special interests include horror and Anne Boleyn. She lives with her wife and is bossed around by her cockatiel named Banakin. Please do not feed her after dark. Please do not let her in your house. creepshannah.com

John Kuyat – The Better to See You With

John Kuyat is an NYC-based horror writer. His writing has appeared in Horror Tree's *Trembling With Fear*. He works full-time at the American Museum of Natural History, passing a video on vampire bats on his way to the office each day. You can find him on Instagram and Threads. linktr.ee/john.docx.

Akis Linardos – A Coat of Mud and Bone

Akis is a writer of bizarre things, a biomedical AI scientist, and maybe human. He's also a Greek that hops across countries as his career and exploration urges demand. Find his words in Apex, Uncharted, Strange Horizons, Heartlines, and more on his website. linktr.ee/akislinardos

S.H. Livernois – In Sickness & In Slaughter

S.H. Livernois lives in rural Northern New York, writing speculative fiction by day and working in food service by night. shlivernoisauthor. com

Matt McHugh – Together Bound Unto Perdition

Matt McHugh was born in suburban Pennsylvania, attended LaSalle University in Philadelphia, and after a few years as a Manhattanite, currently calls New Jersey home. His fiction has appeared in *Analog, The Saturday Evening Post*, and *Dream Forge*. His story "Burners" won the 2019 Jim Baen Memorial Award and "Jennifer Gives Her Heart to Radioland" is PARSEC's 2021 Short Story Contest winner. In 2022, he was a grant finalist for The Speculative Literature Foundation. mattmchugh.com

Aggie Novak – The Fate in Your Flesh

Aggie (she/they) lives with her wife by the beach in Australia, where she spends most of her time hiding from the sun and heat. She writes around studying for her pharmacy degree and entertaining her three dogs. She loves all kinds of speculative fiction and often draws inspiration from Slavic folklore and mythology. When not writing, she can be found drinking tea and reading everything in sight. Her work can be found in *Hexagon* and *Mystery Magazine*. aggienovak.com

Mir Rainbird – Wolves at the Fair

Mir Rainbird is composed primarily of words. Mir's other interests include arguing with cats and being mediocre at art. For more words, read *Cosmic Horror Monthly, Trollbreath*, or *Inner Worlds*. For good cats and bad art follow @mir_rainy on Instagram.

Michael A Reed – The Last Bus out of Black Mouth Canyon

Michael A. Reed is a speculative fiction writer and dyslexic English teacher. He loves to think about ghosts, disappearing cities, and talking rats. mike-cant-reed.bsky.social

Elysia Rourke – Crepi Il Lupo

Elysia Rourke lives in Almonte, Ontario with her husband, two sons, and dog. She has a weakness for London fogs, Christmas morning, and a salty ocean breeze. Publication of her debut middle grade novel with Penguin/Nancy Paulsen Books is planned for 2026. Her writing can be found at elysiarourke.com.

J.F. Sebastian – Fire and Fangs

J.F. Sebastian is a queer, autistic writer originally from the South of France, now residing in Toronto, Canada. Writing in English, and under various pen names, is not merely a creative outlet but also a way for them to delve into and express the layers of their multifaceted identity. @space-irukandji.bsky.social

C. W. Stevenson – A Damnable Life

C. W. "Clint" Stevenson is an award-winning author residing in Central Texas with his wife, sons, and their retinue of furry companions. When he's not writing, he's reading or spending time with his family. Clint's work can be found in *Alien Dimensions, Illustrated Worlds Magazine*, and *Creepy Pod.* Facebook page

AM Sutter – A Horse Walks Into a Bar

AM Sutter has been fascinated with storytelling ever since she snuck downstairs as a child to watch The Twilight Zone with her father. She currently works as a zoo and exotic animal veterinarian, and whenever she's not arm's deep in tiger guts or elephant poop, she enjoys hiking with her Shih Tzu, who fully believes he is a wolf. Website. amsutter.com

Mark Towse – Time for a Change

Mark Towse is an English horror writer living in Australia. He left it very late to begin this journey, penning his first story since primary school at the ripe old age of forty-five. *Chasing The Dragon*, his debut novel from Eerie River Publishing, was released in March 2024. marktowsedarkfiction.wordpress.com.

J. Weintraub – Midnight Run

J. Weintraub has published fiction, essays, and poetry in numerous literary places. A member of the Dramatists Guild, he has had one-act plays produced throughout the world. As a translator he has introduced the Italian and Swiss horror writers, Nicola Lombardi and Davide Staffiero, to the English-speaking public. jweintraub.weebly.com

Scott Weisser – Big Dog

Scott Weisser lives and writes in Goshen, Ind. His fiction has been featured on the *No Sleep* and *Creepy* podcasts and in the online magazine *Flash Bang Mysteries*. He has been a committed fan of short horror fiction since receiving a copy of *Night Shift* during the Reagan administration.

Vincent West – Foxglove Manor

Vincent West is a trans author with a keen interest in fantasy, horror, and romance. A writer since childhood, Vincent lives in Ontario, Canada, with his partner and pets. linktr.ee/VincentWest

THANK YOU!

CONTENT WARNINGS

Please note: because this is a horror anthology, it should be assumed that the basic horror tropes will apply. These include death, gore, and violence.

A Damnable Life – torture, incest

Big Dog – death of a loved one, child endangerment

Crepi Il Lupo – death of a pet (off-page)

Entry of the Gladiators – disturbing violence

Fire and Fangs – child slavery and abuse

Foxglove Manor – mild body horror, transphobia (off-page/implied)

How Afraid – insects, death of a loved one

In Sickness & In Slaughter – depictions of a woman unconscious, loss of bodily autonomy

Kindertransport – child death

Midnight Run – death of a loved one, attempted assault

Moth{er} – implied miscarriage

The Better to See You With – implied animal abuse

The Fate in Your Flesh – mild body horror

The Salt Circle – death of a loved one

Time for a Change – domestic abuse (mostly off-page)

Together Bound unto Perdition – loss of a loved one, death of a child

Wolves at the Fair – transphobia